ENZ(

A MALLERY & HOBB

BY

A.J. GRIFFITHS-JONES

Copyright 2021 A.J. Griffiths-Jones

Cover Image by iStock Photos

Cover Design by Emmy Ellis

Edited by Lorna Read

FOR PAUL RIX

A DEAR FRIEND & AVID READER

CHAPTER ONE – AN IMPATIENT PATIENT

Doctor Juliette Lafoy tapped a pen against the thick file on her desk and leaned back with a sigh, pondering what mood her Friday patients would leave her in by the end of the day. The diary in her computer system showed six sessions, three before noon and the rest between one and four, each case different and equally complex, every one of them demanding her full attention. Madame Lafoy could already feel a headache building and prayed that there would be little drama that morning, although she never could be sure, and popped a couple of aspirin before swallowing them down with a tumbler of water.

For a few moments, the woman allowed her mind to wander, drinking in the smell of lilac trees and freshly mown grass that wafted in through the open window of her spacious office. The perfectly manicured lawns outside sprawled around the building like a thick green safety blanket, silently marking its parameters for the private sanatorium residents within, a visual reminder that they were free to roam but not to step over the boundary, into the real world.

Juliette looked forward to her weekend with relish. She envisaged forty-eight hours of mostly lounging in the garden of her rented cottage, sipping local wine, and ridding herself of the stuffy suit and sensible shoes that she was obliged to wear on weekdays. She looked at the ticking clock; five more minutes. The doctor released her feet from the confines of tightly fitting new shoes and wiggled her toes. Tomorrow she would wear nothing but flip-flops, Juliette promised herself.

Doctor Lafoy glanced at the upright fan in the corner of the room, weighing up the option of a cooler and more comfortable working environment, or the still open window that allowed nature to lap at the edges of her office, bringing with it the occasional welcome breeze and distant chatter from outside. She opted for the latter and inhaled the heady lilac once more with closed eyes.

Juliette winced as she slipped her feet back into the leather court shoes and stood up, anticipating a knock on the door at any moment. It came, brisk and short, accompanied by murmurs of conversation as the nurse and her charge waited for admittance. The psychiatrist checked the buttons on her blouse and smoothed the back of her pencil skirt before sitting once more, poised for her first session of the day.

"*Entrez*," she called, watching the brass handle as it turned slowly in a clockwise direction. "*Bonjour, Enzo.*"

Fran Shepherd closed the office door and turned left along the corridor, leaving the patient to his private discussion with Doctor Lafoy. She had a soft spot for Enzo Roche and wondered how long it would be until the psychiatrist signed the enigmatic man's release papers, allowing him to return to a life beyond the confines of the hospital. In Fran's opinion, Enzo was the most rational and undisturbed of all the private facility's residents, despite his eccentricity, although she never would have dared to challenge the esteemed doctor's professional diagnosis. For all Nurse Shepherd knew, the conversations behind closed doors might reveal a more unstable side to the ex-ballet dancer's psyche, but she very much doubted it.

Fran silently counted the doors on the right-hand side of the long landing, stopping when she reached the fourth. A brass nameplate read *E. Butler*.

"Edwina?" the nurse ventured, tapping gently before going inside. "Would you like to go down and sit in the garden?"

A genteel Englishwoman sat powdering her face in front of a small antique dressing-table, puffs of loose dust settling on the glass as she liberally patted her cheeks. Edwina smiled, she liked Nurse Fran.

"Good morning," the sixty-year-old trilled, watching the woman in the mirror's reflection. "Have you come to bring me my pills?"

Fran picked up a discarded pink frilly nightdress from the floor and shook her head. "No, Edwina, don't you remember? You had your medication with breakfast this morning, as usual."

Miss Butler frowned. "I don't think I did, dear."

Used to the older woman's memory loss, the nurse smiled patiently and placed a reassuring hand on her arm. "I promise you, I gave them to you myself."

Edwina crinkled her eyes, the confusion still there, as she struggled to recall the few hours since waking. Fran lifted a large cosmetic brush from the pot and began lightly flitting it over the patient's brow and nose, in an attempt to rid Edwina of the clown-like appearance that she had unwittingly created, before dabbing at the garish red lipstick with a tissue.

"There, that's better, isn't it?" she asked, finally satisfied with the results.

Miss Butler smiled. "Can I go and sit in the garden now?"

Fran nodded. "Of course you can."

Enzo Roche sat with one leg carefully crossed over the other, both hands clasped around his knees as he watched Doctor Lafoy scribbling on her notepad. He was used to the routine, twice weekly sessions, month after month, sometimes more often if the psychiatrist deemed it necessary. Enzo fought back the urge to tut at the woman's bitten fingernails and slightly creased blouse, subconsciously glancing down at his own perfectly manicured hands. She was different to the last doctor, more probing with her questions, often stepping over the line into the personal territory that Enzo preferred not to discuss.

"How are you sleeping?" Juliette queried, speaking smoothly in French, her words unfaltering. "Any bad dreams?"

Enzo shrugged, the folds of his elaborate Japanese kimono lifting and falling gracefully on slender shoulders, the brightly coloured cranes seeming to momentarily spread their silken wings as the material shifted slightly.

"The same as usual," he replied, lips pursed. "You know me."

"Well, that's just the thing, Enzo," Juliette explained, "I don't really know you, do I? You've been seeing me for what, two months now? And we seem to be making little progress. You've hardly told me anything."

Monsieur Roche adjusted the elasticated headband that kept his hair from falling onto the perfectly made-up face, and then placed a finger on his lips, causing the silk sleeve to fall below his wrist.

"Doctor Lafoy, there really is nothing to tell, I'm perfectly fine."

Juliette smiled tightly. She had caught sight of the scars on the man's arm, albeit a quick glimpse before he had hidden the skin back under the folds of fabric.

"Have you felt any urges to self-harm?"

There was a sharp intake of breath, indignant, displeased, as Enzo averted his eyes. It was the same every time.

"No, Doctor Lafoy, as I told you, I am fine."

"Can you tell me about the last time you thought about hurting yourself? How recent was it?"

There was a knock at the door, causing Enzo Roche to glance at the clock.

"Sorry, it looks as though our time is up. Good day, Doctor Lafoy."

Having settled Edwina Butler on a bench in the grounds, a shady spot where the patient could watch an ensuing game of croquet without catching the sun on her skin, Fran Shepherd returned to her duties in the main building.

At thirty-five, the nurse was agile and youthful, easily climbing the grand staircase that swept upwards from the main entrance hall as she made her way back to the dispensary, her neatly bobbed chestnut hair brushing against her neckline as she hurried to check the inventory.

Edwina had put doubt in Nurse Shepherd's mind and the younger woman needed to ensure that it was nothing more than the patient's memory playing tricks on her. Fran clearly recalled watching the stroke victim swallowing her epilepsy prescription during her rounds that morning, yet she had been so stressed lately that her mind had been elsewhere. It was better to be safe than sorry, that's what her gran had always said, and there was certainly no harm in checking, just to be on the safe side.

As she reached the dispensary, Fran paused, letting her fingers stray to the folded envelope in her uniform pocket. Although it was still unopened, the registered nurse knew what the letter would say and vowed to put off the reading of it until she had time to really digest the contents. She would wait until her lunch break, find a quiet spot, and swallow the bitter news with a cup of strong coffee.

Lifting the black folder from its shelf, Fran flipped the pages to 'B' for Butler.

There it was, Clonazepam. Administered at seven-forty by F. Shepherd, her signature bold and clear. Fran blew out a breath of relief. She should have known better than to let Edwina's confusion rattle her.

"*Est-ce que tout va bien?*" a voice called out from the doorway, startling Fran and causing her to drop the ring binder onto the desk.

She turned, the look of fright switching to one of relaxation as she saw the hulking form of orderly Raymond Verdin watching her.

"*Oui, bien,*" Fran replied, picking up the folder and replacing it.

"*Café?*" Raymond enquired, a dimple appearing in his cheek as he smiled.

Nurse Shepherd looked at her watch. "*Non, merci.*"

It was time for her to collect Enzo Roche from the doctor's office.

Doctor Lafoy followed her patient to the door, carefully side-stepping the trailing ends of kimono as Enzo Roche sashayed towards freedom, frustration etched upon her features.

"Think about what I said, won't you, Enzo?"

The ex-dancer swirled around dramatically, one hand already reaching for the door handle. "About what, Doctor?"

Juliette sighed. "About opening up to me, letting your emotions out. It will be helpful to your mental well-being."

"I'm perfectly fine," the man replied tersely, "or at least I will be when you sign my release papers. Good day, Doctor Lafoy."

In one swift motion, Enzo Roche had exited the room, greeting the nurse who waited outside with far more zeal than he had shown in the past hour.

"See you on Tuesday," Juliette called, turning a thin smile towards Fran Shepherd, who looked back over her shoulder as she escorted a chattering Enzo back to his room, although it failed to reach her eyes.

"Oh, darling," Enzo cried, spreading his arms wide, "look at all these gifts. Are they for me?"

Nurse Shepherd suppressed a giggle as the effeminate man twirled and danced around the room, her eyes taking in the beautifully wrapped presents that had been brought to the patient's room during his absence.

"I guess so," she replied, lifting a label on a particularly pretty box to take a peek, "it is your birthday, isn't it?"

"Yes, Fran darling, it is," Enzo confirmed, clapping his hands together. "These must be from my adoring fans. How wonderful! I'll open them later."

The nurse laughed as her charge rattled a box, trying to guess its contents. "You're a very lucky man."

Enzo's face beamed, eyes tearful as he drank in the dozens of multi-coloured packages. "Yes, I suppose I am, aren't I? Although Lafoy didn't remember."

"Come on," Fran urged, "let's go outside and get some fresh air with Edwina."

Despite it only being just after ten that Friday morning, Edwina Butler has nestled herself into the crook of the bench and fallen asleep. Her wide-brimmed sun hat had slipped forward, and the slight figure resembled a rag doll as she slumbered peacefully in the warm September sun.

"Sssshhhhh," Enzo whispered, tiptoeing across the grass to sit beside his friend, "we don't want to wake the dear soul."

Fran walked silently behind, watching Roche's graceful steps as he slithered towards the bench, the ends of the black kimono trailing in his wake.

"I'll ask Raymond to bring some tea," she said quietly, once Enzo had seated himself next to Edwina, "then I really must go and check on old Monsieur Grimond's blood pressure. Will you be alright here?"

"Of course, Frannie darling. Off you go, we'll be fine."

Nurse Shepherd winced slightly at the affectionate use of her name. That was what Neil used to call her, before things went terribly wrong.

Juliette Lafoy stood at the window looking down. Her ten o'clock patient was recounting a particularly dull recollection from his childhood and the psychiatrist had found her own mind beginning to lose focus momentarily. She nodded now and again, encouraging the young man to continue the diatribe against his mother, but gravitated towards the fresh air and laughter. She could see a patch of shade below, the end of a bench just in view, with an arm dangling down limply. A trickle of animated chatter floated upwards as Enzo Roche and the English nurse came into view, wittering like old friends, until they neared the lilac tree where the sleeping person lay.

Doctor Lafoy turned to check that the patient in the room was still looking down at his hands as he unburdened himself, and then returned to her spot to watch. Enzo was out of view now and the nurse was retreating, coming back indoors, her face glowing. Juliette wondered how it was that Enzo Roche would confide in Nurse Shepherd when she, with all her years of professional training in psychiatry, found it almost impossible to get answers from the ex-principle dancer.

She spun around, noting the absence of a voice in the room, and turned her attention to the blubbering man who gripped a handful of tissues between wet fingers as he slouched in the chair.

"There, there, Rafael," Juliette soothed, "I think that's enough for today."

As Fran Shepherd made her way towards Monsieur Grimond's room, a portable blood-pressure monitor in her hands, she glimpsed the stocky figure of Raymond Verdin coming up the far staircase and paused in the doorway.

"More gifts for Monsieur Roche?" she asked in French, nodding at the numerous beautifully wrapped parcels in the orderly's arms.

"Yes, this is the last of them, thank goodness," Raymond smiled, coming closer, "Enzo certainly has a lot of admirers."

Fran glanced at the topmost box, balanced precariously on top of the others. The stiff white cardboard was topped with a huge lime green ribbon. It looked rather garish compared to the others.

"He hates green," she commented, twitching her nose as the aroma of freshly baked chocolate cake hit both nostrils, "but it's the thought that counts."

"It smells absolutely delicious," Verdin grinned, sniffing hungrily.

"Well, if we're lucky Enzo might share it," Fran replied. "See you later."

"I certainly hope so," the large man winked, "I'm a glutton for cake."

The orderly's footsteps disappeared along the highly polished corridor as he headed towards Monsieur Roche's room, the rumbling of his stomach thankfully disguised by the squeaking of his rubber-soled shoes.

Fran Shepherd knocked at Monsieur Grimond's door and went inside, cursing herself for forgetting to ask the orderly to take drinks to the patients outside. *Never mind*, she told herself, *I'll check on the old man and then do it myself.*

It was after one by the time Fran found herself a quiet spot in the hospital grounds to take a well-earned lunch break. With a carton of orange juice by her side and a plastic lunchbox in her lap, Fran took a deep breath and felt in her pocket for the envelope. The postmark was from England, the handwriting familiar. She would recognise her ex-husband's scrawl anywhere, with its looping characters and sloping capitals. A knot began to form in the woman's stomach as she slowly peeled back the flap and extracted the letter. There was no return address. Neil had obviously moved away from the home that they had shared together for over ten years. The words were brief, and scathing.

A trickle of laughter echoed across a lawn and Fran lifted her head, tears streaming down both cheeks as she looked over to the dining room window. Residents were enjoying their lunch, unaware of her emotional distress outside.

"Come on," the nurse whispered, "hold it together until you get off shift."

Replacing the lid on her lunchbox, the uneaten tuna sandwich abandoned inside, Fran stood, brushing the loose grass clippings from her white uniform as she rose. She had wondered whether the rumours were true and now her ex-husband had confirmed that they were, although she couldn't help but wonder at his motives for telling her now. It seemed as though salt were being rubbed into an old wound, a wound that Fran Shepherd would rather have put a bandage on and forgotten about.

Enzo Roche had enticed his friend Edwina upstairs to help unwrap a few of the cards and gifts that had been sent in by his adoring fans. Despite having been an icon in the world of dance over a decade earlier, Enzo had lost none of his charm and ballet lovers the world over still fawned over his performances and recital reruns. Had it not been for a cruel twist of fate in which Enzo was seriously injured, there was no doubt that the ex-dancer would still have been gracing the stage with his unique talent.

"What's in here?" Edwina asked, picking up a small box and looking at it curiously.

"Go on, dear, open it," Enzo urged, coming closer to take a peek and smiling when his friend lifted the lid, revealing a box of biscuits topped with artistically moulded ballerinas made from icing sugar.

Miss Butler grinned. "Ooh, I say, how wonderful."

"Would you like to try one, dear?" Enzo offered.

Edwina shook her head, greying curls quivering. "Oh no, certainly not, it will spoil the party."

"Party?"

The moment was gone, Edwina Butler back to her forgetful self, the details of the afternoon's activity arrangements already a distant memory. It was too late, however, and Enzo Roche was smiling. Despite having not heard a whisper from the staff or patients that day, the man was satisfied that there was going to be a birthday celebration after all.

Nurse Shepherd headed upstairs, determined not to allow the contents of the letter to distract her from the afternoon's duties. There was medication to be dispensed, rooms to check and charts to fill in, and it was a hard fact of life that she had no time to wallow in the self-pity that was brimming in her mind.

"Is something wrong, Nurse Shepherd?"

Fran looked up and came face-to-face with Juliette Lafoy, the doctor's stern features detracting from her natural beauty.

"No, Doctor, why do you ask?"

The psychiatrist sniffed, allowing her eyes to drink in the younger woman's pale cheeks and puffy eyes before answering. There was something about Fran Shepherd that she disliked, although, if put on the spot, the doctor would have been hard-pressed to tell you exactly what it was that she found so objectionable.

"You might want to wash your face before seeing to the patients, we do have standards to uphold, after all."

Fran cursed under her breath. She had removed the residue of mascara from her tear-stained face after coming inside but hadn't had time to apply fresh make-up. Trust Juliette Lafoy to be the one to notice.

"I had something in my eye," she lied, after an obvious pause. "I'll go and rinse my face again. Thank you for letting me know."

Doctor Lafoy watched the nurse scurry away with an air of superiority, intent upon finding the reason behind Fran Shepherd's obvious distress, and then glanced down at her designer watch. The psychiatrist had popped out to use the toilet between appointments and was eager to see the afternoon schedule over. If it wasn't for Enzo Roche's 'surprise' party, Juliette would have had her feet up with a gin and tonic by five. As it was, she was being forced to take part in what she considered nothing more than a charade to pander to one of the hospital's most lucrative inmates. The doctor shrugged, reminding herself that it was partially due to patients like Enzo that the private facility could afford to pay her handsome salary.

***

At four o'clock, sanatorium manager Leon Cassel called everyone back into the dining room. A tall and formidable figure, the patron stood proud at the centre of the assembly, his crisp beige linen suit oozing quality tailoring. Bunting, balloons and coloured ribbon had been strung up around the room in honour of the birthday party and now a beaming Enzo Roche entered the grand salon to a round of applause. The dancer was dressed in a billowing blue silk shirt and tight-fitting trousers, an outfit more suited to the opening night of a Hollywood screening rather than afternoon tea in a rural sanatorium for the mentally ill, although nobody would comment. They knew Enzo well and were used to his eccentricities. The patients who could walk stepped forward to kiss the guest of honour on both cheeks, while those who had limited mobility waited their turn until Enzo embraced them one by one.

A buffet of delicacies had been assembled on the centre table and in the middle sat a sponge cake decorated with fresh fruits and frosting. Being a man who always embraced every opportunity to turn on the dramatics, Monsieur Roche flitted around, cooing and gesticulating, allowing all to believe that the gathering was a complete surprise. Enzo would never let on that his dear friend had already given the game away, he adored Edwina far too much for that.

Monsieur Cassel clapped his hands together and made a short speech, as was the custom for any of the residents' birthdays and, with Enzo Roche having been a longer-term patient than most, wished the birthday boy a joyful year ahead.

"Now, Enzo," Leon announced, "would you like to cut your cake?"

There were cheers as the dancer took an elegant bow, thanking Monsieur Cassel for his generous and kind organisation of this special event.

With a flick of the hand and a few graceful steps forward, Monsieur Roche took up his place at the central table and cast a practised eye around his audience, knife poised over the sponge, before stopping stock still, open-mouthed.

"Where's Edwina? I couldn't possibly cut the cake without my dearest friend."

Fran Shepherd was standing at the back of the dining room, her personal woes pushed aside for the time being as she smiled at Enzo Roche enjoying his moment of glory. As a murmur went around the room, the nurse searched the group for the missing patient. It was unlike Edwina to wander off. As she exited the party and began climbing the stairs towards Miss Butler's room, heavy footsteps thudded down the upstairs landing, causing Fran to look upwards. Raymond Verdin was racing towards her, his face ashen.

"Come quickly," he panted, "Edwina has had a fit."

All too aware of the sixty-year-old's epilepsy, the nurse quickened her step, following Verdin back to the patient's room as fast as her feet would allow. The strong stench of faeces filled the bedroom, causing Fran to gag involuntarily.

"Get Matron," she told him, looking at Edwina Butler's ankles poking out from the far side of the woman's bed and panicking. "Quickly!"

As Raymond hurried away to locate the head of medical staff, Nurse Shepherd knelt down beside her patient, noting the putrid brown stain on the older woman's pink dress, planning to turn Edwina's head to one side in order to prevent the woman from choking on her own tongue. As she stooped to get closer, however, Fran could see that it was too late. Besides the usual frothing at the mouth that Edwina's epilepsy usually caused, her lips were forced into a rictus grin, her features tight and unmoving.

Fran suppressed the urge to cry out, pressing her fingers to the side of Edwina Butler's neck and feeling for a glimmer of a pulse as several panicked voices approached. There was no doubt about it, the adorable stroke victim who had been a bundle of joy just an hour before, was dead.

Gabriella Dupont slid a key into the lock and pressed her left hand against the door to push it open, fingers splayed, a half-carat diamond sparkling in the sunlight on the young woman's ring finger. She glanced back over her shoulder to where Roberto Mazzo was struggling with two heavy suitcases.

"Welcome home," Gabi smiled.

"Stop, stop," the handsome Italian shouted, dropping the luggage and racing forward, "I need to carry you into the house."

Gabriella continued on into the narrow hallway, laughing. "That's after we're married, Roberto, not yet. Let me make some coffee, I'm so thirsty."

Turning to retrieve their cases, her fiancé looked slightly dejected as he watched the familiar blonde ponytail swish against Gabi's shoulders as she disappeared from view, calling for him to hurry. Roberto stood for a moment, reminding himself that it had only been a month since the female detective's involvement in an anti-terrorism surveillance operation, one which had seen Gabriella taking a personal interest in a young Muslim woman and ultimately being at the scene of the girl's death. He knew that it had affected his girlfriend badly, hence the hastily arranged holiday at Inspector Mallery's insistence, followed by the realisation that Mazzo couldn't imagine his life without this beautiful, sensitive Frenchwoman.

Once inside, Roberto made his way to the kitchen, eager to relax.

Gabriella was filling the kettle and grinned broadly. "Back to work on Monday, so we had better make the most of the weekend."

The Italian moved forward, slid both arms around her waist and nuzzled his face into his future wife's neck.

"I know, don't remind me," he murmured. "Let's just stay in, watch some films, and if you're really lucky I'll make my mamma's special ragù."

Gabriella placed a finger under her lover's chin, forcing his head upwards. "Speaking of your mamma, Roberto, that was quite a grilling she gave me before we left."

Mazzo groaned. Having just spent two weeks travelling around Italy, which had culminated in a stay at his family home in Milan, he had hoped that he and Gabi would have been able to avoid this conversation for a while. As matriarch, Signora Mazzo held firm her rigid beliefs and had imparted them to her son's intended bride in no uncertain terms.

"It's just her way," Roberto pleaded, "take no notice."

Gabriella raised her eyebrows. "When she insisted that I give up my career almost immediately to focus on bearing you half a dozen bambinos?"

The Italian grinned. "Well, perhaps we need to practise some more first."

Leading his beloved towards the bedroom, Roberto sighed. "I love you, Gabriella, don't you ever forget that."

Before she could answer, a buzzing in the detective's pocket caused the pair to stop mid-clinch. Gabi pulled out her phone and looked at the flashing screen. "It's Max."

"Go on, answer it," Roberto told her. "He wouldn't call unless it was urgent."

Without further hesitation, Gabriella pressed the green button.

Thierry Moreau carefully tore a strip of paper from his notepad and balled it up, before hurling it across the room at his red-haired colleague.

Jack Hobbs cursed as the missile landed in his coffee mug, causing the contents to spill out over a report that he had been pondering over.

"Pillock," he swore, turning to glower at the other detective.

"*Pill-uc*?" Thierry repeated. "What is that?"

"It's a plonker, a stupid person," Hobbs grunted.

Moreau swivelled his chair around and got up, striding across to the Englishman's workspace. "What's wrong with you today? Had an argument with Angélique?"

The reddening of the Englishman's cheeks gave Thierry his answer and he sat down on the edge of Jack's desk.

"Want to talk about it?"

Hobbs shook his head. "No, mate, it's fine, just a tiff."

"*Tiff*? *Mon dieu*, there are so many English words I need to learn."

As the pair laughed, Max Mallery walked into the room, hands in pockets, his lips fixed in a tight line.

"No work to do?" he asked, noting the air of joviality.

"Yes, plenty of petty crimes to log," the Yorkshireman replied, "but nothing of any significance."

"Where's Luc?" Max continued, his eyes scanning the Incident Room.

"He's nipped out to the library. He was due a break."

The inspector looked at the clock on the wall. "Can you give him a ring, Jacques, I need everyone ready for a meeting at two."

"A new case?"

Mallery shook his head. "*Non*, a new commissioner."

Hobbs worked his mouth, but couldn't find the right words, so instead reached for his mobile phone. As he did so, Max retraced his steps and went to stand at the waist-height windows that covered the entire corridor outside. He looked down into the car park and then up at his own reflection. Handsome, rugged features stared back. Mallery was on form.

Gabriella hastily discarded her creased travelling attire in the laundry basket and turned her thoughts to the fact that a new chief was on the way. If she wasn't mistaken, Gabi considered, there had been tension in Mallery's voice as he'd requested her to come in for a short meeting, and she wondered what Commissaire Ozanne's replacement would be like. Roberto lay on the bed watching as his fiancée buttoned up navy linen trousers and reached for a blue patterned blouse to complete the ensemble.

"Do I look okay?" she inquired, pulling a brush through long golden locks.

"Of course," Mazzo replied, drinking in the detective's natural beauty. "How long will you be?"

"Max said no more than an hour, it's just a quick introduction. I guess we'll get our proper orders on Monday."

The Italian swung his legs off the bed and reached for a long, lingering kiss. "Right, so I'll go to the supermarket and start preparing dinner, the sauce needs at least four hours to cook."

At quarter to two, the team found themselves waiting with bated breath, Max had told them nothing about the new arrival, wanting to keep the identity of the new commissioner a surprise, and murmurs around the room debated whether they might actually recognise the new arrival.

"I reckon it's Nathan Ferreira," Jack told his colleagues. "You know, Max's old friend from Paris, the one who handled Nicholas Lavigne's murder."

Thierry wasn't so convinced. "No way. Ferreira wouldn't want to move down here, he's settled in Paris. It's more likely to be some old guy on the verge of retirement, sent off to spend his last few working years here, due to the low crime rates."

"The low-level criminal activity is only due to our efficiency," Luc Martin pointed out. "I don't understand why Max didn't take up the position."

Hobbs tutted. "He enjoys the thrill of the chase too much, that's why."

There was a squeak of hinges as the outer door in the corridor swung open and three pairs of eyes turned in unison, expecting to see their boss walking in side by side with the newly relegated commissioner. Instead, a tanned face beamed at them as Gabriella entered the incident room bearing gifts.

"*Bonjour,*" she grinned, setting down four items wrapped in colourful tissue paper, "I'm back."

Thierry tore at the paper on his present, revealing a brass replica of a Ducati motorbike.

"It's a lighter," Gabi explained, as she passed the next gift to Luc. "I know you don't smoke, but you can use it to light the candles around your bath!"

The dark-skinned detective grinned. "It's great."

Luc Martin came over to kiss his colleague on the cheek. "Italian chocolate, you know my weakness. Thanks, Gabi."

Jack took the heavy item from his friend's outstretched hands and removed the wrapping to reveal a hand-painted salad bowl.

"Wow, this is brilliant," he enthused, "really thoughtful."

"And perfect for your next garden party," Gabriella chuckled.

She laid Mallery's present to one side and stood with her left hand pressed against her cheek. It took a few seconds for the three men to register the diamond on her finger but, when they did, there was an almighty cheer.

A black Mercedes-Benz swung through the gates of Bordeaux Police Headquarters at five minutes to two that Friday afternoon. The woman sitting in the back seat was dressed in formal uniform, a hard-topped hat on her lap. As the driver brought the vehicle to a stop at the foot of the front steps, she placed the cap on her head and waited for the rear door to be opened.

Max Mallery was pacing the reception area, determined to make a good impression upon his new superior. In recent talks, the inspector had found himself impressed with the new commissioner's plans and vowed to welcome her with an air of positivity. Despite having no regrets at having turned down the promotion himself, Max was still feeling cautious about the changes that lay ahead, especially after the previous commissioner's dealings with the underworld had been exposed, a travesty that Ozanne had been caught up in for no other reason than to line his own pocket.

Spotting the unfamiliar saloon just before the hour, Max straightened his tie, stepped out into the sunlight and headed down the steps. The woman who faced him was not how Mallery had imagined. On the telephone, his new boss's voice had been soft and slightly musical, yet the steel-haired, slender woman in front of him now suggested that she would stand for no nonsense. The commissioner's frame was shapely, yet slender, her uniform void of creases, despite the morning's long car journey down from Paris.

"*Commissaire Rancourt*," he said, smoothly extending a hand, both to help the woman out of the car and to welcome her, "*bonjour*."

Audrey Rancourt nodded, mentally comparing her impressions by phone with the man who now stood in front of her. She had been so far off the mark. Inspector Mallery was both far more sophisticated and much more handsome than she had imagined, his inherent good looks catching the woman off guard for a moment.

"*Inspecteur*," the policewoman replied, suppressing her delight. "*Bonjour*."

A waft of expensive perfume momentarily pervaded Max's nostrils as the commissioner came alongside, causing him to breathe in the aroma without thinking. It was the same blend of vanilla and bergamot that his ex-lover had been fond of. It seemed that Audrey Rancourt had expensive tastes.

"I have heard so much about you all from Inspector Mallery," the new arrival told Max's team. She assessed the row of faces in front of her before continuing, "All good, of course, and an impressive resolution rate on your casework."

There was a shuffle of seats and nods of approval as the detectives listened.

"Of course," Rancourt smiled, turning to Jack Hobbs, "it is most unusual for a French police force to employ a foreigner, but I'm sure that you are used to the laws of our country by now and I won't hinder your progress."

She turned her gaze away, letting it settle on Gabriella. "That goes for all of you. I am here to make your jobs easier, and I'm sure we will all get along well. One of the first implementations will be better technology for this division, which will include interactive iPads, a measure to increase the effectiveness of meetings and transferral of critical information."

The group murmured their approval, warming to Audrey Rancourt's positive first speech, with Luc Martin looking particularly delighted with the news of more gadgets to be tried and tested.

The commissioner glanced at the ageing clock on the wall, noticing that the shortest hand was nearing three. "Well, it's Friday afternoon, and I'm sure you all have plans for the weekend, so let's hope there are no serious incidents requiring your attention over the next couple of days. I will leave you to it now and look forward to getting to know you all in due course."

She raised her thin, pencilled eyebrows at Max and nodded towards the door. "Shall we have a quick chat in your office?"

Mallery was on his feet in a flash, steering his new boss towards the end of the corridor, where the infamous state-of-the-art coffee machine awaited them.

***

Doctor Brijesh Singh replaced the telephone on its cradle on the wall and rubbed a hand over his long, coarse black beard. It just didn't make sense, he brooded. The coroner would usually want to check any death under eighty years of age as a matter of due diligence, but Jean Blanchet, the medical examiner covering for Paul Theron that week, had seemed more interested in his drive back home to Aurillac than in checking over the recently departed.

Doctor Singh turned away from the wall and walked back over to the hospital gurney, where the lifeless body of Edwina Butler lay covered with a green surgical sheet. Carefully lifting the covering, the medic looked down at the woman's face. Her mouth was pulled into an almost clown-like rictus grin, the lips tight, exposing the female's small, yellowing teeth. A small amount of foam residue still sat in the open cavity and a slight smell emanated from the tongue. Brijesh leaned closer, closing his eyes to try to figure out what it was.

"Celery?" he muttered. "Or parsley perhaps?"

Reaching for a cotton swab, the astute doctor took a sample from Edwina's mouth, sealing the specimen in a zip-lock bag and labelling it. Doctor Singh took no chances where the dead were concerned. Mistakes simply didn't happen on his shift. This might be nothing more than an epileptic seizure as reported by the staff at the sanatorium, he told himself, but better safe than sorry. Besides, Coroner Theron would back from his holiday on Monday and would be keen to check over any recent mortalities.

Closing the mortuary door behind him, Brijesh returned to his office and picked up the notes for *E. Butler*, his eyes quickly scanning the information.

Something didn't feel right. Call it a gut instinct, but the nurses had sworn that Edwina had been given her regular Clonazepam at breakfast. If that really was the case, it should have prevented a fit, or at the very least have prevented such a severe one. The woman was sixty, with severe palsy and memory loss following a stroke according to her records, yet she hadn't had one epileptic seizure since entering the care of the private hospital four years prior.

"Is everything alright, Doctor Singh?" a deep voice called from the open doorway. "I'm about to lock up."

Brijesh nodded, giving his secretary a weak smile. "Yes, Jeanette, thank you. I lost track of time. I'm all done here."

The woman stepped closer, gesturing at the folder. "An unexplained death?"

"No, in fact it's just the opposite. There is a perfectly plausible reason for this poor woman's demise, yet... well, I don't know, it just seems a bit premature."

Jeanette's expression turned to one of sympathy. "Every death comes far too soon, Doctor, I've learned that even more so since coming to work here."

Singh rose from his chair and raised his eyes heavenwards. "You're right. Somebody up there obviously has greater plans for Madame Butler."

Coroner Jean Blanchet pulled his car into the garage forecourt at Libourne and climbed out into the heat of the afternoon to fill up the tank. Clasping the handle in his right hand, Blanchet looked out across the road, calculating the amount of traffic heading towards Perigeux and wondering how many of those same vehicles would be travelling onwards to Aurillac. On a good day, the journey would take him just under four hours, but, given the heavy loads thundering by and the fact that it was Friday rush hour, he didn't give out much hope of arriving back home before ten that night.

Entering the small shop to pay for his fuel, the coroner wondered whether his wife would leave him some supper in the fridge. Perhaps she had gone to visit their daughter and forgotten all about him. Anticipating the latter scenario, Blanchet reached for a chilled energy drink and a prawn baguette, sliding his purchases over the counter with credit card at the ready.

Having returned to the car some minutes later, Blanchet checked his phone for missed calls. There was only one and he immediately recognised the area code for Bordeaux. It was probably that doctor again, he grumbled, starting the engine, trying to look for problems where there were none. The car pulled out onto the main road, a motorcyclist blasting his horn as the coroner swerved to miss him, and Blanchet continued on towards the next town.

"What the hell can he want now?" the medic cursed, recalling the curt conversation with Brijesh Singh less than an hour ago. "It was an open and shut case of death by SUDEP – Sudden Unexplained Death in Epilepsy."

Blanchet had no regrets over his decision not to examine the body, it was a straightforward death, easily explained away. There was absolutely no need for him to go trekking off across the city to see the corpse, it would have been a total waste of time and he had conveyed his thoughts to Singh in no uncertain terms. More than likely, he pondered, the nursing staff were simply too late in reaching the victim and if the doctor had checked, he would probably have found that she had swallowed her own tongue.

The medical examiner turned up the Audi's air-conditioning and leaned across to open the glove compartment, throwing his phone inside whilst steering the vehicle precariously with his left hand. As far as Jean Blanchet was concerned, his temporary cover in Bordeaux had come to an end. Anything that occurred after five was now the responsibility of Coroner Paul Theron.

Enzo Roche was inconsolable. Lying on his bed facing the window, the dancer hugged a satin pillow and sobbed loudly, tears streaming down his cheeks in rivulets. Not only had his friend been pronounced dead that afternoon, but she had died alone and very obviously in distress.

Nurse Shepherd sat down on the edge of bed, leaning forward to bring her face close to that of her patient. She gently slid an arm around the man's shoulder, attempting to supply some comfort to his grief.

"I'm so sorry, Enzo, it must have happened really suddenly," she soothed.

Enzo turned his face upwards, running a finger along his eyelid to wipe away the blotchy mascara that had settled there.

"But why, Frannie? Edwina took her pills every day and I've never known her to have a seizure, not in all the time I've been here."

The registered nurse shook her head. "I've been asking myself the same question, but apparently these things do happen. I'm so sorry for your loss, Enzo. Is there anything I can do? Would you like a cup of sweet tea?"

"Or something to help you sleep?" Juliette Lafoy asked as she stepped into the private suite without knocking. "You look rather pale, Enzo."

Fran stood, embarrassed to have been caught in what might have been misconstrued as a hug by the psychiatrist. "Sorry, Doctor Lafoy, I didn't see you there."

Juliette blinked twice. "No need to apologise, I can see you are trying to help."

Enzo rolled himself over so that he was facing the doctor. "Would Edwina have suffered?"

Lafoy shrugged her narrow shoulders. "I doubt it, but who knows?"

Fran Shepherd could feel her cheeks burning as the frustration rose. What on earth was Juliette Lafoy playing at? She could have at least told Enzo that the death would have quick and painless, regardless of her own professional opinion. Straightening her dress, the nurse patted Roche's arm gently.

"I'll get you that tea now, and I'll ask Monsieur Grimond to come and sit with you for a while, just until I finish my rounds, okay?"

Enzo smiled weakly. "Thank you, Frannie."

Outside in the corridor, Juliette Lafoy caught Fran by the elbow before she could make her way to the kitchen. The doctor's face was stern.

"It really doesn't help to get so close to the patients, Nurse Shepherd. After all, they're all here because of their fragile mental state."

Fran narrowed her eyes. "I'm well aware of that, Doctor Lafoy, but Enzo Roche and Edwina Butler were inseparable, so the least I can do is offer him some comfort."

"Yes, well, just ensure to keep it on a professional level, won't you?"

Fran almost laughed out loud at the irony of the psychiatrist's comment. Enzo Roche was the most self-assured homosexual she had ever met, and that was saying something. If Lafoy was inferring that anything improper might happen between the pair of them, she could think again.

Biting her lip and holding back the harsh words on the tip of her tongue, Fran excused herself and turned away. Whatever the doctor was up to, she was having none of it.

Juliette Lafoy returned to her office and found the imposing figure of Leon Cassel waiting for her. The tall, hulking man was sitting in the chair opposite her own, his fingers pressed together at his mouth as though in contemplation. His suit was far more creased than it had been at the party some time earlier, yet the hospital manager still managed to looked well-groomed and smart.

"Ah, Juliette, there you are."

"Monsieur Cassel. I was just checking on a patient."

"Please, call me Leon, you've been here long enough now," the man enthused, getting up to greet her. "I was just wondering if you're alright."

Juliette raised a hand to her throat, swallowing hard. "Me? Yes, of course. Why wouldn't I be alright?"

Cassel gestured for the doctor to sit. "Well, you know, the unfortunate death of Madam Butler this afternoon, it's bound to be a stressful time. Everyone is very sad, very sad indeed."

Doctor Lafoy studied her boss's face for a few moments, wondering what the real reason was that he had invaded her private space,

"Of course it's distressing, but these things happen and we have to stay strong for the other patients, don't we… Leon?"

His name dropped off her lips uncomfortably, Juliette finding the familiarity too suffocating and unprofessional under the circumstances of her employment.

"Yes, of course. I have informed Edwina's next of kin. Naturally they are distraught, but anyway…"

The psychiatrist waited, head cocked. "Yes?"

"I wondered if you might do me the honour of dining with me this evening. I know a very good bistro not too far, and of course I'll drive."

So, there it was, the real reason behind Leon Cassel's intrusion. The gentle giant wanted to ask her out on a date!

Juliette scrambled her thoughts, searching for a suitable excuse. She could hardly tell her employer that she was already planning an enjoyable evening of her own, one that included a bottle of Bombay Sapphire and a pizza.

"I'm sorry, Leon," Lafoy said sweetly, forcing her mouth upwards and almost tasting the insincerity as she spoke, "I have promised to work late tonight, to keep an eye on Enzo Roche in case he should need grief counselling. Nurse Shepherd told me she had concerns that he might self-harm. He's in a bit of a state, you see. Maybe some other time?"

The lie was so natural and smoothly delivered that Leon Cassel fell for it, hook line and sinker, never doubting that the psychiatrist was portraying anything more than her devotion to the job. His face relaxed, the gratitude evident.

"I must say, Doctor Lafoy, your dedication is highly commendable. Thank you, this will not be forgotten when the review of your trial period comes up. In fact, I will personally see to it that that the board offers you a permanent place here."

"Thank you, Leon, I'm very grateful."

Juliette watched as the large man licked his lips and bid her goodnight, before cursing under her breath. Thanks to Enzo Roche, she had inadvertently given herself unwanted overtime on a Friday night!

CHAPTER THREE – A SECOND TRAGEDY

Maurice Fabron climbed out of the dark blue Citroën van and leaned in through the open window to speak to his son.

"*Dix heures, d'accord?*" he shouted over the noisy engine.

Telo nodded, his long fringe falling down over one eye. "*Oui, Papa.*"

The boulangerie owner stood at the kerb watching the vehicle disappear into traffic, before turning to look at the frontage of the wine bar in Bordeaux.

It was rare that Maurice ventured into the city on a Saturday night, but Max Mallery had been persuasive, insisting that his friend could do with a change of scenery. Now, Monsieur Fabron stood on the pavement in blue jeans and a crisp white shirt, wondering whether the police inspector had already arrived and was waiting inside. After a moment's hesitation, he pushed open the door and was greeted by incessant chatter in a variety of languages and mellow pop music.

"*Maurice!*" an instantly recognisable voice called across the crowded room.

Max was seated at the bar, a glass of coke with ice in front of him.

Fabron strode over, pulled out a bar stool and climbed on.

"*Bonsoir, Max,*" he grinned, nodding at the soft drink. "*Une bière?*"

Max gave a wry smile. He was officially on duty, but they hadn't had a Saturday night call-out for weeks and he felt it unlikely that there would be one that weekend, either. He nodded in the affirmative and watched as the barman poured an ice-cold foaming lager.

In the picturesque village of Saint Margaux, Jack Hobbs was sitting in the back garden with an ice-cold lager in his hand. Having settled their son down for the night, the Englishman and his wife, Angélique, were enjoying a rare moment of uninterrupted relaxation, although Jack could sense that a torrent of questions about the new commissioner were on the tip of his spouse's tongue. He waited and, sure enough, ten minutes later the probing began.

"Is she married?"

The red-headed detective swallowed a mouthful of beer and considered the answer. "I have no idea. Probably."

"Why do you say probably?" Angelique pressed.

"Well, I'd guess that Audrey Rancourt is in her mid-fifties, so I imagine she's married. You're itching to see her, aren't you? I can tell!"

"Of course! It's only natural to be curious about your new 'big boss'."

Hobbs licked his lips and reached for the bowl of peanuts on the outdoor table. At least now, after weeks of speculation, they knew who it was filling Commissioner Ozanne's boots.

"Just promise me you're not going to try to match-make with Max."

His wife laughed, throwing her head back and chuckling loudly. "No, I have no intention of fixing Max up with an older woman. Look what happened last time, with Vanessa Chirac. He needs to find a woman his own age, or younger."

Jack raised an eyebrow. "Don't tell me, you have just the woman in mind."

Angélique's lips formed a tight line, but her eyes sparkled.

"No, but I'm sure I'll find one."

Jack cast his mind over the unattached women in the village. Apart from the gift shop owner, Dominique Fabre, who was bordering sixty, he couldn't think of a single female who met the criteria. He looked at his wife, bewildered.

"Where? This place isn't exactly teeming with single women, or are you planning to sign him up to an internet dating site?"

"There are one or two women who come into the village for coffee sometimes, to Maurice's, and they're always alone."

Jack Hobbs flipped the cap off a second bottle and shook his head. "Max is meeting Maurice for a drink in the city tonight. Maybe they'll both get lucky, who knows?"

Angélique shook her head. "Quoting my funny English mother-in-law, that's a recipe for disaster."

Doctor Brijesh Singh adjusted the stethoscope around his neck and drew back the flimsy cotton curtains on his patient, simultaneously telling the duty nurse to phone through to the x-ray department. The young teenager on the gurney grinned as the effect of the gas took hold, easing both the pain of his broken fibula and the concerned looks on his parents' faces. A few moments later, the doctor was moving on to his next casualty. Since the start of his shift at six, there hadn't been a moment to just sit and relax and Singh was running out of steam.

Brijesh consulted the chart of the elderly man in the next cubicle and stifled a yawn. Having worked a full week on his regular shift, the doctor was now having to cover for a colleague who had called in sick with the flu, and he was beginning to feel the toll on his body. On any other Saturday night, Doctor Singh would either be playing badminton with his ten-year-old son, or having dinner with his family at a pizza restaurant. Now, stuck in the Accident and Emergency Department until midnight, the medic had visions of himself spending most of Sunday in bed. Taking a deep breath to clear his mind, Brijesh pulled back the curtain and greeted his next case with a broad smile.

Meanwhile, Max Mallery and Maurice Fabron had moved on to a sports bar and were chatting in French whilst drinking beer and eating fried chicken. A game of football aired on the huge screen above their heads and the lively bar crowd cheered loudly when the one of the Bordeaux strikers scored against rivals Saint Étienne.

"How long is it since you came out for a drink in Bordeaux?" Max shouted over the roar. "Must be a while."

Maurice nodded and pretended to count the years on his fingers. "Yes, you could say that. I usually just stay home to keep Telo company, or drink at the bistro in Saint Margaux."

The boulangerie owner fiddled with a beer mat, thinking.

"Do you mind me asking…" Mallery began.

The detective could see from the expression on his friend's face that Maurice knew exactly what was coming.

"You're wondering if I've dated anyone, since my wife," he said simply.

Max nodded. "Yes, I know it must be hard…"

Fabron shook his head and sipped at his dark, malty beer. "Not really. I loved my wife unconditionally, but it's been a long time since she passed away. Of course, you know that I used to be close to Simone Dupuis."

Mallery traced a finger around his glass, recalling the murder of Cecile Vidal a couple of summer's before when he had been new to the area. He found it easy to recall Madam Dupuis, the flower shop owner who had duped them all, including her closest friends. Max chose his next words carefully.

"But you haven't met anyone special since?"

Fabron turned the question over in his mind for a while. It was a subject that he often contemplated, especially lying alone at night in his king-sized bed at the grand *maison du maître*.

"I'm open to a new relationship," he said honestly, looking Max in the eye, "but what about you? You're only a couple of years younger than me and still no family of your own."

Mallery drained his glass and gestured to the waiter for two refills.

"You know my track record, Maurice," he sighed, "but I'm actually more than ready to settle down if the right woman comes along."

Raucous laughter caused the two men to look towards the door as it swung open to admit half a dozen giggling middle-aged women, who were tottering towards the bar in high heels. The youngest of the group, a dark-haired woman in her early thirties, wore a banner over a tight-fitting pink dress, announcing that she was the 'Bride to Be.' As the ladies searched for seats and ordered bottles of sparkling wine, Max and Maurice registered that the place was now packed and moved along the bar in order to create room to accommodate the group.

"*Merci*," a bleached blonde cooed at Maurice, as she slid her ample form onto a bar stool next to him, her auburn friend honing-in on Max and flashing him a broad grin. The inspector flushed pink under the attention.

"It could be a long night," Maurice told his friend. "I think she'll eat you alive!"

Max tutted and rolled his eyes dramatically. "I don't like your chances, either."

A few minutes later, the two men had been urged into conversation with the hen party and found themselves the objects of much admiration amongst the apparent divorcees. Both men agreed that the sudden onslaught of females was a welcome distraction from their nonexistent love lives, but the fad was short-lived, causing them to make their excuses and leave. At ten o'clock, the appointed hour that Telo Fabron had driven back to Bordeaux to collect his father, the pair stood on the pavement saying their farewells.

"Will you drive over tomorrow for lunch?" Maurice asked. "I will do a roast on the barbecue."

"I'm officially on duty again," Max replied, turning down his mouth in mock disappointment, "but as long as there are no urgent disasters, I'll come over for an hour or two. Thanks."

He waved at Telo who was sitting patiently in the van and watched as Fabron climbed into the passenger seat, his heart swelling with pride that he had found such an amazing circle of friends since relocating from Paris.

It was only on his walk home minutes later that Inspector Max Mallery noticed three recent missed calls on his phone.

***

An hour earlier, Doctor Brijesh Singh had heard the ambulance siren. Not long after, the emergency department doors flew open to admit paramedics running alongside a metal trolley on which lay a large, muscular man in obvious distress. Dr Singh instructed one of the duty nurses to take over the removal of splinters in an old woman's hand and made his way towards the registration desk.

"What do we have?"

"A thirty-nine year-old gentleman named Raymond Verdin," the lead paramedic said rapidly, steering the gurney into the only empty cubicle. "He appears to be having some sort of fit, although there's no medical history of seizures."

Doctor Singh drew the curtains across and pressed his fingers to the man's pulse. An oxygen mask had been placed over Monsieur Verdin's mouth, but Brijesh could see that the man was having severe respiratory failure.

"Doctor, his heart rate is really erratic," the medic continued, "it was highly elevated when we arrived at his home, but now it's slowed to just thirty beats per minute."

Doctor Singh nodded and raised his voice. "Nurse, hook up the ventilator."

Raymond Verdin began to tremble, his muscles spasming involuntarily as he jerked under the blanket covering the lower part of his body, a white foam beginning to froth on his lips.

"Help me to turn him!" Brijesh shouted, dipping his head to look at the patient's pupils. "Raymond, can you hear me?"

Singh frowned. He could smell the distinct aroma of herbs and recalled the same parsley tang having touched his senses the day before, when a dying Edwina Butler had been brought into the hospital with epilepsy.

"I don't think this is a fit," he announced, "I think this man has been poisoned."

Max dialled police headquarters, wondering if he should risk driving if the case required him to travel outside the city. He briefly contemplated stopping for a kebab, at least that might absorb some of the wine and beer that was in his system but, after speaking to the duty officer, he decided that time was of the essence. This sounded urgent.

Hailing a taxi and directing the driver towards the local hospital, Max pulled out a filtered cigarette. He figured that the smell of nicotine might at least mask the odour of the ale that he had imbibed over the last three hours, and it might also sober him up slightly. Although not drunk, the inspector's responses might be compromised somewhat. Walking towards the Accident and Emergency Department, Mallery showed his identity card to the young receptionist and followed her through to a large open-plan area where sections had been curtained off.

"Doctor Singh is in the office, just there," the woman told him.

Inspector Mallery tapped at the door, looking through the glass at the bearded Sikh pacing the room inside. He wore a tightly-wound blue turban and had his eyes fixed on a spot on the ceiling.

"*Inspecteur Mallery?*" the medic asked, snatching open the door as soon as he heard the knock.

Max answered in the affirmative and eyed a full coffee pot on the edge of the doctor's desk.

"*Entrez, s'il vous plaît,*" Singh sighed. "*Café?*"

Ten minutes later, the severity of the case had sobered Max up considerably.

If Brijesh Singh's instincts were right, Raymond Verdin had been poisoned. Having suffered terrible muscle spasms and constriction to his lungs, the hospital orderly now lay dead in the basement mortuary. There had been little the medical team could do in their attempts to save the man's life. They simply hadn't known what was harming him and therefore couldn't hazard a guess at an antidote. Doctor Singh had felt utterly helpless.

Mallery listened intently, sipping the thick dark coffee as he made notes.

"What do we know about Monsieur Verdin?" he queried.

Singh pulled a file closer and flicked the cover open. "He worked at the private sanatorium between Saint Margaux and Riberon. Do you know it?"

Max shook his head. "No, can't say I do." He rubbed his fingers through his hair, thinking. "You say you have no idea what could have poisoned him?"

The doctor didn't answer straight away but averted his eyes and glanced up at the ceiling again before answering.

"Look, this might just be a complete coincidence, but a woman was brought in yesterday afternoon. She was a patient at the same hospital and was taking medication to prevent epileptic seizures. It's just…"

"What?" Max shuffled in his seat, waiting.

"Well, I noticed a strange smell on the woman's breath, something herby, like parsley or celery, and Raymond Verdin's mouth emitted the same odour."

"Her name?"

"Edwina Butler."

"Sounds English, was she?"

"I believe so, yes."

The inspector frowned. "But you called the coroner yesterday, right?"

"That's just the thing, Inspector Mallery. Coroner Theron is on vacation until Monday and the man standing in for him brushed it off as SUDEP. He said there was absolutely no need to conduct an autopsy on such a case."

"SUDEP?"

"Sudden Unexplained Death from Epilepsy."

"Right, and is that common in your experience?"

Brijesh rubbed his forehead. "No, Inspector, it isn't. Of course, I learned about it at university, but I've never actually seen a case of it myself. In fact, neither have any of my colleagues here."

Max clicked the top of his pen and bit down on it. "So you're not convinced that this woman's death was caused by epilepsy?"

"Edwina Butler was taking a drug called Clonazepam, to prevent fits, and she hadn't had an episode for years. The poor lady had suffered a stroke, but as far as epilepsy was concerned, the drug was just a precaution."

"So, what are you saying, Doctor?"

"I just find it too much of a coincidence that two people connected to the same facility turn up here and die within minutes of arrival, both foaming at the mouth and both smelling of a strange herb."

"What about Verdin's medical history?"

Brijesh shook his head. "That man was fitter than me, Inspector."

Max's fingers were worrying the curls at his temple, an unconscious habit when he was anxious, or deep in thought. "I must say it's unusual for the city coroner not to want to take a look. Who was on duty?"

Singh opened his desk drawer and consulted another set of notes. "Coroner Jean Blachet, he's from Aurillac."

Mallery made a note of the name and raised his eyes to meet those of the medic. "I guess I'd better take a quick look at Raymond Verdin, if you've got time."

Doctor Singh finished the dregs of his coffee and stood. "I'm on shift until midnight, but things have calmed down so I'm sure the staff can cope."

"Lead the way," Max answered, opening the door.

Taking the steps down to the basement at a steady pace, the two walked in silence, each lost in their own thoughts, both trying to work out a scenario where two people connected to one place could be poisoned in two completely unrelated incidents. It wasn't as though they had been eating dinner together on the same night.

The mortuary was cold and airless, the temperature kept at a consistent low level. On one side of the room, a row of metal doors housed the dead, whilst in the centre of the room the recently departed Raymond Verdin lay on a trolley, his body covered with a green sheet, a cardboard tag attached to his big toe.

Brijesh pulled back the coverlet and stood back.

"I took a swab of his mouth after death," he told Max, "exactly the same as I did with Madam Butler yesterday. It's just a hunch but there's something odd about both deaths. I'll get the samples sent over to the lab first thing on Monday morning."

"His mouth," Mallery observed, "almost like he was laughing… Is this normal?"

"Risus sardonicus," the medic confirmed, "it's caused by a spasm of the facial muscles in death. This is usual at the final stage, when the victim is struggling to breathe."

"But you have no way of confirming whether both Butler and Verdin were poisoned?"

Singh tilted his head. "Not yet, but I'm hoping that when Coroner Theron returns to work, he'll order full autopsies on both."

Max leaned over the corpse of Ray Verdin, wrinkling his nose. "I smell it. You're right, it is something like parsley. Any idea what type of plant could be so toxic? And how it might be used?"

Brijesh considered the question, stroking his long beard.

"No, not at all, sorry."

***

Inspector Mallery consulted the calendar in his phone, checking that he had the right shift rota, before dialling Officer Jacques Gibault's number.

"*Inspecteur?*" the young recruit answered eagerly on the second ring. "*Quoi de neuf?*"

Max could hear the sound of late-night city traffic as he explained his plight to the patrol officer, having to raise his voice to be heard over the hubbub.

"*Nous sommes en route*," Jacques assured him.

Mallery stood at the hospital main entrance smoking his second cigarette of the night as he waited for Officer Gibault and his colleague to arrive. It wasn't standard protocol to phone a police officer on duty, normally dispatch would have come to Mallery's aid, but he wanted someone astute and familiar to help him tonight and, in his opinion, Jacques Gibault had great potential to make the grade as detective. It would most likely take the officers ten minutes to arrive and another fifteen to get to Riberon; Max just hoped that they weren't too late.

Raymond Verdin lived in a modest two-bedroomed semi-detached house with his wife and teenage daughter. Most of the lights in Riberon village were turned off as the patrol car approached the orderly's home, as streetlamps were few and far between. In the Verdin household, however, bulbs burned brightly as Chloe Verdin waited patiently for news. As soon as she caught sight of the marked vehicle, the front door was pulled open and a distressed middle-aged woman ran outside, tears streaming down her face.

"*Non, non, non!*" she cried, staggering on unstable feet, realising that the three officers came bearing tragic news.

Mallery took Chloe Verdin in his arms and walked her back inside, glancing upwards to where fourteen-year-old Elise sat at the top of the stairs.

Having instructed Gibault's colleague to make a pot of tea, the inspector settled the woman on the sofa and called her daughter to come downstairs.

"I am so very sorry for your loss," he said solemnly, as soon as the sobbing subsided, "but I will do everything in my power to find out what happened to your husband."

"He was fine up until half past eight," Chloe Verdin stammered, clutching her daughter tightly. "I just can't believe that my Ray is dead."

"Madam Verdin, this might sound like an unusual question, but what did your husband have to eat this evening?"

Jacques Gibault was poised with his notebook and Max nodded his approval, pleased that the young officer had take the initiative to allow Mallery to interview the family without the encumbrance of having to write things down.

Chloe Verdin looked at Elise before responding, "Why, was it food poisoning?"

"We are just trying to rule it out, at the moment," Max explained. "Did you all eat the same meals today?"

"Yes, we had chicken on the barbecue, with salad," Elise offered, holding her mother's hand. "Papa cooked it."

She could see the police inspector gathering his thoughts and wiped away a tear.

"I don't suppose there is anything left?" Max queried.

"My Ray was a big man, Inspector Mallery," Chloe replied quietly, "there was never anything left over."

"Did you notice your husband, your Papa," he continued, looking from mother to daughter, "eating or drinking anything else at all, perhaps something that you didn't eat? A dessert, a beer?"

Madam Verdin shook her head. "No, we shared a bottle of wine. Elise?"

A look of confusion came over the teenager's face just then, as though realisation had dawned. "The cake!"

Mallery was on the edge of his seat. "What cake?"

Chloe Verdin was on her feet and, rushing to the kitchen, pulling the refrigerator door wide. "Here, it's still wrapped in foil."

The officers watched as the housewife lifted a silver parcel from the shelf and placed it in the centre of the kitchen table.

"Ray cut a piece off this and ate it just as we were finishing clearing up. Elise and I said we'd wait until later to try it, but my Ray, well, he never could resist chocolate gateau."

"And this is the only thing he ate that you didn't?" Max reiterated.

Mother and daughter were nodding, all eyes on the offending package.

Mallery gestured to the younger officer who stood idly waiting for instructions. "Get an evidence bag, please, Marcel."

Closing the door on the fridge, Mallery slid a finger under the lip of the foil and sniffed. Could he really smell parsley in the chocolate sponge, or was it just his senses working overtime?

"Madam Verdin, where did this come from? Did you make it?"

"Ray brought it home from work last night. There had been a party to celebrate one of the patient's birthdays, you see."

Finally, the connection.

"Madam Verdin, has your husband ever mentioned the name Edwina Butler?"

"Yes, Inspector. She died on Friday. Ray was devastated about it, such a lovely lady, he said."

Max's thoughts were racing ten to the dozen. What if the cake really had been poisoned? How many other people were likely to end up with food poisoning?

"Madam Verdin, this is very important. Do you have any idea how many people attended the party? Or how big the original cake was?"

Chloe looked confused, her mouth tightening into a tight line. "Well no, not really, there are about thirty residents and ten staff, I think. Usually, when one of them had a birthday Monsieur Cassel makes a real fuss, putting balloons up and arranging afternoon tea for them all."

"Monsieur Cassel?"

"Leon Cassel, he's the manager."

Jacques Gibault's pen could be heard scratching the paper as he made a note of the name, allowing Max time to consider his next move.

"Thank you, Madam Verdin, Elise," he said eventually, stepping into the narrow hallway, "I'll be in touch soon."

As the trio walked back towards the patrol car, Mallery weighed up his options. Was there a case of death by poisoning to be reported here? Or had Doctor Singh been overreacting? The only man to give them their answer was Coroner Paul Theron.

"Well," he announced brightly, "there's not much else we can do here, tonight. Any chance of a lift home?"

English nurse Fran Shepherd was enjoying a Sunday cycle ride in the countryside surrounding Riberon in the hope of finding a cottage or, failing that, a room to rent. Her position at the private hospital was to be made permanent and she couldn't be happier. This was what she needed, Fran told herself, breathing in the scent of wildflowers and fresh grasses; a new life away from old friends and bad memories.

A couple of miles down the winding lane, the nurse pricked up her ears as the melodic sounds of singing from the Saint Augustin monastery floated towards her. A little further, she reached a narrow bridge straddling a river and stopped to check that no traffic was coming in the opposite direction. From her vantage point on the curve of the elevated bridge, Fran could see the church of Saint Margaux, a huge, light grey structure with immaculate grounds.

Pulling her bicycle onto the verge and leaning it against the fence, Fran climbed the stile and found a spot on the riverbank to rest her legs. Anticipating a long trip that morning, the Englishwoman had packed some snacks and a bottle of fizzy water but craved the caffeine hit of a strong coffee. After a few minutes, Fran mounted her bike once more and headed for the village bakery, hoping above all else that the place would be open.

Maurice Fabron was just locking the front door of the boulangerie, several fresh baguettes in his arms, as Fran Shepherd cycled up.

"Are you closed?" she called, quickly dismounting.

Maurice turned, curious at the spoken English, and came face to face with a tall, slender woman. She had the most beautiful green eyes he had ever seen.

"Sorry, Madame," he replied, "I do not open on Sundays." Maurice juggled the bread in explanation. "I was just picking up bread to take home."

"Oh, what a pity!" Fran smiled, showing perfect white teeth. "Never mind, I'll have to pop back another day."

"Was there something in particular you required?"

She shook her head, slightly embarrassed. "No, not really. I missed breakfast and fancied a coffee and pain au chocolat."

Monsieur Fabron slid his key back into the lock. "And so you shall have one."

"No, no, I couldn't…" Fran started, but it was too late, Maurice wasn't taking a blind bit of notice, and had left the boulangerie door open for her to follow.

"They were made yesterday," he told her, as she entered the dark interior, "but still delicious. Take a seat."

An overhead light blinked and came on, illuminating the quaint interior of the shop. Fran pulled out a chair and sat down, feeling slightly embarrassed.

"Monsieur, I, erm… I really didn't mean to inconvenience you."

Maurice studied the slender neck and the way that the woman's neat dark bob ended exactly in line with her jaw.

He switched on the coffee machine and glanced at the clock. "I have another half hour before church service, so why not spend it having a coffee?"

Fran blushed. She calculated that the baker must be ten or twelve years her senior, but he was handsome and charming, exactly what she imagined in a Frenchman that might wish to sweep her off her feet.

"Do you attend church?" Maurice was asking.

Fran could feel her cheeks turning pink again under his scrutiny. The magnetism between the pair was electric. "No, I'm afraid I'm not very religious."

"Neither am I," the Frenchman confessed, "but my son likes to go, and I find it helps to clear my mind. Besides, the communion wine is delicious!"

"Is it local?"

"Of course!" Maurice chuckled. "It is provided by Vidals' Vineyard in the village."

A steaming cup of coffee accompanied by a jug of cream and a sugar bowl were placed down on the table, together with the chocolate pastry which appeared to be perfectly shiny and crisp.

"Wow, thank you so much," Fran enthused. "Are you joining me?"

Fabron lifted his own cup and saucer. "I was waiting for an invitation."

The nurse pushed out the chair next to her, a move that even she felt stepped over her own personal boundaries. "I'm Fran, lovely to meet you."

Leo Cassel turned the cup around on its saucer, causing the bone china to squeak. "This is really tragic news, Inspector. Raymond Verdin was a greatly valued member of staff, his professionalism was second to none."

Max Mallery listened, wondering whether the hospital manager had ever actually said those words to the deceased in his time working there. He decided to move the conversation along.

"The reason that I came in person, rather than phoning, is that the duty doctor seemed to think there could be a connection between his death and that of a patient who died on Friday, Edwina Butler."

Cassel appeared horrified at the suggestion and his face paled. "That can't be! Madam Butler had a seizure, an epileptic fit."

"Unfortunately, Raymond Verdin was admitted to hospital with the very same symptoms," Max explained, taking a sip of the lukewarm tea. "What I need to know is, did Edwina Butler eat any of the cake at the party?"

"No, she didn't come down. It was Enzo Roche's birthday, you see, and he refused to cut the cake before Edwina arrived, they were very close friends. Anyway, Nurse Shepherd went upstairs to get Edwina and found her collapsed in her room."

Mallery was making notes and stopped. "I'll need the names of everyone who attended the party, please."

"Of course, I'll get my secretary to draw up a list."

"Has anyone else been taken ill? Perhaps with food poisoning?"

Leon shook his head, thinking. "No, everyone else is fine."

"If Doctor Singh is correct in his findings, we'll need to know who ate a slice of the chocolate cake and if there's anything left, I'll need to confiscate it."

"Wait," Cassel said abruptly, narrowing his eyes, "you said chocolate cake."

"Yes, I did why?"

"Enzo Roche's birthday cake was most definitely a vanilla sponge."

Climbing back into his car, Max Mallery was perplexed. According to Leon Cassel, the description of Roche's cake didn't match that of the one found in Verdin's refrigerator, nor did he know where it could have come from. At least now it was safely at the laboratory and marked for Roberto Mazzo's attention first thing Monday morning.

To the right of the driveway, a large, immaculate lawn spread to the boundaries, where rose bushes, rhododendrons and dahlias were in bloom. A smartly dressed group of people were playing boules, congratulating each other every time the shot rolled close to the jack. Max watched the scene thinking that, apart from their clothing, it looked more like a scene from a period drama than Sunday morning at a private hospital facility.

On arrival, he had asked Cassel about the people who stayed here, some of whom had been admitted years ago, and the various reasons for their ongoing treatment. The manager had replied honestly, in the detective's opinion, and explained that many had nowhere else to go and others were on the long road to recovery after mental and physical breakdowns.

The detective cast his mind back to the conversation with Brijesh Singh the previous night. The clinician was adamant that both Butler and Verdin had been poisoned by the same method, although the doctor had openly admitted that he had no clue as to the specific toxin. Max concluded that there was little he could do right at that moment, especially as Leon Cassel had insisted that the cake in question was vanilla sponge and definitely not chocolate. There was also the fact that the hospital manager could find no evidence that Edwina Butler had eaten anything at all that fateful afternoon.

"Leave it until tomorrow," Max told himself wearily. "Paul Theron will have all the answers we need in the morning."

Starting the engine, Mallery checked his watch. It was too early to arrive at Maurice's for lunch but, on the other hand, not worth driving back into Bordeaux just to return in an hour. At a guess, both Maurice and Telo would be on their way to church right now. He put down the automatic soft-top roof and looked up at the clear blue sky; a walk around Saint Margaux would do him some good.

*****

"I'm so sorry that we have to cut our conversation short," Maurice Fabron was telling Fran in English. "It's just that we French like our routine and Sunday service is one of the things that I never miss."

The young woman tilted her head, blinking in the sun as they stepped out through the boulangerie doors. "It's quite alright. It was very kind of you to provide my breakfast, I feel so much better now."

"And the apartment upstairs?" Maurice prompted as he turned the key.

"I'm sure it will be perfect, Monsieur Fabron."

"Maurice, please. So, you will come back to take a look?"

Although Fran hesitated for a second, her indecision was lost on the baker, whose heart was beginning to miss a beat as he looked at the striking woman.

"How about I come over tomorrow after work?" Fran heard herself saying. "I can be here by six-thirty."

The smile reached Fabron's eyes. "Perfect."

As Fran Shepherd collected her bicycle and prepared for the gentle ride back to Riberon, the roar of an engine caused her to look up. A red sports car was pulling into the village square, a dashingly handsome man at the wheel.

Goodness me, she thought, her lips quirking in a smile, *it really is true that France is full of good-looking men!*

A second later, Maurice Fabron was waving to the driver and beckoning Fran to follow him.

"This is my dear friend Max, he's our Police Inspector. Max, meet Fran."

Mallery closed the car door and lifted his sunglasses onto the top of his head, ears pricking up as he noted Maurice was speaking in English.

"*Bonjour, Madame*," he grinned, "Or should I say good morning?"

"*Bonjour,* Inspector."

Fran held out a hand, intending for it to be shaken, but Max lifted the fingers to his lips. "*Enchanté.*"

Maurice coughed, breaking the silence. "Fran was just heading home. She's thinking about renting the apartment above the boulangerie."

"So, we'll be seeing more of you?" Max retorted cheekily.

"Let's see. Perhaps..." The nurse smiled, mounting her bicycle. "Lovely to meet you. See you tomorrow, Maurice."

With a quick farewell wave, Fran was gone, disappearing into the greenery of the lanes just as unexpectedly as she had appeared.

"You're a sly one, Maurice," the detective laughed, giving his friend a hug, "she's stunning."

The boulangerie owner was standing proud as a peacock, but he was giving nothing away. "I'm also going to be late for church. Are you coming?"

Mallery reached inside the car for his lightweight linen jacket. "I have nothing else planned, so I might as well. It doesn't look as though Fran wants to keep me company while you go and confess your sins, does it?"

Maurice laughed. "She's a nurse working twelve-hour shifts and is no doubt desperate to enjoy her day off."

Max turned his head, just managing to catch sight of the dark-haired cyclist disappearing from view. "Where? In Bordeaux?"

"No, at the private hospital in Riberon."

Fran Shepherd arrived back her cottage fifteen minutes later, having cycled at a leisurely pace to allow the coffee and pastry to settle. As she steered her bike around the side and into the small garden shed, the nurse looked at the quaint, century-old building. She'd been happy here over the past six months, but the rent was rather expensive for a single person and, being someone who rather enjoyed their own space, Fran didn't feel the urge to look for a lodger to occupy the spare bedroom.

Entering the kitchen and laying her bag on one of the pine chairs, the young nurse reached for the kettle and filled it. A second coffee was in order, but no doubt it wouldn't be half as delicious as the one recently served up by Maurice Fabron. While she waited for the appliance to boil, Fran cast her mind back to the events of that morning.

Monsieur Fabron was a real catch. Not only was he handsome and funny, but she had felt a real sincerity in his words, as though he was truly interested in her babbling conversation. And babbling it had been, Fran reflected. In her eagerness to get to know the boulangerie owner, the nurse had inadvertently poured out her life story within fifteen minutes of idle chatter. Well, not all of it. She sighed, looking at the opened letter on the kitchen table. At least she hadn't poured out her heart about her devastating recent romantic failure.

And then there had been Max, the police inspector, Fran reminisced, glancing at the tips of her fingers where the dashing, curly-haired Frenchman had brushed his lips against them.

"Damn," Fran giggled, reaching for a mug, "I forgot to check whether either of them was wearing a wedding ring!"

Maurice, Telo and Max had been back from church just twenty minutes before the doorbell rang on the Fabrons' *maison du maître*. Despite Angélique Hobbs insisting on attending the local church most Sundays, her husband couldn't be tempted and had stayed at home playing with their son and getting young Tom ready for lunch at their friend's.

It wasn't long before laughter could be heard coming from the rear garden, and glasses clinked together as Telo ferried plates of delicious food to the trestle table under his father's instructions.

"I'm sorry, everyone," Maurice apologised, carrying a large joint of ham and placing it centre stage, "it's a cold lunch today, but there's plenty of salad, bread, and pickles. Please, help yourselves."

"This looks amazing, as always," Angélique gushed, eyeing the array of dishes in front of them. "I don't know how you do it, Maurice."

"He cooks for us more often than you do," Jack quipped, gasping as he received a slap on the leg from his miffed wife. "Ouch."

"Cheeky!" She frowned. "At least I try."

Hobbs passed around a dish of warm potato salad and wondered what his mother would make of this. Every Sunday without fail, no matter the weather outside, Jean Hobbs would serve up a full roast with three vegetables and the largest Yorkshire puddings her son had ever seen. Jack let the moment pass, promising himself that a trip back to Yorkshire was on the horizon.

Clearing up the plates a while later, as was their general ritual whenever Maurice had hosted, Max stood with his hands in the sink while Jack dried up the crockery. As Mallery related the events of the past twenty-four hours to his colleague, a look of concern began to show on the Englishman's face.

"So, this Doctor Singh... How sure is he that both of them were poisoned?"

"Well, to be honest, without a toxicology report, it's not definite, but he's an experienced medic. Besides, the hospital orderly, Raymond Verdin, had no history of fits and he was the only one at home that had eaten some cake."

"It sounds dodgy to me," Jack agreed, putting down the tea towel, "but why hasn't Paul Theron ordered an autopsy?"

"That's just it, Jacques. Paul's been on vacation in Portugal for the past week and his... erm, how to say... stand-in?"

Hobbs nodded.

"Well, he said he didn't think there was any need for concern, but Singh's personal opinion was that the man was more interested in getting home."

"So, he's not a local coroner?"

"No, but he's not so far away. I checked and he lives in Aurillac. It's about a three and a half hour drive, or two hours in my car."

Hobbs stifled a laugh, remembering the last time he'd been a passenger in Max's BMW. They'd taken some of the country lane bends so sharply that he'd ended up holding on to the seat with both hands for most of the journey. He could well imagine his boss cutting the journey time to Aurillac in half.

"I guess we'll be paying Paul a visit in the morning then," he replied, after some reflection, "but it's not a great start to his first day back at work."

"No, but better we check out both deaths, *non*? I have a feeling that there's more to it than food poisoning."

"What makes you say that?"

Mallery shrugged and tapped his nose. "That's for you to know and me to find out, my friend."

Hobbs grinned. It wasn't the first time Max had got his English sayings mixed up and it was a part of the reason why they got along so well. The odd blast of humour in their line of work was essential.

"What's taking you two so long?" Maurice asked, as he entered through the patio doors and made for the huge fridge. "Gossiping?"

"Thanks for reminding me," Max answered, winking at his friend, "I almost forgot to tell Jacques about your new lady."

Fabron clicked his tongue and leaned into the appliance, selecting a bottle of chilled wine. "There's nothing to tell, Max, and you know it."

Mallery was undeterred, enjoying the topic far too much to let go now. "Even though you're seeing her again tomorrow?"

When Maurice pulled his head out of the chiller, his face was quite flustered, despite the low temperature. "She's coming to look at the flat over the shop, that's all. Will you stop trying to play matchmaker, Max?"

"But you do like her?" Jack ventured.

Fabron gave in, resigned to the banter. "Yes, I think I do."

Leon Cassel was sitting at his desk with a rather grim look on his face. Having checked the list of names against those in the patient register and a second list of the staff, he was finally satisfied that nobody had been missed and began drafting an email to the police inspector. In all his years at the facility, Leon had never found himself questioned by a detective before, and certainly not over the demise of two people in his care. The large man took his responsibilities very seriously and was appalled that the circumstances under which both deaths were now to be scrutinised very closely.

Leon thought back to Friday afternoon, retracing his every move and comment as best as he could recall, but could find no reason for anyone to have poisoned dear old sweet Edwina Butler. Given, the sixty-year-old was eccentric and frail, but she wouldn't harm a fly, certainly not since the stroke had left her partially paralysed.

And then there was Raymond, the gentle giant who would have given his right arm just to help someone in their hour of need. Surely the inspector must have been mistaken, the duty doctor too! There had been mention of a chocolate cake, so no doubt the kitchen staff would come under scrutiny.

49

Perhaps the detective was getting ahead of himself, Leon pondered, staring at the hastily written email; maybe this Max Mallery had jumped on the deaths as a means of looking proactive when he had little else on his plate.

Monsieur Cassell pressed the 'send' button and straightened his tie. He would have to gather the staff for a meeting and inform them of Ray's death. For now, at least, he would put it down to a seizure, although goodness only knew how long it might be before the grapevine started saying otherwise. Perhaps it might be wise to ask Juliette Lafoy to come in, brief her on the deaths and ask advice on how best to break the news to the rest of the staff and patients. Some of the people under their care were highly strung, others dependent upon mood-altering medication, so a careful approach was needed to avoid hysteria.

Leon flicked through his black book of staff contact numbers and dialled the psychiatrist.

Juliette Lafoy was sitting on her small terrace with a murder mystery, a large glass of white wine on the table at her side. As her mobile trilled loudly, the woman scanned the last few sentences of her novel, determined to reach the end of the page before turning her focus to the unwelcome interruption.

"*Oui?*" she answered abruptly, searching the seat underneath her for the bookmark that had gone astray. "Juliette Lafoy."

The doctor bristled on hearing her employer's voice, expecting some pathetic excuse as to why Cassell might be calling on a Sunday – a dinner invitation perhaps, or the ruse of trying to locate an errant patient file. Within minutes, however, Juliette's demeanour had changed significantly, turning to one of alarm as she listened to the intimate details surrounding Monsieur Verdin's death.

"As you can imagine," Leon continued, "I think it imperative that you and I get together at your earliest convenience, to discuss how to handle the situation."

Doctor Lafoy crinkled her brow. "But surely Raymond's death was natural? There's nothing to suggest otherwise, is there?"

"I'm afraid there is," the manager explained steadily. "Both the duty doctor and Inspector Mallery seem to think it might be a case of poisoning. Of course we will have to wait for the coroner's verdict, but nevertheless…"

"I see," Juliette whispered, eyeing her glass of wine. "I'll come at once."

Up in his spacious bedroom, Enzo Roche was sitting quietly at the open window staring at the gently swaying trees beyond. Tchaikovsky's *Waltz of the Flowers* from *The Nutcracker* played in the background, giving the room a far more jovial ambience than its occupant felt. Enzo's red-rimmed eyes moved upwards, momentarily fixing on a buzzing hornet on the sill, the creature's yellow and black striped body reminding him of a dress that dear Edwina had always worn on Sundays. How he missed the mild-mannered woman already.

Fresh tears began to well up, causing Enzo to reach for a box of tissues. As he did so, the dancer's gaze moved to the walls above his bed. There, in glorious colour, were posters from his heyday, the time before the accident. Clad in long leather hose and the shimmering silver sequined costume of his stage character, the Mouse King, Roche looked both elegant and poised, his handsome dark features and slight frame suiting the role to perfection.

To the left of the stage stood the heroine, Clara. Enzo studied the pale white face of Marianne Ogier, statuesque and exquisite in her leading role, and wondered where she was now. Once a force to be reckoned with, the duo had been inseparable, joined together by the passion of their trade. These days, however, weeks would pass without communication, Marianne too busy following her dream to spend time with her newly crippled friend.

Enzo climbed up onto the bed, his injured leg causing both hindrance and pain as he tried to balance and steady himself, fingers desperate to remove the framed pictures from their hooks. Sweat began to trickle down the former *danseur's* neck, such was the exertion required to lift the heavy artwork from its prominent place, Roche's arms trembling from the sheer weight of the task.

Finally, he sat back, exhausted, the images turned to the wall. The posters had been a cruel reminder of Enzo's achievements, his distinguished career and adoring fans, but nowadays all that had changed. He wondered how long it would be before the letters stopped coming, the notes of encouragement, the occasional bouquet and warm wishes. Just how much time did a lover of the arts need to forget their idol? Would it be just a few more months? Were they waiting patiently for Enzo's grand recovery and return to the spotlight?

Flinging himself onto the bed in anguish, Roche allowed the tears to return, his greatest fear bubbling to the surface. Would he ever be ready to return?

Luc Martin trudged up the internal stairs of police headquarters, navigating a series of empty cardboard boxes as he neared the Incident Room. A rather hot and sweaty delivery man was exiting the room with a clipboard as the techie arrived. Commissioner Audrey Rancourt stood in the centre of the room, hands on hips as though surveying a coveted cache of stolen goods.

"Bonjour, Commissaire. C'est quoi tout ça?" Luc asked, scanning the half dozen iPads and HD screen that sat prominently clustered on a desk.

Rancourt tapped her nose, smiling softly. *"Tu verras bientôt."*

Martin didn't have to wait long. Max Mallery strode into the room oozing his usual Monday morning joviality, closely followed by Detectives Dupont, Moreau and Hobbs. Rancourt couldn't wait to announce the purchases.

"Voilà," she smiled, changing to English on meeting Jack Hobbs' eye, "I am going to bring this department into the twenty-first century!"

Max inspected a silver-cased iPad and raised his eyebrows. "Interesting."

The Commissioner was in her element, picking up one of the devices to explain.

"With new technology, these will enable every one of us to update information on new and old cases, share with others, access files and have more productive meetings. Everything stored on here can be shared on the main screen."

Rancourt pointed at the HD television, smiling broadly. "Imagine not having to write up all your notes on the whiteboard. Superb, yes?"

"Incredible," Max offered, feeling cynical, "but has this used up our overtime budget for the next twelve months?"

"Well, we will obviously need to tighten up a little in other areas," his boss agreed, "but think of the speed with which we should be able to solve cases with all this at our fingertips!"

Mallery noted the use of 'we' and 'our', wondering whether Audrey Rancourt intended to be a lot more proactive than her predecessor. He looked at his watch, noting that it was now almost nine.

"Thank you, Commissioner, this is incredible. Perhaps Luc, being our computer whizz, can set everything up. I'm afraid that Jacques and I are due at the coroner's office. I also need a quick briefing with Thierry and Gabi, there was a new case in over the weekend. Okay if I catch up with you on our return?"

The steel-haired woman nodded. "Of course, I wasn't aware of any reports, so it looks as though I have some catching up of my own to do."

Rancourt turned to Luc, her eyes fixing on him in earnest. "Let's get to work, shall we?"

As Detectives Moreau, Dupont and Hobbs followed Max to his office, the new commissioner stood watching them retreat from the room, curious as to what might be more important than updating their technology.

Coroner Paul Theron was whistling as he hung up his light jacket in the office. Two weeks in Italy had worked wonders to relieve the everyday tensions of his occupation and he was now ready to return to his tasks with gusto.

Two thin grey folders sat on the top of the tray on Paul's desk, and he nimbly lifted them with interest, noting several items of unfinished paperwork underneath. He took a sharp intake of breath, wondering how much unfinished business Jean Blanchet had left in his absence. A few minutes later, a knock at the door caused a brooding Theron to lift his head from the file.

"Ah, Max, Jack, good to see you both. I take it you haven't just called in for a cup of coffee. What's up?"

The detectives entered the office and Max quickly explained about the two strange deaths that had occurred and how he felt that they were connected.

Paul nodded thoughtfully and tapped the document in front of him. "I was just reading up Edwina Butler's hospital notes. Doctor Singh has written a very detailed report on her admission to the emergency department, but that's as far as I've got so far. Do you know if he called Blanchet?"

"He did," Max verified, taking a seat, "but the coroner didn't seem to think it was worth doing an autopsy. He put it down to an epileptic seizure."

"I suppose Madam Butler did have a history of fits, albeit some years ago."

Mallery noticed the second file and lifted it up. "Take a look at this one, too. Raymond Verdin died of the same symptoms and worked at the private hospital where Edwina Butler was a patient."

"A coincidence?"

"Brijesh Singh doesn't seem to think so."

"Have you any reason to think his death was foul play?"

"Singh noticed an unusual smell on both Butler's and Verdin's breath, he said it was similar to parsley. We recovered a small quantity of chocolate cake from Raymond's home. Apparently it was the last thing he ate and the only food that neither his wife nor daughter consumed. I sent it to the lab."

Paul Theron stood, his long legs creaking slightly as he stretched them out. "Let's go and take a look at our cadavers, shall we?"

Edwina Butler lay as still as a marble statue on the steel gurney, her pale skin almost as white as the sheet that covered her. The small, bird-like features were framed by a nest of soft, greying curls, although the fixed rictus grin that had appeared close to death gave the Englishwoman a sinister mask.

Paul Theron popped a mask over his face and leaned in closer, examining the way in which the corpse's lips were pulled back over her teeth. The woman's tongue was visible, and the coroner quickly swabbed around the organ for traces of anomalies.

"Mmm, interesting…" he said, noncommittally. "Let's put Monsieur Verdin alongside her and see what similarities there are."

Jack turned to the second trolley in the room, helping Theron to guide it along on squeaking castors until it was a metre away from the first.

As the sheet was removed, Mallery gasped in shock. Paul Verdin also hosted a menacing smile, forced as though his cheeks had been injected with Botox to stop them from relaxing.

"Wow, the expression on his face at the moment he died is almost identical!"

"Rictus sardonicus," Paul explained, "very commonplace with poisons such as strychnine. The victim's lungs and airways are restricted and eventually they suffocate. A very painful and agonising death."

"Strychnine?" Hobbs muttered. "So you think this is murder?"

Theron clicked his tongue, "Well, of course I can't be certain yet, not until I examine the stomach contents, but if I were you I'd pop over to the lab and see what Roberto can tell you about that chocolate cake."

Roberto Mazzo was working with a permanent grin on his face. The recent trip to Italy and his proposal to Gabriella Dupont had boosted the Italian's morale no end. He felt that life was perfect, all the pieces slotting together like a puzzle. Marriage, children, career prospects, who knew what the future might hold, but with Gabi at his side, Roberto knew that he would be content.

Pulling a slide out from under the microscope, Mazzo turned as Max and Jack appeared in the doorway. Typical of Max, he thought, impeccable timing.

"Hey, guys," the lab technician smiled, "I guess this isn't a social call?"

"No," Mallery returned, "but congratulations on your engagement, it's fantastic news. You and Gabi are perfect for one another."

Jack Hobbs leaned forward to shake Roberto's hand. "Congrats, mate."

Max allowed his eyes to wander, fixing on the sample that Mazzo had been inspecting. "It that what I think it is?"

"Yes, this is a part of the cake that you sent us, and very interesting it is, too."

"How so?"

"It contains toxins, certainly enough to kill a person, but it's definitely not your regular poisonous substance."

"Oh? What is it then?" Jack enquired, frowning slightly.

"Well, I can't be sure yet, we need to run a few more tests to work out exactly what it is, but the compound is plant-based."

Mallery stepped forward, looking more closely at the crumbling mixture. "Seriously? Do you mean something natural?"

"Exactly that. Could be poison ivy or something. We'll know by tomorrow."

"Tomorrow? No sooner?"

"Sorry, Max, it's going to take a while to figure out. Do you know how many different species of toxic plants there are? It could even be a type of fungi."

"But someone definitely put it there with the intent to kill?"

Mazzo stroked the stubble on his chin. "Oh, yes, definitely. Whatever this is, the perpetrator mixed it into the cake alongside the flour, eggs and cocoa powder."

"*Merde*," Mallery sighed, "we'd better inform Paul Theron."

On Mallery's instructions, Gabriella Dupont had driven Thierry out to the private hospital facility in Riberon. The building was white and imposing, built in the style of a Caribbean plantation house from the nineteenth century. A long lawn stretched out in front, bordered by thick bushes and beyond that, trees both to the side and rear of the property. The Mini's tyres crunched to a halt on the gravel drive as they pulled up, causing curious glances from the few residents who sat outside enjoying the morning sunshine. A large metal sign pointed to the main entrance, announcing that the reception area lay beyond.

As they entered, Gabriella's phone sprang to life.

"It's Max," she told Thierry, turning away to answer the call.

A minute later, her pretty features now taut, Detective Dupont was updating her work partner on the latest news.

"It's poison, in the cake. We need to find the source, and quickly."

Leon Cassell was stirring cream into a cup of coffee as his secretary entered, closely followed by two strangers. The darker skinned of the two was holding out an identity card.

"Please excuse the interruption," Thierry told the manager, "but we need to speak to you as a matter of urgency."

Cassell removed the gold-rimmed spectacles from the top of his head and placed them on his nose, looking closely at the man's wallet.

"Detective Moreau," Thierry continued, "and this is my colleague, Detective Dupont. I'm afraid we have some bad news concerning the recent deaths of your patient and orderly."

"I see," Cassell replied calmly, gesturing towards the two chairs that sat on the opposite side of his desk. "Please, take a seat."

It didn't take long for Thierry and Gabriella to relay the seriousness of the situation and Cassell looked visibly shocked to find out that the two deaths were connected. He gulped a mouthful of coffee, his hand shaking slightly.

"This is terrible, just terrible. Who could do such a thing?"

Gabi glanced at Thierry, eager to move the conversation along. "Monsieur Cassell, before we can find out, we need to locate the source. Did you check with the hospital kitchen as to whether they baked a chocolate cake on Friday?"

"Yes, yes, I did, and as I told Inspector Mallery, the only cake created for the party was a vanilla sponge, which most of the residents here had a slice of."

Thierry was consulting his notes and looked up, "And this was for... erm, Enzo Roche's birthday?"

"Yes, that's right."

"Is it possible that Monsieur Roche had a second cake?" Gabriella queried. "One that wasn't shared with everyone else?"

"Well, I suppose so," the manager considered, "but I'm not aware of one."

"Perhaps we could speak to him?" Thierry offered.

"Oh, now, I'm not sure. Enzo Roche is one of our most delicate patients. He was distraught on finding out about Madam Butler's death and we haven't dared tell him about Ray Verdin yet, they were very close, you see."

"But you have told the rest of the staff and patients?"

"Yes, Doctor Lafoy and I made an announcement yesterday afternoon but Enzo refused to come out of his room, so we let him be."

"He's bound to find out eventually..." Gabi observed, watching the large man as he pushed the coffee cup to one side. "What do you suppose his reaction will be?"

Leon pressed his fingers together, thinking. "I should imagine that Monsieur Roche will be distraught, that's why Doctor Lafoy has arranged a session for this afternoon, to break the news to him privately."

"In the meantime, could we take a look around Roche's room? Just to check there are no edible items?" Thierry pressed.

"I'll see if Juliette Lafoy is available to accompany you," Leon offered, pressing a button on his phone extension. "She knows Enzo well and will be able to ensure his wellbeing."

Gabi shot a look at Thierry, wondering what kind of man Enzo Roche was and why he needed such pandering.

Despite only being a fraction shorter than Juliette Lafoy, Detective Dupont found herself having to quicken her pace to keep up with the psychiatrist as she strode out of Cassell's office and up the stairs towards patients' quarters. The doctor had given the police officers only a cursory glance as the reason for their visit was hastily explained, giving the air of one with a hectic schedule.

"I have appointments from ten onwards," she told them, checking her watch and calling back over one shoulder, "we will have to be quick."

Thierry took the steps two at a time, arriving on the landing ahead of the woman.

"We will try not to take up too much of your time," he promised. "However, we do need some answers, especially if there is a chance of contaminated cake being circulated on the premises." Moreau had purposely avoided using the word 'poison' for fear of causing alarm or being overheard by the patients.

"In here," Lafoy gestured, knocking at a door with the name *E.Roche* engraved upon it. "I'll check on him first."

After a couple of minutes of muffled conversation, the doctor reopened the door and beckoned the detectives inside. Neither was prepared for the sight that greeted them.

Enzo Roche was seated at a large dressing-table, hair pulled back off his face by an elasticated band, an array of cosmetics scattered in front of him. The man had applied a pale foundation and white powder to his face, giving both a deathly and dramatic appearance. Ever the performer, Roche was robed in a black turquoise kimono emblazoned with large cranes in mid-flight. A pair of piercing dark eyes met the visitors in the mirror's reflection.

"Enzo, these are Detectives Moreau and Dupont, they would like to ask you a few questions about Friday afternoon."

The ex-ballet dancer sniffed, patting his heavily made-up face with a tissue. "You mean the day that dear Edwina died?"

Juliette Lafoy nodded, placing a hand upon the slightly built man's arm. "Yes, that's right. They need to know if you remember Edwina eating a piece of chocolate cake."

It was as though a charge of electricity had been connected to the dancer's nervous system, so dramatic was his response.

"Why yes, of course I do, but how is that connected to her death?"

"We'll come to that in a minute," Gabi told him softly. "Monsieur Roche, do you know where your friend got the gateau from?"

Enzo blinked, a smudge of mascara appearing on his otherwise perfect features. "From me…"

Thierry looked slightly confused and looked around. "And where is it now?"

Roche pointed to a shelf near the door where an array of unopened boxes were stacked, the top one, a vibrant forest green, being tied with a lime-coloured ribbon. "In that box there."

Moreau lifted the topmost parcel and carefully lifted the lid. Inside sat a heavily iced chocolate fudge cake with what appeared to be two slices missing. Gabriella peered over her colleague's shoulder to look inside.

"Monsieur Roche, has anyone else taken a piece of this? Have you eaten it?"

With a flick of his head, Enzo sighed, waving a hand over his slender waistline. "Goodness me no, I can't bear it. I gave dear Edwina a piece, to save for her supper. Surely you're not suggesting…?"

Lafoy detected a hint of a distress in the man's tone and quickly jumped in to diffuse the situation. "No, nothing of the kind, Enzo. It just might have upset her stomach, that's all."

"Oh, I see."

"Do you happen to know where it came from? Was there a card?" Gabi pressed.

"No, sorry. I received a lot of gifts on my birthday, as I do most years. They're usually from loyal fans and close friends."

Gabi sensed that the patient was losing focus as he dwelled upon his friend's death. "Monsieur, just one more question and then we will leave you to rest. Who had the second slice?"

Enzo seemed to brighten slightly, placing a hand on his cheek. Both Thierry and Gabi noticed the red scars that seared through the man's otherwise perfect skin.

"Monsieur?" Gabi prompted.

"Why, Raymond did, that's who. He took a slice home to eat after dinner and he's perfectly alright, isn't he?"

The cautionary exchange between the detectives wasn't lost on Roche and his voice quivered as he repeated the question.

"I said, Raymond is fine, isn't he?"

Juliette Lafoy tilted her head towards the door, signalling for Gabi and Thierry to leave. "I think it's best if I take things from here," she whispered.

Carrying the pretty green box, its lid replaced for safety, Thierry led the way outside into the wide corridor. As soon as they were a few metres away, an audible cry came from Enzo Roche's room.

"Sounds as though he and Ray were close, too," Gabi commented, leading the way back downstairs to the entrance hall. "Poor Enzo must be devastated."

"Did you see the marks on his arms?" Thierry asked quietly. "Self-harm by look of it. Why was he admitted here?"

"I'm not sure, we'll have to check with Max, but if Roche has a tendency to hurt himself under pressure, it's lucky he has Doctor Lafoy to watch out for him."

"I wouldn't mind being in her care," Thierry scoffed, laughing weakly. "She's very pretty."

Gabriella tutted and pulled out the car keys. "Put that box in the boot and I'll open all the windows, we don't want to risk getting poisoned."

It was almost eleven by the time Mallery reconvened with the team, with the coffee pot brewing and a brand-new iPad sitting on every desk. Luc Martin stood proudly next to the new large screen on the wall, demonstrating how the photos of the two victims could now be brought up for them to see collectively.

"If you check your folders on the device," he explained, "everything can be updated and shared with one another without the need to use our desktops."

"Let's hope this can save us some time," Max nodded, "then we can focus on catching criminals instead of writing up reports."

"We'll still need to do that…"

"I know, Luc, it was just wishful thinking."

"Okay, boss."

"Now, let's see what we have on these new cases so far, *oui?*"

Thierry pulled out his notepad and read the information that he'd updated on the drive back from Riberon, including the fact that they'd dropped the chocolate cake off at the lab on their return to Bordeaux.

"Good, good, at least now we know that there aren't any more potential victims," Max told him, "but unfortunately it does mean that the perpetrator obviously intended to poison Enzo Roche. We need to find out why."

"I'll do a search into his background, "Luc offered. "It shouldn't be too difficult considering how famous he was in his day. Hospital records, however, might prove to be a touch more difficult."

"I'll speak to Juliette Lafoy again, see what she can tell us. They must have historical case notes on Roche."

"Great, don't forget to upload it onto the new system."

Mallery rolled his eyes, wondering how long the new gadgets would remain an obsession with their resident techie.

"What clues do we have regarding the packing of the cake?"

"There weren't any obvious clues," Gabi answered. "No card with it or shop name on the box. My guess is that it was homemade."

"And the delivery?"

Gabriella looked at Thierry. "Sorry, Max, we didn't ask."

"Well, find out. It must have been dropped off in person or by a courier."

Jack Hobbs sat dunking a digestive biscuit into his coffee and looked up. "Just a thought... if the poisoner failed this time, how do we know that Enzo Roche isn't still in danger?"

"Good point, Jacques," Max agreed. "He's going to need round-the-clock surveillance. I'll see if uniform can free up some officers."

"Do you think we have the budget?" Luc scoffed cheekily. "After all, this new equipment must have cost a fortune!"

"Don't you worry about that, I'll clear it with Commissioner Rancourt."

"Rather you than me," Jack grinned.

"Madame Rancourt hasn't yet experienced my charm," Max retorted, smiling broadly. "She'll be a pussycat, you wait and see."

A loud cough behind him caused Max to turn.

"Commissioner!" He flushed. "How long have you been there?"

"Long enough, Inspector Mallery. Would you mind stepping into my office for a few minutes?"

As Mallery followed Audrey Rancourt out of the room, stifled laughter erupted.

"Commissioner Rancourt," Mallery began, pulling out a chair opposite the slightly bemused looking Audrey, "what I said back there, I didn't mean to disrespect you."

"No offence taken," she replied steadily. "I can take office chatter as well as anyone. I just wanted an update on these two murder cases. Anything to report yet?"

Mallery's cheeks were still pink as he shared the findings with his boss, emphasising the need for extra bodies during the investigation.

Rancourt listened, watching the way in which Max spoke with fluidity and momentum as he warmed to the subject.

"And how do you plan to proceed?" she queried at last. "Time is imperative."

"I agree, Commissioner, that's why I need officers to keep watch on Enzo Roche. As soon as the lab have identified the source of the poison we'll have an idea of where to start looking. Unfortunately, that won't be until tomorrow."

"Did Madame Butler have family? I'm guessing that if she did, they were in the United Kingdom."

"An elderly brother, Arthur Butler," Max verified, "we've asked the Thames Valley police to notify him."

"Good. Well, it seems you have everything in hand. Don't let me hinder you any longer, I'm sure you want to press on."

"Thank you, I'll let you know if there's significant progress."

As Mallery got up, a smile played across Rancourt's lips. "Don't be fooled into thinking I'm a pussycat, Max, I'm most definitely not."

The inspector felt himself heating up under scrutiny. "Sorry, I don't believe for one moment that you are, Madame."

Audrey placed her hands on the desk in front of her and resumed an air of authority. "You would do well to remember it. Neither am I a pushover nor a corrupt officer, unlike my predecessor. Do I make myself clear?"

"Absolutely, good day."

"Everything alright?" Hobbs asked, turning around as soon as Max returned. "Did she slap your wrists for you?"

"No, certainly not, the commissioner simply wanted to know what is happening with the investigation."

"And she's okay with us drafting in a few more bodies?"

"Absolutely."

"Great. What now then, boss? Do you want me to come out to Riberon with you to talk to Doctor Lafoy."

Mallery considered the question for a moment, turning it over in his mind. "Do you know what, Jacques? I think it might be a good idea if I handle Juliette Lafoy by myself."

"Do you reckon she'll open up more if you're on your own?"

"Something like that, let's see, but I don't intend to count my ducks just yet."

"Chickens, Max."

"What about them?"

"The saying is 'don't count your chickens'."

The inspector shrugged his shoulders and grabbed a jacket from the back of a chair. "Whatever, my friend. Ducks, chickens, geese, no matter."

Before heading out to the sleepy village of Riberon, Max made a detour to the general hospital, intent upon finding Brijesh Singh. Driving with the soft-top of his car down, the inspector's thick brown curls ruffled in the breeze, causing Max to check himself in the rear-view mirror before getting out of the BMW. Always a stickler for an immaculate appearance, the Frenchman cursed under his breath at not having a brush to hand.

Doctor Singh was on duty, thankfully, and Mallery waited in an uncomfortable plastic chair whilst the medic finished consulting with a patient. Despite tired eyes, when Singh finally drew back the curtain, he looked jovial and upbeat.

"Inspector Mallery, good morning." Brijesh consulted his watch. "Sorry, I mean afternoon, it's gone twelve. I take it you have news?"

Following the doctor into his cramped office, Max closed the door and took a seat. "I'm afraid it's not good. Turns out you were right, both Edwina Butler and Raymond Verdin were poisoned."

Singh stroked his beard and looked thoughtful. "I see. Any idea what the substance was?"

"No, not yet. The guys at the lab are working on it but they suspect some kind of herb or plant."

"Do you think it was an intentional poisoning?"

"That's what we need to find out, but at the moment it looks as though the toxin was mixed into a chocolate cake. I'm afraid there are some sick people in the world nowadays."

"Did you mention to the coroner about the distinct smell of parsley on the victims' breath? I don't think I put it in my report," Singh queried.

"No, come to think of it, I didn't. I'll ring Theron and our chap at the lab now, it might help them to narrow down the plant."

"Well, thank you for letting me know, I appreciate it."

"I'll keep you up to date with any progress. Thanks to your vigilance we now have a murder case to solve."

The doctor swung his chair around so that he was directly facing Mallery. "Please do. I'm utterly shocked, Inspector, truly I am. Do you have any clues to go on so far?"

"Not a great deal," Max admitted, "but hopefully, staff at the private facility will help us to pinpoint when and how the cake arrived there."

"I take it they have a resident doctor of some sort?"

Mallery was nodding in the affirmative. "Yes, a psychiatrist. I'm just going out to speak to her now, a Doctor Juliette Lafoy."

"Juliette Lafoy?" Singh repeated. "Wow, that's a name I never thought I would hear again in connection to a medical centre."

Max leaned forward, hands between his knees. "You know her?"

"I know *of* her," Brijesh went on. "We were at medical college together. Juliette had a complete breakdown at the end of her second year and I haven't seen or heard from her since."

"Any idea what happened?"

"No. Of course there were rumours, the usual stuff about pressure and boyfriends, but I couldn't say for sure."

Max was alert, absorbing the information. "What was she like back then? As a person, I mean?"

Doctor Singh shrugged. "I didn't know her terribly well, we just took a few classes together. I guess you could say she liked to party, so we didn't hang out in the same social circles, due to me not drinking."

The inspector presumed that Singh meant for religious reasons and didn't press the matter further. "Was she popular?"

"Oh yes, definitely. Always the centre of attention, that one."

Mallery stood up to leave, shaking the tall man's hand. "Thank you, you've been a great help, Doctor. I'll be in touch."

The drive out to Riberon took Max straight down the highway and then through a warren of country lanes. The distinctive smell of cow parsley pervaded his nostrils as the sports car navigated narrow roads with overgrown hedgerows, reminding the police officer of the unusual aroma that Brijesh Singh had noticed on the breath of the two fatalities. Mallery couldn't imagine anything commonly found amongst the wildflowers in France being poisonous, but he was no expert and was eager to find out what Roberto Mazzo had to say on the matter.

Life at the sanatorium was continuing as normal, despite the tragic deaths over the weekend, although the inspector's gut told him to suspect everyone inside the grand facility. As he locked the BMW, Max watched a group of patients playing croquet on the lawn, their faces etched with concentration as the ball was putted through small metal hoops. He entered the reception area and immediately came face to face with a familiar figure.

"Ah, Madam Shepherd, isn't it?" He smiled, noting how smart the young woman looked in her nurse's uniform. Her neat dark hair was swept back off her face, enhancing her pretty features.

"Inspector Mallery, good afternoon."

Fran was carrying a small file which she handed to the receptionist before holding out her hand. "Good to see you again. I presume you are here to see Monsieur Cassell?"

"No, actually, I was hoping to speak to Doctor Lafoy."

"In that case, you've probably come at the perfect time." Nurse Shepherd smiled, showing slightly crooked white teeth. "She'll be on her lunch break."

"Great, does that mean she'll be in the dining room?"

Fran stifled a laugh and put a hand over her mouth. "No, the doctor prefers to take her meals outdoors. If you look out there," she told him, pointing to a bench at the far corner of the lawn, "you'll find her."

Mallery thanked the nurse and turned to go, pausing as a thought struck him. "By the way, have you moved into the apartment over the boulangerie yet?"

The Englishwoman's face dropped slightly. "Not yet. I was hoping to move in on Wednesday afternoon, when I get some time off, but... well, Ray Verdin was going to help me, he had an estate car, but now..."

Max could see tears welling up in the nurse's eyes and felt slightly guilty at having incited her grief. "I'm so sorry. Listen, let me speak to Maurice later, I'm sure he could use to the bakery van to help with your things."

Fran seemed to brighten slightly, although her eyes were still moist with genuine sorrow. "Would you?"

"Of course, leave it with me. Take care."

Watching the police inspector step outside into the sunshine, Fran felt a soft warmth envelop her. It wasn't often that you met people who were naturally kind and supportive, and now she had encountered two such men in one week.

In stark contrast to Fran Shepherd's pleasant demeanour, Juliette Lafoy scowled as Mallery's torso cast a dark shadow across the book that she was reading. A pair of glowering eyes looked up sharply, annoyed at the intrusion.

"I'm very sorry to interrupt you, Doctor Lafoy," Max smiled softly, despite the unfriendly reception, "but I wondered if you have time to answer a few questions."

The psychiatrist made a show of slowly placing a bookmark in the page and smoothing down the cover of her novel. "I'm afraid I'm due back at my office shortly, Inspector. Perhaps you could make an appointment for later in the week."

Max went on, unperturbed. "This won't take long, just a few minutes. As I'm sure you will appreciate, it's important that we speak to everyone involved in the current investigation."

"You mean the deaths of Madame Butler and Ray Verdin?"

"Murders," Max clarified, "they were both poisoned."

As he watched the doctor bite her top lip, Mallery wondered if Lafoy adopted this brusque manner with her patients. He couldn't imagine her having much success in therapy sessions if she did.

"Very well, what is it?" Juliette answered finally.

"I wanted to ask you about Enzo Roche, off the record so to speak."

Perfectly manicured hands spread wide, showing dark painted nails. "You are aware of patient confidentiality, I take it?"

"Yes, and I don't need to know anything medical just yet. Can you tell me about Monsieur Roche's visitors, anyone he has regular contact with?"

There was a loud sigh, Juliette beginning to warm to the conversation. "There isn't anyone, not these days. Enzo used to receive flowers and letters from a friend, Marianne something or other, another dancer, but they seem to have stopped over the past few weeks. It's almost as though she's moved on and forgotten about him."

"I see, and are you able to tell me the reason for his admission to the facility?"

Arched eyebrows raised, the cold front coming down like a curtain of ice. "All I can tell you is that Monsieur Roche was involved in a serious car accident, it affected his mobility. After surgery, he became depressed and was admitted here as he began to self-harm."

"How long ago was this exactly?"

"Six months, I think," Juliette replied thoughtfully, her eyes drifting over to the laughter on the other side of the lawn, "before my time."

She shifted on the bench, squinting up at Max in the sunlight. "Is that all, Inspector? I really do need to get back to work."

"Just one last thing, before you go. Can you think of anyone who might want to harm Enzo Roche? Anyone at all?"

Lafoy snatched up the paperback and stood, pulling down her navy shift dress as she did so. "No, I can't. Now, if you don't mind, I must get going."

Mallery turned, watching the shrink stride off across the pristine grass in her kitten heels. He couldn't imagine the confident psychiatrist having a meltdown, no matter how long ago it was, and wondered if Brijesh Singh had got the right woman.

Fran Shepherd discreetly watched the exchange between Juliette Lafoy and the dashing police inspector from an upstairs window, noting the psychiatrist's defensive body language and taut features.

"Anything interesting?" a voice asked from behind her.

"Sorry, Monsieur Cassell, I was looking for Bernard, I couldn't find him in his room."

The manager pursed his lips and tapped at a gold watch. "I suspect he will be in the dining room at this time of day, don't you think?"

"Yes, of course, how foolish of me," Fran replied, turning to go.

"Nurse Shepherd," Leon went on, stopping the woman in her tracks, "what was that all about?"

The tall, bald-headed manager pointed out through the window, to where Max Mallery was watching Juliette tramp back across the lawn.

"I'm sorry, but I have no idea."

Cassell nodded, but continued to observe the police officer. "Very well."

Fran returned to the upper floor nurse's station, aware of the sanatorium manager rushing downstairs behind her to intercept the policeman as he returned to the main building.

I wonder what's going on? Fran mused. *Cassell looks like he's seen a ghost and the doctor looks furious.*

As Max reached for his phone, it trilled to life, flashing up Mazzo's identity.

"Roberto. Oui?"

The lab technician explained that they had worked all morning to get results and could now confirm the origin of the plant species that had poisoned both Edwina Butler and Raymond Verdin.

"You're one hundred per cent sure?" Mallery reiterated.

"Absolutely no doubt," the Italian told him. "You just need to find it."

As Leon Cassell stood waiting at the entrance for Max to reach him, the manager straightened his tie and tidied the gold cufflinks at his wrists.

"Inspector," he said politely, "back again, I see."

Max wiped his feet on the doormat and stepped inside. "I just had a few things to clear up with Doctor Lafoy. I'm glad I've caught you though, Monsieur Cassell. Perhaps a few words in your office might be appropriate."

Ushered into the spick and span sanctuary of the hospital manager, Max was relieved to be offered coffee almost immediately.

"Thank you, that would be great."

"I'll get my secretary to see to it," Cassell smiled. "Now, you have an update?"

"Yes, and it's not good, I'm afraid. We have confirmation that both Butler and Verdin were poisoned. It seems that the chocolate cake delivered to Enzo Roche last Friday was laced with a toxic plant."

Cassell looked visibly shaken. "My goodness, how terrible! What was it? Are you able to tell?"

Mallery sat weighing up his options. Should he tell Leon about the lab results and risk the news spreading like wildfire, or hold back on the details and see if the culprit could be flushed out first? He decided on the latter.

"I'm afraid we're unable to say at the moment," he lied, pressing his fingers together against his lips in an attempt to mask the untruth, "but officers will be arriving shortly to keep a close watch on Roche. It seems obvious that he was the intended target and will need some form of protection."

Cassell opened his mouth to speak but was unable to utter a word.

Max watched the hospital manager with interest. No doubt the scandal associated with two murder victims under his care had shaken Cassell to the core and Mallery could understand why.

Back outside, the inspector was just about to climb into his car when a second vehicle arrived. The familiar figure of Jacques Gibault was in the driving seat.

"Inspector Mallery," the young policeman smiled, ushering his female colleague forward, "this is Caterina. We're taking the first shift to watch Roche."

"Great," Max replied, glancing up towards the second floor of the hospital, "You'll find him in his room upstairs, although beware the resident psychiatrist, she won't be happy if you upset her patient. If I were you, I would avoid getting into a conversation with Roche, your job is to observe and keep him safe. Okay?"

"Yes, boss," the pair answered in unison.

Then Caterina lowered her voice to ask, "Is he… you know… alright up there?" She tapped the side of her head.

"Yes, from what I can tell," Mallery assured her, "it's not that kind of hospital. Enzo Roche is here to recover after an accident and some depression, so bear that in mind. Also, anything delivered here has to be checked with caution. Whoever sent that cake to Roche didn't succeed in poisoning him, so there's no telling whether they'll try again."

"Any idea why someone would want to harm him?" Jacques queried.

"No, I don't," Max confessed, "but I'm going to find out."

"And the staff and patients here, sir? Are they suspects?"

Mallery cast an expert eye over the huge white building, then brought it down to the lawn and its resident croquet players. "Unfortunately, until we find out who tried to poison Roche, we must treat everyone here with suspicion. Keep your eyes and ears open, and your mouths shut, do you hear? I don't want anyone finding out about the poison and I certainly don't want any more of it to enter the hospital. Got it?"

Both uniformed police officers looked sheepish as they nodded in agreement. Jacques Gibault had experienced Max Mallery's wrath on previous occasions, but he also knew that the inspector was a fair man and a competent one at that.

"Just one thing before you go, Inspector," he ventured. "When you say everyone is under suspicion, does that mean the doctor and the manager too?"

There was a slight pause as Max considered the question. "Yes, Jacques, absolutely everyone."

Leaving the uniformed officers to their duties, Max took a short drive to the nearby village of Saint Margaux. The square was lively for a Monday, with both locals and tourists doing their shopping and milling around in the sunshine.

The boulangerie was particularly busy, with customers sitting both outside and in. Telo was moving swiftly between tables, delivering cups of coffee, iced tea and pastries with practised ease. Several heads turned as Mallery switched off the engine, his dashing figure a cause for gossip amongst the women.

"*Maurice, bonjour*," he called, taking the only available seat at the rear.

Monsieur Fabron raised a hand and continued to place crusty rolls onto a tray, his eyes lighting up on seeing his close friend.

It wasn't until Max had finished a bottle of sparkling water that Maurice managed to grab a few minutes to join him.

The baker grinned. "What brings you here? Not enough work?"

"Quite the opposite," the inspector retorted, "but I promised to speak to you on behalf of that young nurse."

"Fran? Oh, what for?"

"She needs help to move her belongings so I said you might be able to use the van. That is alright, isn't it?"

"Yes, of course. I did offer, but she said that a work colleague was coming over with his estate car, but no matter…"

Mallery dropped his voice to a whisper. "I'm afraid the man in question is now lying in the mortuary."

"You're not serious! Who was it?"

"Raymond Verdin, he was an orderly at the sanatorium. Did you know him?"

"Verdin…" Maurice muttered, thinking. "Oh, yes, my goodness, I do. I believe he and his family come to church service here on occasion. What happened?"

"Let's just say the investigation is ongoing…"

The boulangerie owner shook his head. "I know you, Max. If you're investigating, it means his death was foul play!"

***

It was two-thirty by the time Mallery returned to police headquarters, a bag of custard tarts in his hand and a thirst for more coffee clawing at his throat.

"How are you getting on?" he asked, glancing around the room before placing the pastries on Luc Martin's desk. "These are for sharing."

74

The techie looked dejected as he licked his lips at the offering.

"Not much, boss," he sighed, "although I've got a pretty good background on Enzo Roche now."

Max took off his linen jacket and leaned back against the desk. "I've spoken to Roberto, we now have a positive identification on the toxin. Apparently, it's called *Cicuta*."

"Water hemlock," Jack Hobbs called across the room, proud of the knowledge that he'd picked up from his green-fingered mother, "it grows near ponds and rivers and has little white flowers that grow in an umbrella shape."

"Thank you, Monsieur Benech," Luc chuckled.

Hobbs was confused and it was written all over his face.

"Louis Benech is a French landscape gardener," Gabriella offered, getting up to help herself to a custard tart.

"I see," Jack tutted, warming to his subject. "Anyway, it shouldn't be too hard to locate the plant locally, we just check the local waterways."

"All one hundred of them," Thierry added.

Hobbs was dumbfounded. "What? There's so many?"

"Maybe not quite a hundred, Jacques," Max told him, "but there are a lot of streams going off the main river and plenty of lakes and ponds, too."

"Well, to ensure the plant was effective, my guess is that it wouldn't have been cut from too far away, the fresher the better."

Mallery shook his head. "That still leaves us with miles and miles of area to cover. It's an impossible task."

"What if we start with the places closest to Riberon?"

"The perpetrator would have to be pretty stupid to use a poison grown on his own doorstep, don't you think?"

Hobbs swung around to face his boss. "Can you think of a better place to begin?"

Mallery walked over to the coffee pot and poured himself a mugful of the thick, strong liquid. "Fine, fine, let's do it, organise a team, but I swear it will be like looking for a pin in a haystack."

"Needle," Jack supplied, suppressing a smile. "Needle in a haystack."

"That too," Max grunted, grimacing as he swallowed the bitter coffee. "Now, Luc, tell us what you have on Enzo Roche."

Luc Martin sat at the small conference table that had been set up close to the new screen, tapping at his much-coveted iPad as he found the file.

"Right, so, as you can see here," he announced, pointing to the dancer's profile as it appeared above him, together with a shot of Enzo Roche at the height of his career, "Roche first hit the headlines with his debut role in *Swan Lake* back in nineteen eighty-four, with the Paris Opera Ballet, aged eighteen. He then travelled extensively to Australia, Canada, the U.K. and then finally Russia, where he played the Mouse King in Tchaikovsky's *Nutcracker* for a season with the Bolshoi."

"Net worth?" Hobbs piped up. "I mean, he must have a bob or two with a career like that, right?"

"Approximately ten million euros, plus a château close to Saint-Emilion."

"Any history of family feuds, blackmail, minor offences?" Max asked, studying Roche's profile photo.

"Nothing. He lost both of his parents to cancer over the past decade and there are no siblings. Everything was looking positive up until the accident six months ago. The contracts were rolling in and he even had a few television appearances lined up."

"Didn't he take part in that reality show last year?" Gabriella inquired, moving closer to the screen.

"Yes, that's right," Luc grinned, glancing over at Jack, "it's the French version of *Big Brother*."

"I can't imagine anyone wanting to put their personal habits on show for the world to see." The Englishman shuddered. "Why would he do that?"

"Because it pays big money," Max offered, finished his coffee. "Thousands, plus all the extra publicity that comes with it after eviction."

Martin clicked onto the next image, the photo of a Range Rover with the front end smashed up against a tree.

"This was New Year's Eve," he explained. "According to witnesses, Roche swerved to avoid a dog in the road, hit the grass verge and skidded into this large oak. His tibia was shattered in two places and surgeons needed to put steel pins in to stabilise the bones."

Mallery was frowning. "What am I missing here? Surely now, six months later, Roche's leg would have healed, and he could start dancing again."

"That's not the end of the story," Luc went on, enjoying his moment in the spotlight. "During his hospital stay, Roche started a relationship with one of the male nurses. We don't have any more specific details, but it seems that, a month after leaving the hospital, Roche became depressed and ended the affair..." he paused to give the punchline the desired effect, "and the nurse committed suicide."

Jack let out a low whistle from between his teeth. "So maybe there is a motive for wanting Enzo Roche dead after all."

Max picked up on Hobbs' thought and ran with it "What was the name of the nurse? Did he have any family?"

Luc let his fingers run across the screen, clicking on a new folder. "Daniel Baur. Elderly parents, both in their seventies, and one sister, Louise, deceased."

The clock on the incident room wall ticked away the minutes as the team sat chewing over the information. Thierry Moreau was the first to break the silence.

"Who stands to inherit the estate if Roche dies?"

"Good question." Max nodded, turning his attention to the techie. "Do we know?"

"Not yet, boss, but I'll find out by the end of the day."

"Good, good. Now let's make a list of suspects, shall we? It seems we have very little else to go on until we find the source of the poisonous plant."

He began writing on the old whiteboard in a clear hand, but Luc coughed and pointed to Mallery's redundant iPad. "If you put the names in there, we can bring it up on the big screen, keeps everything in one place. See?"

Max sighed and picked up the device. "Okay, now how do I turn the damned thing on?"

Luc shifted from his seat and pressed a button on the side of the iPad, causing it to spring to life with the Apple logo. "I'll give you a quick run-through."

Mallery's shoulders hunched as he bent over the desk to watch Luc type in a code and then click on various icons.

"We'll leave you to it then," Hobbs coughed, watching with amusement.

"Where are you off to?"

"We thought it best to give the area around the sanatorium a quick once-over, while it's still light," Jack explained, grabbing three bottles of chilled water from the fridge, "see if we can find any water hemlock."

On Tuesday morning, Jack Hobbs entered the incident room to the sound of loud conversation, causing him to pause and look at his watch. It was almost eight, his usual time of arrival, yet the second floor was already a hive of activity. The Yorkshireman slung the rucksack off his shoulder and peered through the open door, his view partially blocked by the formidably wide shoulders of Coroner Paul Theron. Further into the room, Audrey Rancourt was talking animatedly, her arms making circles in the air as the newly appointed commissioner explained a point to the medic. On seeing the detective, she immediately switched to English.

"Ah, Jack, good to see you so early." The senior police officer smiled politely. "I was just explaining to Monsieur Theron that you were out until dusk looking for the toxic plant – the, erm, water hemlock – yesterday."

Hobbs pulled out a chair and pushed his bag under the desk. "Yes, but to no avail, I'm afraid. We followed the riverbank from Riberon to Saint Margaux but found nothing. Max has a team of officers scouring the area today, so they'll cover the opposite direction, from Riberon to Salbec."

Audrey nodded thoughtfully, her neat, steel-grey hair bobbing up and down. "I have every confidence that something will be found, but time is of the essence right now, we need to locate the source."

Jack wrinkled his nose, confused. "But couldn't the plant have come from almost anywhere?"

Paul Theron unfolded his arms and put his hands in the pockets of his pin-striped trousers. "Actually, no. I completed the autopsies on both victims yesterday afternoon and discovered that the water hemlock must have been extremely fresh when it was added to the cake batter. If it had come from further afield, well, I think it would have started to dry out and the toxins rendered less effective."

The trio were slightly distracted as Mallery entered, his ears pricked up on hearing the mention of the poisonous substance. "What's that?"

"The water hemlock, Max," the coroner explained, "It must have been picked locally, there's no doubt about it. It has to be within a few miles' radius."

"Well, the team are outside now, ready to go, so let's hope they find something. I'll keep you posted with any progress."

Theron pursed his lips. "Thanks, Max, I'd appreciate it. The method used by our poisoner is a particularly cruel and sadistic one. No one should have to suffer as Madame Butler and Monsieur Verdin did. They must have died in agony."

As he turned to leave, picking up his briefcase from the floor, Max lowered his voice and caught his friend's elbow. "Have you spoken to the relief coroner yet, Jean Blanchet? What did he have to say for himself?"

"Oh yes and believe you me, I'll wager that his ears are still ringing."

The inspector conjured up an image in his mind, imagining an irate Paul shouting down the phone at his colleague with gusto, heart pounding.

"I'll call you later," he winked, raising a hand in farewell as Theron's bulky frame reached the wide corridor outside.

"Meet you at five, usual place," Theron returned, "the wine is on me."

Audrey Rancourt watched the exchange with interest, wondering how close the two professionals were. They seemed unlikely friends, yet the playful body language between Mallery and Theron suggested that they were much more than two individuals brought together by their chosen careers. She was about to speak, but Luc, Gabriella and Thierry arrived, causing the commissioner to sit back and listen as Mallery gave his morning instructions.

"Right, just a quick one, as we need to get moving," Max called out over the chatter, which soon settled down. "As you probably saw on your way in, we have a team going out to search the ponds and streams leading from the hospital facility out to Salbec. Thierry, Gabriella, I want you two to go out to the sanatorium and take statements from the staff, find out exactly who was on duty last Friday and get their home addresses. Somebody must know something."

"Yes, boss," the detectives replied as one.

"Jacques, I want you to liaise with Thames Valley Police, find out all you can about Edwina Butler and why she was here in France rather than at a facility in the UK." He turned to face Luc. "Anything on Roche's will yet?"

Martin was already allowing his fingers to race over the silent keyboard of his iPad. "Yes, I have it here, one second… Roche has left everything to charity."

"*Merde*," Max muttered, "another dead end."

Fran Shepherd was just about to go through the door when her phone rang. Juggling a lunchbox, door-keys and a light sweater, she pulled the device from her pocket and looked at the screen before answering. Leon Cassell; what on earth could he want at this time in the morning?

"Monsieur Cassell," she said politely. "Is everything alright?"

Leaving the cottage door ajar as she listened, Fran added the odd affirmative comment to the conversation and then closed the call.

Great, that was all she needed. One of the nurses had phoned in to request a change of shift due to a hospital appointment and Cassell had requested that Fran swap. Naturally she had agreed, but then cursed as she clicked off the phone. Now she would be off today and working tomorrow, the day that she had arranged with Maurice Fabron to move her belongings to the apartment above his boulangerie. The only thing for it was to ring him, in the hope that it wasn't too inconvenient to change her plans. The Englishwoman suspected that the kindly baker would work his day around the move, yet she couldn't help but feel a pang of guilt at the unexpected request.

"Perhaps I could treat you to supper at the bistro," she suggested, trying to sugar-coat the reason for her call. "It's the very least I can do."

Fabron laughed nervously. "We'll see, Madame Shepherd. Telo will look after the shop for a while, so I'll see you around eleven, if that suits you?"

"Perfect," the nurse grinned, "that will just give me time to pack the last few boxes. See you later and thanks again, Maurice."

Max Mallery placed the press release on Audrey Rancourt's desk and stepped back. "I really appreciate you handling this," he told his superior, "there's enough to do without me having to face those bloodhounds."

The Commissioner lifted the papers and scanned the brief details. "It's the least I can do. I can see that you're extremely busy with this double murder, and don't worry, I'm used to handling the big boys in Paris, so these local reporters will be easy."

"Rather you than me, Commissioner, it's a part of the job I find to be the most tedious."

"Please, call me Audrey. If we're going to be working closely side by side, the very least we owe one another is to become allies, don't you think?"

There was a glimmer of mischief in Rancourt's eyes and Max smiled. "I agree, so please call me Max."

Audrey nodded her approval and moved back to the matter at hand. "How are you getting on with the new technology?"

"It's great. I just need a bit of time to adjust to the new system."

The commissioner tapped her pen on the papers in front of her. "Well, don't take too long. I think having every detail at your fingertips should have this case closed within the week. Thank you, Max."

Realising that he was being dismissed, Mallery headed for the door.

Is that what she really expects? An open and shut case within seven days?

Maurice Fabron brought the Citroën delivery van to a stop outside Fran's rented cottage just before the appointed time. The nurse was ready, waving at him from the doorway as he climbed out and reached for the gate. Maurice felt an unfamiliar sensation of delight, his heart skipping a beat as he headed towards his new tenant. It had been a long time since anyone had touched the boulangerie owner in such a way and Maurice wondered whether leasing his apartment to Fran Shepherd might bring some unexpected challenges.

"Maurice, thank you so much," the dark-haired Englishwoman called as he approached, her slender body clad in a pair of denim shorts and navy vest.

"It's my pleasure," he said honestly, kissing her on both cheeks. "Now let's get these boxes loaded and settle you in to your new home."

The cottage had been fully furnished when Fran had taken over the tenancy six months previously, but the dark interior and low ceilings lacked a homely feel, and she was glad to be moving to a brighter, much airier residence. Besides, despite the house being convenient for her work in Riberon, Nurse Shepherd looked forward to being in the more vibrant hub of Saint Margaux with its chic range of shops and eateries.

It didn't take the pair long to load up the van, most of Fran's belongings being clothes and books, and they were soon on their way out of the village with the windows wound down and the radio on full.

"What's going on down there?" Maurice shouted over the music, pointing towards a police transit parked on the grass verge further down the lane. "What are they looking for?"

"No idea." Fran shrugged. "I didn't notice it there earlier when I went out to fetch some milk. Maybe someone's horse got loose or something."

"Oh well," the baker sighed, "I'm sure Max will tell me all about it later."

Henri Coutillard raised a meaty hand and waved at his colleague. "*Ici.*"

The day was hot, causing sweat to trickle down the side of the man's face and down into his collar. He grumbled under his breath, wondering which clever designer had decided to create their uniforms in navy blue, a colour that not only attracted the heat, but held it there for what seemed like eternity.

The younger police officer ran forward, his heavy boots swishing through the overgrowth as he headed for the edge of the stream.

"*C'est là,*" Henri told him, pointing up the incline to where an abundance of green foliage with delicate white flowers was taking over the hedgerow. The tall stalks continued upwards, climbing into the garden of a nearby property.

His colleague nodded, his usually cheerful features now tense and serious as he made a call to headquarters. "*Oui, Inspector Mallery s'il vous plaît.*"

Max put down the phone and headed to the incident room to find Jack Hobbs. "Fancy a ride out to Riberon with me, Jacques?"

The red-haired detective was out of his chair and crossing the room before Mallery had chance to say another word. "Sure, what's up?"

"They've found the plant, at the back of a cottage in Riberon."

"Is there anyone at home?"

"I don't know yet. I've told the officers to hang back until we get there. I don't want their presence frightening off whoever is in residence."

"Good idea," Hobbs agreed, following his boss downstairs to the car park. "By the way, there's not much to tell you about Edwina Butler. She's lived in France for over forty years, hence her admission to a facility here, and her care was paid for by savings and her widow's pension."

"No dark past? Nothing to antagonise anyone?" Max asked, as he unlocked the BMW and clicked a button to collapse the soft top.

"Nothing at all, she was a music teacher and much loved by everyone, by all accounts. Seems she must have just been in the wrong place at the wrong time. I reckon that cake was intended to poison Enzo Roche and Edwina just happened to eat it instead."

Mallery lowered his sunglasses onto his face as the engine roared to life. "One thing bothers me, though, Jacques."

"What's that?"

"Roche was very clear about not liking chocolate cake, in fact that's why the hospital chef made him a vanilla sponge on Friday, so whoever it was that wanted to poison him, didn't know that. Don't you think that someone close to him would be aware of his likes and dislikes?"

"You're right. I'd say it's unusual for someone not to like chocolate, so the perpetrator simply presumed that the gateau would be well received."

"Exactly, so let's keep that fact in mind as we move forwards, *oui*?"

Henri Coutillard stood mopping his brow next to the transit, the overweight police officer feeling the strain of being outside under the midday sun instead of out on the beat in the shaded passageways of the city. He considered the hour and snorted. Round about now, he would usually be tucking into a fresh baguette at Gigi's bistro, accompanied by a pint of cola and a view of the best-looking waitress in Bordeaux. Henri turned as an engine became audible in the distance. So, here was the man himself, the infamous Inspector Mallery in his top-of-the-range sports car. The officer straightened, stuffing the handkerchief into his trouser pocket as he anticipated the arrival of the suave detective.

Mallery made a few quick introductions and then asked some preliminary questions, rubbing his chin as the officers gave him the answers. No, they had not approached the cottage, no they hadn't seen anyone arrive or leave from there, and yes, they were certain that the plant at the rear of the property matched that of the image provided with their instructions earlier that day.

"Right," Max decided. "Come on, Jacques, we'll take the front door, while these officers wait around back. Let's see what we can find out."

Unlatching the gate, Jack Hobbs looked around the neat front garden, observing that the water hemlock hadn't become prevalent in this part of the patch. He stepped onto the doormat and rapped hard, once, twice, three times.

Meanwhile, Mallery was peering in through the front downstairs window, scooping his hands together to block out the bright sunlight streaming in.

"I don't think anyone is living here," he called, "it's furnished but there are no personal items. Perhaps it's used as a holiday gite."

Jack tried the doorknob, but it jarred under his grasp. "It's locked. Can we get Luc to do a quick search on ownership?"

"Yes, call him. I'm going around back to check that those two monkeys have got the right plant, although Luc did provide a clear picture."

Hobbs took out his phone, but called out as an afterthought, "Whatever you do, don't touch it!"

***

Fran Shepherd was enjoying unpacking her belongings, hanging up the loose summer dresses and colourful tops that she had bought from various boutiques in Bordeaux. Already she had filled two bookshelves and the bottom of the closet was now lined with sandals and trainers in various styles. This apartment was such a contrast to her previous home. She could feel the difference already, simply from the long windows filling the rooms with sunlight, to the compact but bijoux kitchen that appeared to be well-equipped for her needs.

Knowing that Maurice Fabron was downstairs working lifted the nurse's spirits, too. Not only was the baker kind and caring, but their conversation flowed easily, as though they were old acquaintances rekindling a friendship.

Fran wasn't one to count her chickens before they'd hatched, but she couldn't help feeling that life was suddenly going to get a whole lot better.

Jack Hobbs rounded the corner of the cottage, watching as the inspector stood giving instructions for the uniformed officers to cordon off the area. Max looked up for a second and, on seeing his colleague's concerned face, began climbing up the embankment, struggling in his smart Oxford brogues.

"Did he find anything?"

"You're not going to like this one bit, Max."

"Go on…"

"The cottage belongs to a couple in Armagnac. However, they have leased it out for the last six months, to Fran Shepherd, that nurse from the sanatorium."

Mallery's jaw slackened as he digested the information. "*Merde, seriously?*"

"Yep, apparently she was due to move out tomorrow, but I'd say, judging by the bare surfaces, she's already done a bunk."

Max gathered his thoughts, recalling the previous day's conversation with the attractive Englishwoman. "It's okay, Jacques, I know exactly where she is."

Maurice opened the door at the bottom of the stairs leading up to the apartment and coughed before calling up to its new resident. "Fran, would you like some lunch? A slice of quiche, perhaps?"

A smiling face appeared on the top step, the woman's hair tied back with a spotted scarf, causing her large, oval eyes to become more prominent.

"Yes, I'd love something to eat, but I'm going to pay for it, Maurice."

The boulangerie owner beckoned, dismissing the offer. "Come on down, and I won't hear of it. Today is my treat, your moving-in present."

Fran made her way down the narrow staircase and smoothed down her crumpled shorts as she reached the bottom. "I hope I don't look too scruffy, some of your customers look impeccably dressed."

Maurice chuckled, enjoying the company of his new tenant. "It's very quiet at the moment. Besides, Fran, you look wonderful, *très chic*."

A short while later, he was in such deep conversation with Fran that he failed to notice the bright red BMW until it stopped on the opposite side of the village square.

"Ah, it's Max and Jack," he sighed, pointing out the detectives, "they've probably come to buy some pastries to take back to the team in Bordeaux."

"They drive all the way out here for cakes?" Fran asked, incredulous. "What's wrong with the bakeries in the city?"

Maurice feigned horror at the mention of his rivals and picked up his new friend's empty coffee cup to refill it.

"*Bonjour*, Max, *bonjour*, Jack."

The stern look on Mallery's face caused Maurice to stop dead in his tracks and, when the inspector pulled out his warrant card, the baker turned deathly white.

"What on earth is going on?"

"I'm afraid I'll need you to accompany me to the station, Madame Shepherd," Max stated, turning to address Fran, "we have some questions for you."

The nurse stiffened, a natural reaction under scrutiny, and tilted her face up to look at the inspector. "Can you tell me what this is about?"

"I'm afraid that the plant used to poison Monsieur Roche's cake, the same one that caused the deaths of Edwina Butler and Raymond Verdin, was identified at the rear of the property that you have conveniently just vacated."

Fran looked genuinely shocked. "What? That's impossible!"

As Maurice stood looking between the two, first Mallery and then to Fran, a police transit van pulled up outside the boulangerie.

"If you wouldn't mind coming with us, Madame Shepherd," Max said softly. "Let's not make a scene."

Fran was dumbfounded, unable to respond; surely there was a misunderstanding? The nurse's legs wobbled slightly as she stood and allowed Jack Hobbs to escort her to the waiting vehicle.

Maurice Fabron slumped into the nearest chair, feeling a dreadful sense of déjà vu. Wasn't this how things had started with Isobel Gilyard, his English pastry assistant, two summers before? Accused of murder on his very doorstep?

"Do you want to call someone to represent you, Miss Shepherd?" Jack asked, setting a cup of water on the table next to their interviewee. "I can see if there's an English-speaking solicitor on duty."

Fran shook her head, fingers shaking slightly as she lifted the paper beaker to her lips. "No, there's no need. I haven't done anything wrong."

On the opposite side of the table, Max Mallery sat with his arms crossed over his chest, causing his short-sleeved shirt to tighten over his biceps. The fixed mouth and dark, brooding eyes told Fran that the pair were intending to play out the usual scenario of 'good cop, bad cop' seen all too often on television dramas.

"Madame Shepherd, do you have any reason for wanting to harm Enzo Roche?"

Mallery's question was delivered deftly, the words soft, as though he might be asking her opinion on a fine wine or a book recommendation.

"No," she said simply, sitting up straight in the uncomfortable plastic chair. "I am very fond of Enzo, as I am of all the patients under my care."

"Can you think of anyone who might want to frame you? Someone with a grudge, perhaps?"

Fran bit her lip, thinking about the unkind correspondence recently received from her ex-husband and then of the frosty exchanges between herself and Juliette Lafoy. "No, not really."

"No, or not really?" Hobbs jumped in, studying the woman in front of him.

"No," she told him emphatically, tears beginning to fall. "I love my job and I've been very happy here in France. Whoever wanted to poison Enzo must have taken the plant from the back of the cottage without my knowledge. I swear I know nothing about it."

Max tilted his head towards the door, gesturing for Hobbs to follow him into the corridor beyond. He let his gaze fall onto the tearful woman. "Excuse us a moment, Madame…

"Well?" Mallery asked, once they were out of earshot, knowing that he could rely on an honest appraisal from his colleague. "Is she telling us the truth?"

Jack didn't hesitate, his gut feeling was serving him well today. "Yes, I think she is. Fran Shepherd could no more kill a man than you or me, Max."

"Very well, then we let her return to Saint Margaux, but we keep a close eye on her, understood? Just in case."

"What about the water hemlock?"

Max considered the question and shrugged. "It's cordoned off and Henri Coutillard will be on watch until we get another officer to relieve him later."

Hobbs stifled a laugh. "He'll be well happy about that!"

"Coutillard could do with losing a few pounds, perhaps in this heat they will simply melt off him, who knows?"

Before Jack could respond, Mallery opened the door to the interview room and leaned in. "Madame Shepherd, you are now free to go."

Fran ran a finger under the track of eyeliner that had smudged her cheek and looked up. "Really? So, you believe me?"

Max was non-committal. "Let's just say that we have other lines of enquiry to pursue, but for the moment, please don't leave the area."

"Okay. I'm on duty at the hospital tomorrow, anyway. Can I leave now?"

The inspector consulted the expensive timepiece on his wrist and raised an eyebrow at Hobbs. "It's almost five. Any chance you could drop Madame Shepherd back in Saint Margaux on your way home?"

"No overtime tonight then?" the freckled Yorkshireman queried.

"Not tonight, Jacques, I think Commissioner Rancourt has used up all our budget on those new gadgets. Besides, I have an appointment with Paul Theron… five minutes ago!"

Jack Hobbs was well aware that at five on Tuesdays, his boss would mull over the current caseload with his good friend, the local coroner. He also knew that more than a few glasses of wine were most likely involved.

"See you tomorrow then, have a good evening." He smiled softly at Fran. "Come on then, Miss Shepherd. If you don't mind a ride in my old Mondeo, I'll gladly drop you off."

Fran was on her feet in seconds, eager to return to her new home and even keener to offer some words of explanation to her new landlord. The look on Maurice Fabron's face had been priceless as she'd been led away, and the least she could do was try to convince him of her innocence.

CHAPTER EIGHT – TÊTE-À-TÊTES

"*Merci.*"

Max smiled at the waitress as she placed a bottle of Chablis and two glasses on the table and watched her walk away. Cute face, great hair and curvy hips. On any other night he might have been tempted to strike up a conversation, but Tuesday was his catch-up night with Paul. As the woman turned and smiled at the detective, perhaps sensing his eyes lingering for a minute longer than necessary, Mallery made a mental note to call back to the same bar on Friday night, work willing.

"Sorry, sorry," Theron called as he lumbered across the space, a raincoat hooked over one arm. "I ran in Roberto and stopped to check on his progress."

Max was immediately back in the moment, all thoughts of a prospective date gone from his mind. "Oh, have they found anything?"

Paul squeezed his ample stomach between the bench and table, laying the coat down beside him. "Yes, actually, but it might not be what you want to hear."

The inspector poured their drinks and waited until his friend had taken a sip before gesturing for him to go on. "Okay…"

"The box that the cake was delivered in was one of those self-assembly ones that you can purchase online from any confectionery supply store. It could have come from any one of twenty-plus retailers. Also, the only prints found on the exterior were those of the delivery driver and the hospital orderly, Raymond Verdin, whom we can assume carried it upstairs to Roche's room."

"What about inside the box?"

"Only the fingerprints of Butler and Verdin, whom we know were the only two to take a slice from it."

Max swirled the pale-coloured Chablis around the glass. "So, not even Roche's fingerprints were on the inside?"

"No, why?"

"No reason, I was just considering that he might have known the gateau was toxic and avoided touching it."

"Maybe, but unlikely, don't you think?"

"I agree. Also, if Roche had purchased the box, who would he have asked to bake it? I think we can disregard that theory, Paul."

"There is just one more thing," the coroner confessed. "Edwina Butler's brother is arriving from London tomorrow. I spoke to him earlier about arranging the funeral. He seems a no-nonsense kind of fellow, so he's bound to want to know what progress you've made in finding her killer."

Mallery groaned and picked up his glass again. "That's all I need right now. Is he planning to bury her here, in France?"

"Yes, it sounds like it. After all, Edwina had lived here for many years and considered it to be her home."

"Can you give me a ring when he arrives, and I'll come over? Better I speak to him at your office than mine, just in case the new boss sticks her nose in."

"No problem. Are you two not getting along?"

Max could feel himself smiling for the first time that afternoon. "Do you know what, Paul? She's alright, very efficient and motivated, it's just…"

"What? You're not used to working for a woman?"

"No, it's not that. Audrey Rancourt deserves the position, she's got years of experience, I just feel that she's wanting to make too many changes, too soon."

Theron looked into his friend's eyes. "She's probably just asserting her authority, it's the settling-in period where she'll make her mark. Give it time and I'll bet you make a formidable team."

"Maybe, let's wait and see."

Whilst Mallery and Theron chatted over their chilled wine, a very different conversation was taking place in the village of Saint Margaux.

Despite his better judgement, Maurice Fabron had reluctantly accepted his new tenant's invitation for a drink and supper at the local bistro. It wasn't that the boulangerie owner worried about gossip in the small community, but rather his concerns were due to Fran Shepherd being unexpectedly escorted to the police station earlier in the day. The whole scenario had reminded Maurice of the Englishwoman who had worked for him a couple of summers before. Isobel Gilyard had been an inspiration to the baker, working hard and bringing an air of warmth to the shop. That was until Max had accused her of murder.

"A penny for your thoughts?" Fran quipped, as she looked up from the menu. "You look miles away there, Maurice."

"No, no, I'm just a little tired that's all," he replied quickly, dismissing the woman's concern. "It's been a long day."

"For you and me both!"

It wasn't until he looked closely at the nurse's tired eyes that Maurice realised just how taxing the inspector's questioning must have been for her and a pang of guilt hit him in the gut.

"I'm very sorry, Fran, I didn't mean to be insensitive, it's just that… well, I didn't want to pry."

Fran closed the menu and laid it next to her wineglass. "Please, ask whatever you want, I honestly have nothing to feel guilty about."

Maurice sensed the feeling of déjà vu once again. Hadn't Isobel told him exactly the same thing? But then, hadn't she been found innocent in the end?

"It's fine, really. Let's just enjoy supper."

The nurse could feel her new friend's attention slipping away. He was so obviously having concerns about meeting up with her.

"I'll make a deal with you," she smiled, tapping a finger on Fabron's wrist. "After we've eaten, let's go for a walk and I'll tell you why Inspector Mallery asked me to go to the police station. It's the least I can do."

Maurice nodded, studying the woman's face as she spoke. Instinct told him to avoid getting involved, but a heavy heart pleaded for more time. He had been single for too long and if there was even an ounce of opportunity for more than friendship with Fran, the baker was willing to risk it.

"Okay, agreed," Maurice heard himself say. "I'll order us some wine. They have some new bottles on display. I can highly recommend the mussels, if you like them, although the chef does tend to be heavy-handed with the garlic."

Fran leaned across the table and replied in a whisper, a cheeky grin on her face, "As long as you're having them, too. That way, it won't matter if I smell of garlic for the rest of the evening!"

"Okay, why not? Let's order some garlic bread to go with them," he chuckled.

"I can see you like to live dangerously, Maurice, go for it."

As the couple conversed, invisible walls crumbled, leaving only good intentions. In fact, they were so engrossed in each other that Maurice failed to notice his closest neighbours until they were seated at the next table.

"*Bonsoir, Maurice*," Angélique greeted. "We didn't expect to see you here."

Fabron was on his feet in seconds, making introductions and kissing the dark-haired French beauty on both cheeks. "How delightful. Why not join us?"

Jack Hobbs was looking down at his feet, embarrassed at coming face to face with a woman he had been interviewing in a murder investigation just hours before, but his wife glanced at Maurice's companion to check whether she minded the intrusion.

Fran smiled. "Yes, please sit down. It would be lovely to get to know some of Maurice's friends, although I've already met your husband."

Angélique looked confused. "You have?"

"Yes, at the bakery," Hobbs replied quickly, saving Fran from further explanation. "Fran is Maurice's new tenant."

Whilst the waiter moved chairs and pushed their tables together, the women took the opportunity to comment on one another's outfits. Both were tall and dark with slender figures, although Fran's short bob was a stark contrast to Angélique's long tresses. Within minutes, they had bonded over a mutual love of fashion and books. Jack sat quietly listening to their chit-chat. There didn't appear to be any animosity on Fran's part, but he considered that she might just be skilled at masking her true feelings.

"Shall we go and have a look at the new wine selection?" Maurice suggested to Jack, aware of the detective's slight awkwardness.

"Good idea." The Yorkshireman nodded, following his friend to the bar. He could feel Fran Shepherd's eyes on them as they moved away.

"I trust it was a mistake," Maurice said boldly, picking up a bottle from a display and pretending to examine the label.

"We're not sure yet," Jack said quietly, "but you know I can't discuss the case with you."

"I know. I just can't help feeling some similarities between this fiasco and when Max arrested Isobel Gilyard. I think Fran is innocent, too."

"Maurice, you hardly know her…"

The older man held up a hand. "I know her well enough to be convinced that she is no more capable of murder than you or I."

"How can you be so sure?"

Fabron tapped the side of his head. "Intuition and, as you English say, touch wood, I am usually right."

Maurice noticed Jack's shoulders loosen up slightly. He hadn't realised that the Yorkshireman had been so tense and nudged him playfully.

"Come on, lighten up, the truth will come out in the end, and you will catch the culprit. There's no stronger team than Max's"

"I certainly hope you're right, Maurice. What is it about Fran than makes you want to trust her?"

"I don't know," the baker replied honestly, "I just feel that she's a good person. Most nurses are, that's why they're so good at what they do, looking after others and making a difference. I could ask you the same thing, Jack. What makes you think that Fran was involved?"

Hobbs lifted the sample of wine that was being offered by the bartender and let the aroma fill his nostrils. "That's just it, Maurice, I don't believe she is."

The bottle of Chablis was three-quarters empty when Paul Theron lifted it and raised an eyebrow at his friend to suggest another.

"Do you want more? I'll have to have a soft drink as I'm driving."

The bar had become quite full, and Max had to raise his voice to be heard over the crowd. "In that case I'll just have a beer, I should get an early night, anyway. I'll order on my way to the gents."

Mallery elbowed his way to the bar, gave the hovering waitress their order and pushed through a crowd of students towards the toilets. As he returned to his seat, the detective noticed a couple of women in nurses' uniforms. A tall, bearded man stood next to them, swigging from a bottle of lager.

"Doctor Singh!" Max called, automatically waving at the medic. "Good evening. What a surprise seeing you here."

The Indian moved forward, greeting Mallery with a strong handshake.

"Inspector," he smiled, "call me Brijesh, I'm off duty after all."

Mallery glanced down at the beer bottle, and a memory tugged at his brain. Two glasses of wine had caused him to shed any inhibitions and the words came tumbling out before he had time to consider any implications.

"I thought you said you didn't drink, Brijesh."

Singh looked down at the beer in his hand and frowned. "Did I?"

"Yes, when you were telling me about Juliette Lafoy. You said you mixed in different circles due the fact that you didn't drink."

Brijesj clicked his tongue, his mouth breaking into a wide grin. "Ah, and you presumed that I abstain for religious reasons."

A pink tinge appeared on Max's cheeks. "Yes… I…"

"No, Inspector. I didn't drink when I was younger as I was in training. I used to keep fit and played a lot of basketball. These days, well, the pressure of the job, etcetera. I do enjoy the odd drink now and again, though."

Mallery started to backtrack as he formed the next sentence in his head. "I see. Look, I didn't mean any offence."

"None taken, it's good to know that our city detectives are alert. It seems you don't miss a trick, which is good, very good."

"Well, I'd better get back to my friend. Enjoy your evening, Brijesh. No doubt I'll see you again soon."

"Let me know if you find out anything," the doctor urged, turning back to his colleagues. "Or if I can be of help in any way."

"I will, thanks."

Mallery made his way back over to the coroner and looked at the cold beer that had arrived during his absence, condensation trickling down the side of the glass. He was tempted to stay for a session but common sense prevailed.

"Just this one, Paul, and then I must get home."

"Me too. If I'm any later than nine, my dinner will be in the dog," Theron joked. "You know, you really must come over one night soon."

Max leaned back against the banquette. "I will, Paul, thank you. Let me just get this investigation out of the way first. I'm guessing that my time is going to be tied up completely until we solve the case."

Theron nodded thoughtfully. "Indeed. Rather you than me, Max. I don't suppose you have a shortlist of suspects yet?"

Mallery snorted. "That's just it. As Jacques would say, every man and his dog is a suspect right now, we just don't know where to start looking."

The coroner could plainly see his friend's frustration. "Sometimes what you are looking for is right under your nose, you just need to step back and look at the whole picture."

"Easier said than done, Paul. Enzo Roche doesn't appear to have an enemy in the world. He's everybody's darling with dozens of adoring fans."

Theron reached for his coat. "I should get going. You'll work it out, you always do. Do you want a lift home?"

Max stretched and looked from his friend's waterproof jacket to the gathering clouds outside. "If you don't mind, it will save me getting wet."

With a last glance at Brijesh Singh, Mallery followed the coroner out to his car. The case really was getting to him, as for one second back there he had even suspected the doctor of lying to him.

At the bistro in Saint Margaux, Jack Hobbs was trying his best to discuss football with Maurice, whilst also keeping track of the conversation between his wife and Fran Shepherd. Angélique was asking the nurse about her job and the Yorkshireman's ears pricked up when the talk turned to her work colleagues.

"Most of them are great," Fran was saying as she scooped a mussel from its shell, "but the resident psychiatrist is hard work. I swear she's got it in for me."

"Any idea why?" Angélique queried. "Do you think it's personal?"

"Not really. It might sound daft, but she seems to disapprove of my close relationship with some of the patients. It's almost as if she's jealous."

"That's weird. You would have thought that, as a doctor, she would be glad the patients trust you."

Fran shrugged. "I know, but anyway, I'm not bothered, I just try to keep out of her way. I'm busy enough with my duties to avoid bumping into her."

"Jack?" Maurice was saying. "You were miles away there."

Hobbs' ears reddened and he shifted his focus back on his friend. "Sorry, what were you saying?"

"I was wondering if you fancy going to a local game one weekend. I'm sure Telo would enjoy it, too, and we could ask Max."

"Yeah, great. I'm guessing we'll have to get this current investigation out of the way first, though. We'll be working right through until it's solved."

"Yes, of course. Are you making progress?"

Jack glanced at Fran, who was now looking at him and waiting for his response with interest.

"Not yet, Maurice, but you know I can't talk about it."

The baker nodded and winked at Fran as though to set her mind at rest. "Let's order another bottle of wine then, to celebrate Fran moving to Saint Margaux."

It was over an hour later that the Hobbs' made their excuses and left the bistro, hurrying home to relieve Dominique Fabre from her baby-sitting duties. Angélique and Fran had promised one another that they would catch up on the nurse's next day off and departed with an air of excitement.

"She's so lovely," Fran gushed to Maurice as she settled their share of the bill, having insisted on treating her new landlord. "I can't wait to have a shopping trip with Angélique, she's so stylish."

"As are you," Fabron appraised. "You are just as elegant."

Fran blushed and followed him to the door, sliding her hand through Maurice's offered arm. "Thank you."

They walked in silence for a while, enjoying the warmth of the evening and stillness of the quiet village, heading towards the riverbank. As they reached the bridge, Maurice stopped, looking down at the trickling water.

"This is my favourite spot," he told her. "If you listen carefully, you can hear the trees in the wood whispering as the wind blows through them."

Fran tilted her head but couldn't make out anything. "Perhaps there isn't enough wind tonight."

"Close your eyes," Maurice instructed, "then you can hear it."

Fran did as instructed, half expecting Fabron to lean in and kiss her. After a few moments she opened her eyes, slightly disappointed when he hadn't planted his lips upon hers. "Yes, I think I heard something."

Maurice smiled. "The more you come here, the easier it will be."

The pair were silent for several minutes, each unsure of how to proceed with the conversation when there was so much that they wanted to ask one another.

"I shouldn't be telling you this," the baker said finally, unable to hold back, "but I think it might help you to sleep easier tonight."

"Go on…"

"Jack Hobbs doesn't think that you are involved in the attempt to poison Enzo Roche, and he's a very good judge of character."

Fran's face gave no clue to her feelings, instead looking completely blank. "I suppose I should be glad," she sighed, letting go of Maurice's arm and placing both hands on the top of the stone bridge, "but I'm still pretty shocked that they took me in for questioning in the first place. I won't lie to you, Maurice, it makes me feel tarnished in a way, being under suspicion."

"Perhaps they are just covering themselves," the baker offered, "for lack of any real clues to go on. I'm sure they will be looking closely at all the hospital staff."

"Maybe… I just wish they'd started with someone else."

Maurice sensed his new friend welling up with emotion and slid an arm around Fran's shoulder as she fought to hold back the tears. "Everything will be alright, I'm sure of it. Just promise to be honest with me."

"I'm sorry, I didn't mean to spoil such a lovely evening, Maurice. I'm truly grateful for your kindness, and your friendship. I have nothing to hide."

As soon as the final word had left Fran Shepherd's lips, both she and Maurice knew that there was much more between them. The chemistry was almost magnetic, drawing them together in an invisible bond. Their lips found each other, growing more and more passionate by the second as the couple's arms locked around each other's bodies in a tender embrace.

Maurice Fabron tried to push the doubt from his mind. He wanted to believe that Fran was innocent, and he would be there to fight her corner.

Relaxing on the sofa in his apartment, Max Mallery flicked through various television channels, unable to settle on any one programme. His mind kept wandering back to the conversation with Paul Theron earlier that evening.

It was true, they did have a lot of suspects, although no motives and very little to go on, and that was without widening the circle to people who might have a grudge against Enzo Roche. Max felt disturbed. What were they missing?

Had he been wrong to dismiss any connection between the murderer and Edwina Butler or Raymond Verdin? No, the target had to have been Roche. There was no way that whoever sent the gateau could have predicted who was going to eat it besides the person they'd sent it to, and that was Roche.

Mallery went into the kitchen and poured himself a glass of water. No more alcohol tonight, he needed a clear head to begin afresh in the morning, and that meant an early start. No doubt Audrey Rancourt would be pressing the team for answers, too; she'd made herself quite clear on that point.

Five minutes later, Max was standing in the shower, face tilted up towards the pounding water, eyelids closed, hands pressing against the walls of the cubicle.

A dark-haired woman flashed into his mind's eye, startling Mallery and causing him to open his eyes wide. There was nobody there, but he was certain that the image was that of the nurse, Fran Shepherd. What was it about her that he found so intriguing? She was definitely hiding something, he knew that much, but whether it was connected to the two deaths was another matter altogether.

"Pull yourself together," Max told himself out loud. "Focus."

Allowing himself ten more minutes under the steaming flow of water, easing the tension from his limbs, the inspector tried to erase both the woman from his mind and the guilt that he'd felt at bringing her in to the station earlier.

Jack Hobbs was unbuttoning his shirt and watching Angélique undress in the dressing-table mirror. He loved the way in which his wife elegantly slipped off her dress and allowed it to slide to the floor in one sweeping motion. It was true what they said about French women being incredibly chic, he thought, as he couldn't recall a single girlfriend back home who would have been able to disrobe in such a naturally sexy way.

Jack stifled a laugh as he recalled one past relationship during his days at police college. The young woman in question had been naturally clumsy, and most probably the pair of them had drunk a fair amount in those days, and she had fallen off the bed in an attempt to untangle herself from the thick winter tights she'd been wearing. Hobbs couldn't imagine Angélique getting into such a pickle, but neither could he recall a time when he'd laughed so much, either. Patsy, that was her name; a fiery redhead like himself, and now a Detective Sergeant in Wakefield.

"Do you like what you see?" Angélique asked provocatively, catching his eye.

"Of course! You looked hot in that dress tonight, it's my favourite colour."

His wife picked up the red cotton shift from the floor and dropped it into the laundry basket. "Hot? Not beautiful or chic?"

Jack could feel himself treading water as he grasped for an appropriate reply.

"You know what I mean. You always look stunning."

There was a playful smirk on his wife's lips. "Good answer. What do you think about Maurice and Fran? Are they getting involved romantically?"

"No, don't be daft, she was just treating him to a meal as a thank-you for letting her rent the apartment. Don't start reading too much into it, Ange."

Angélique waved a hand to dismiss his response. "Didn't you see the way that they were looking at each other? Are you blind?"

"No, she spent most of her time talking to you about clothes. I didn't notice any connection between them."

A pillow flew through the air and just missed Jack's head by an inch. "Really? Thank goodness you are a better at solving crimes than match-making!"

Hobbs' mouth fell open. "You don't seriously think that..."

"Yes, I do, and do you know what else?" Angélique put a hand to her ear as though straining to hear something. "I think there will be wedding bells!"

Jack shook his head, "Get into bed, you've gone mad, woman!"

The Frenchwoman slid under the covers and smiled. "Wait and see."

"Did you enjoy your breakfast, Enzo?"

Nurse Shepherd smiled at the patient as she counted out two Diazepam tablets from the portable drugs trolley and then leaned over to pour a glass of water.

"I can't eat, Frannie darling," the ex-dancer responded, hunching down in his chair. "It's just not the same in the dining room without Edwina."

"You have to eat something," Fran warned, tilting her chin to indicate that she needed to watch Enzo swallow the pills. "What about a pancake?"

"Really, I couldn't. I'll try something later."

Checking the man's pulse and temperature, the nurse seemed satisfied that missing a meal would do him no harm and made to leave the room.

"Can't you stay a while?" Enzo pleaded, as he picked at the loose threads on a cotton blanket.

"You know I've got my rounds to finish, I'll come back later, on my break. Besides you've got your appointment with Doctor Lafoy at ten."

Glancing at the police officer on duty just outside the door, the patient lowered his voice and beckoned Fran closer. "I don't trust her, Frannie. Three months now and she still won't sign me out. I'm well enough to go home."

The nurse considered the statement as she closed the lid on the trolley. "Have you asked her why?"

"Oh, yes, plenty of times. She just says I'm not stable enough and she needs to keep an eye on me. You know, I wouldn't be surprised if it was Juliette Lafoy who was trying to poison me."

Fran glanced at the officer, but he hadn't turned around, so she guessed that he had been unable to hear the accusation. "Whatever makes you say that?"

"Just a hunch, but my instincts are usually spot-on."

Nurse Shepherd placed a hand on Roche's arm and whispered in his ear, "I'll keep an eye on her, okay? Is that the real reason why you're not eating?"

Enzo nodded. "She could tamper with anything that comes from the kitchen."

"Will you eat something if I fetch it myself? Please?"

"Alright, darling, if you insist. I trust you."

Fran wheeled the wooden cabinet out of the room and stopped next to Officer Jacques Gibault. "Monsieur Roche has an appointment with Doctor Lafoy in half an hour, perhaps you would be good enough to accompany him?"

Gibault was surprised at the Englishwoman's excellent French and nodded enthusiastically. "Of course, but I will need to wait outside, surely?"

"Most probably, but just make sure he returns here fit and well."

Jacques looked confused as he watched Fran walk down the corridor, but he mentally made a note of her words and vowed to call Mallery at the end of his shift.

Juliette Lafoy was dressed in a red and white polka-dot shirt and black trousers, an outfit that was far too stifling for the warm summer's day, yet she insisted upon maintaining a semblance of professionalism, even at the cost of feeling uncomfortable. Her hair was tied back in a chignon at the nape of her neck and the only visible jewellery was a smart gold watch with which she measured each patient's session to the minute. It was now a minute before ten, the second hand ticking away the time until her first patient, and then, as though programmed to arrive dead on schedule, there was a knock at the door.

"*Entrez.*"

Officer Gibault pulled at the handle and ushered Enzo inside, smiling at the psychiatrist as he closed the door behind him and left.

"*Bonjour, Enzo,*" Juliette began, watching the man like a hawk.

Roche placed his hands in his lap and met her gaze. "*Bonjour, Doctor Lafoy.*"

Outside the door, Jacques Gibault could faintly hear the muffled conversation and wondered if he was breaching some kind of patient confidentiality by being there. Still, it had been the English nurse who had insisted upon him accompanying Roche to the doctor's room, so she must have her suspicions about the female psychiatrist. He wondered what to do. Mallery had told the officers to keep an eye on anyone going to or from Roche's room, especially if they were carrying food or gifts, but he had mentioned nothing about going to the patient's therapy session. Gibault checked the time and made up his mind. In two hours he would be finishing his shift and would call into the station on his way home to report Fran Shepherd's suspicions.

Paul Theron smoothed down his tie and stepped forward to shake hands with Gerald Butler. The tall, gangly Englishman looked pale, no doubt upset by his sister's death and also tired from his journey over to France. He was dressed formally in a black suit, a crisp white shirt and a patterned grey tie.

"Good of you to see me," Butler acknowledged, his fingers cold and bony against Theron's warm skin. "I expect you're terribly busy."

"I can always find time to see the family of the recently departed," Paul assured him. "Besides, these are rather unfortunate circumstances."

"I rather thought that the police inspector in charge of the case might be joining us. I would have liked him to bring me up to date with progress."

As the coroner was opening his mouth to respond, the steel entrance doors clattered open and Max Mallery hurried inside.

"Sorry, sorry, my apologies," he called out, striding across the tiled floor, "I got held up in the traffic. Monsieur Butler? I'm Inspector Mallery."

The man stretched out his hand and made a quick assessment of the suave inspector, noting his impeccably tailored jacket and leather brogues.

"How do you do? Very glad to meet you, Inspector."

Theron coughed and gestured towards his office at the other end of the corridor. "Shall we take coffee in my office? We can speak privately there."

The coroner's receptionist took the hint and moved towards a side kitchen to prepare a cafetière as three sets of footsteps clip-clopped down the hall.

As soon as they were seated, Gerald Butler turned to Max and adopted a stern tone. "Have you found the person who did this to my sister?"

"Not yet, Monsieur, but we are pursuing several lines of inquiry. Please rest assured that we will find the person who murdered Edwina."

Butler took out a white handkerchief and dabbed at his lips. "It's been five days, Inspector Mallery, surely you must have something to go on?"

"As I said, Monsieur, we are looking a several possible suspects."

"Mmm, very well, but I have no intention of laying poor Edwina to rest until her murderer is behind bars. Understood?"

Max glanced at Paul and ran a hand through his hair, the habit that Mallery always adopted when feeling under pressure. "I'm sure that Coroner Theron is happy to release your sister's body as soon as you wish."

Butler shook his head, undeterred. "That may well be, but I'll be staying right here in Bordeaux until the case is closed. I want to see justice done, Inspector Mallery and I'm not going anywhere until I'm certain that it is."

Max took a deep breath and exhaled slowly through his nose. "Of course, as you wish. Do you have a contact number here in Bordeaux?"

"I'm staying at the Hilton Garden Inn, Room 511."

Mallery plucked a card from his inside pocket and passed it across with two fingers. "My number, Monsieur Butler, call me any time."

As coffee was brought in and placed on Theron's desk, a silence descended upon the trio. The coroner wondering how long it would be before Edwina Butler was laid to rest, Gerald contemplating the competence of the distinguished-looking police detective in front of him, and Max hoping that Gerald Butler wasn't the kind of man to ring him at all hours of the day and night demanding answers.

Enzo Roche returned to his room a minute after eleven, Doctor Lafoy having finished their session on the dot. As promised, Fran Shepherd had been watching for his return and was pleased to see Officer Gibault following Roche back to his room at a discreet distance.

"How was it?" she asked, slipping in through the door behind Roche. "Did you ask why she won't sign your release papers?"

Enzo dabbed face powder over his nose and looked at Fran in the reflection of the mirror. "She gave me the usual bullshit about not being ready. I feel worn out, Frannie, I really do. Lafoy kept pressing me about my childhood, asking whether I was happy as a young boy."

"Hasn't she ever asked you about your background before?"

"Yes, she has, several times, but I told her that everything was completely normal. I don't understand why she keeps coming back to the same question."

Fran shrugged. "Maybe it's just part of the therapy, I wouldn't worry about it."

Enzo frowned, wrinkling up his small nose. "It's more than that, Frannie, she's digging for dirt."

The nurse was confused. "Why on earth would she do that?"

"I don't know, but she's definitely up to something."

In an attempt to steer the conversation away from Juliette Lafoy, Fran laid a hand on Enzo's shoulder and met his gaze in the mirror. "Dorothy has gone down to the kitchen, she's fetching the pancakes that I persuaded chef to make for you, they're filled with bananas and honey."

Roche lifted his fingers to his mouth and blew a kiss at Fran. "You do spoil me, Frannie, thank you. You're sure they'll be safe?"

The nurse pointed to Officer Gibault, who stood close to the door with his hands in his pockets. "I'm sure that we can ask this kind officer to try them first."

Jacque's Adam's apple lifted in his throat as he gulped at the words.

Both nurse and patient burst out laughing, only stopping when Fran realised how panicked the policeman really was. "I'm only joking. Dorothy has been in the kitchen the whole time, the pancakes are quite safe to eat."

Luc Martin lifted his head as a packet of chocolate cookies slid into view.

"Where is everyone?" Max asked, leaning on the edge of the computer whiz's desk as he watched Luc deftly rip open the biscuits.

Luc counted off the team on his fingers. "Thierry is speaking to the letting agent who rented out the cottage, Gabi is out in Riberon talking to Raymond Verdin's wife and Hercule Poirot is out fetching lunch."

Mallery laughed at the comparison between Jack Hobbs and the Belgian detective. They couldn't be more dissimilar in looks, yet the English detective certainly had a nose for sniffing out trouble, just like Agatha Christie's creation.

"Anyway," Luc continued, "you might want to sit down for this."

Max was intrigued and reached for a swivel chair, pulling it up alongside Martin's desk. "I'm listening."

"It's Juliette Lafoy, there's something you need to know about her."

Luc tapped at his keyboard and turned the screen for his boss to see. "She applied for the position at the sanatorium three months ago. Before that, she was working at a day clinic."

Max waited patiently, aware that it was Luc's habit to build up the story to a grand finale for which he would almost expect a round of applause.

"Well, guess who regularly went to the clinic for counselling after his relationship breakdown?"

Mallery had already clicked on to where this was going. "Enzo Roche?"

"Correct. Although Lafoy didn't see him personally, she did try to get Roche transferred to her patient list. However, he was under the senior psychiatrist and her request was refused."

"So, it might not be a coincidence," the inspector mused, "that she is now working at the same facility where Roche is an in-patient?"

"I doubt it, boss. She applied for the position straight after Roche was admitted, but it took a while for the reference checks to go through and then, naturally, her predecessor was working his notice period."

"What game is she playing, Luc?"

The techie filled his mouth with a cookie and gave a muffled reply. "I don't know for sure, but it certainly looks dodgy."

Max was rubbing the bristly stubble on his chin. "The question is, do I ask her straight out, or do we dig a little bit more?"

"Why not ask Leon Cassell about it? He hired her, so he must have known."

"Good thinking. When the others get back, tell them I want a team meeting at four. No excuses."

"Yes, boss. Thanks for the snacks."

"You deserve it, Luc. Just keep searching, see what else you can find out."

"Oh, by the way," Martin called as the inspector reached the door, "Jack had something for you on that nurse, too – Fran Shepherd."

Mallery stopped in his tracks. "Did he say what?"

"No, but I should think he'll be back…" Luc's voice trailed off as Hobbs appeared in the corridor carrying a takeaway sandwich.

"With me," Max told him. "You can eat that on the way."

Mallery collapsed the BMW roof as he waited for the sports car engine to warm up, eyeing his colleague's lunch as he did so.

"I'm not driving out to Riberon with the smell of egg mayonnaise up my nose. You could have chosen a less offensive sandwich, Jacques."

The Yorkshireman chuckled and began to peel off the wrapper. "Sorry, it was just what I fancied. Do you want half?"

Max wrinkled his nose in jest. "No, I certainly don't!"

The car pulled out of the police headquarters car park and joined the long queue of traffic heading towards the highway. The inspector fiddled with the radio as he waited for the cars in front to move down the road.

"Luc said that you've found out something about Fran Shepherd."

Jack licked a piece of watercress off his top lip and nodded. "Yes, she's married."

"*Married*? But I thought you said that she and Maurice…"

"I don't know for sure, but they seemed pretty close at the bistro. I hope she's not messing him about."

Max could feel the hackles rising on his neck in defence of his friend. "I think we'll have to tell Maurice, it's only fair."

"Don't you think that she should tell him herself?" Jack reasoned. "After all, everything else about her checks out. She's had a successful career and is more than qualified for her job at the hospital in Riberon."

"She's lying to one of my best friends."

Hobbs lifted a finger. "Ah, we don't actually know that, do we?"

"Well, there's only one way to find out."

The rest of the journey was spent in silence, with Mallery brooding over the secrets that Fran was keeping and Hobbs wishing that he'd had a chance to speak to the nurse before his boss went blundering in with both feet. Knowing Max, it wouldn't be long before he was demanding answers and warning Fran to keep well away from their mutual friend.

Leon Cassell rose from his chair and removed the gold-rimmed spectacles from his nose. "Inspector Mallery, Detective Hobbs, what a surprise, I wasn't expecting to see you today. I didn't see a scheduled appointment..."

Max was still irritated and had adopted a no-nonsense attitude, every inch of his body and expression taut and defensive.

"Monsieur Cassell, we can never predict when new information is uncovered. We have a few questions that cannot wait. Is now a good time?"

Cassell made a show of shuffling papers on his desk. "As you can see, I'm up to my eyes in work, but I suppose I can spare a few minutes."

Mallery didn't wait to be invited to sit and pulled out a chair opposite the hospital manager, gesturing for Hobbs to do likewise.

"We would like to ask you about Doctor Lafoy and her tenure here. Did you offer her the position yourself?"

"Yes. Yes, I did. Our resident psychiatrist, Doctor Blume, had given his notice, he was taking up a lecturing post at the university, you see. Juliette Lafoy was one of three candidates whom I interviewed."

"And you deemed her to be the person who was best suited for the job?"

A crimson flush appeared on Leon's cheeks as he considered the question. "Yes, I did. She's well-qualified, and had very good references."

Max narrowed his eyes, trying to gauge the truthfulness in Cassell's next response. "Are you aware that Doctor Lafoy worked at the same clinic where Enzo Roche was being seen as an outpatient after his accident?"

The large man's jaw dropped open and Mallery could see that the question had come as something of a shock. He studied Cassell's face carefully.

"I had no idea, Inspector. Of course, I knew where Juliette was working, but I hadn't a clue that Enzo was having counselling there. Do you think it's relevant?"

Mallery opened his palms. "I have no idea yet, but it seems rather too much of a coincidence to me. This is, of course, just between us, for now."

"Indeed." Cassell was almost lost for words. "You don't think…"

Max got to his feet and held out his hand. "I don't know what to think yet, Monsieur, but perhaps you will let me know if anything comes to mind."

As the detectives were leaving Leon Cassell sitting in a thoughtful, if not agitated state, another familiar figure was descending the grand staircase. Nurse Shepherd raised a hand at Jack Hobbs and then glanced at her boss, who was still reeling from the inspector's recent interrogation.

"Good afternoon." She smiled politely on reaching the bottom step. "Long time no see. I didn't expect to see you again so soon."

"Perhaps too soon," Max grumbled, as he stood indignantly with his hands in both trouser pockets. "Are you free for a moment, Madame Shepherd?"

"I was just about to take my lunch break," she answered, holding up a plastic lunchbox, "but you're more than welcome to accompany me outside."

Jack Hobbs was inwardly groaning, hoping that Mallery wasn't going to go charging into Fran's private life like a bull in a china shop.

"Maybe now's not the time..." he started, tugging at Max's sleeve.

"Wait for me in the car, Jacques," Mallery grunted through gritted teeth. "This won't take long."

From the front seat of the BMW, Jack could see Fran walk over to a bench positioned in the shade under an apple tree. Max walked silently alongside, glancing across at the nurse every few seconds. At first, they looked like any normal adults having a polite conversation, but then Fran stood, hands on hips as she wagged a finger at the seated inspector. Despite not being able to hear raised voices, Hobbs could tell by the Englishwoman's face that she was not amused by the way in which the police officer was speaking to her.

111

A few minutes passed and Max leaned back against the bench, his face becoming placid as he listened. Fran was animated for a while, but then dropped down beside him and rubbed her cheek. Jack wondered whether she was wiping away a tear or trying to cool down her fraying temper. As the altercation came to a close, the inspector put a hand on the nurse's shoulder and rubbed it gently. It looked as though Max Mallery was apologising.

Then, leaving Fran Shepherd to eat her lunch in peace, the police officer strode back to the car and climbed in, looking several shades whiter than he had a short while ago. Hobbs could see his boss's shoulders visibly sagging.

"Jacques," he said quietly, "next time, stop me from making a fool of myself."

Fran Shepherd returned to the building through the back, making a detour to the staff locker room before resuming her duties. Turning the lock on the metal door, the nurse immediately reached for her bag and, before tucking her uneaten lunch inside, pulled it towards her and recovered the familiar white envelope. It was looking slightly dog-eared by now, the letter within having been removed several times over the past few months, and Fran sighed as she stared at the small, untidy handwriting. *Better to put it in the incinerator now*, she told herself, *there's no point in keeping it.*

"Is there a problem, Nurse Shepherd?"

Juliette Lafoy's slightly high-pitched voice was close by. Fran turned, at the same time pushing the correspondence out of sight.

"No, Doctor, why would there be?" she asked innocently.

Juliette displayed a smear of lipstick on her teeth as she spoke. "I thought I saw you talking to that police inspector just now."

"Yes, I was, but there's no problem. Just a few questions to clear up."

"About the patients?"

Fran bit her bottom lip before blurting out the lie. "Yes."

"Well, perhaps you would direct them to me in future. After all, I do know far more about our inpatients than the rest of the staff here."

"I'll bear that in mind, Doctor Lafoy."

Sharp, red-painted nails dug into Fran's arm unexpectedly. "We wouldn't want them getting the wrong information now, would we?"

The nurse pulled herself from Lafoy's grip and watched as the psychiatrist forced her mouth into a sneer. "Just watch your step, that's all I'm saying."

Fran waited until Juliette had stormed off before retrieving the letter once more, running a forefinger over the unsteady lettering as she took it through the back kitchen and out to the incinerator where bandages, used medical supplies and other toxic waste were regularly burned. With a flick of the wrist, it was gone, smoking hot in the cinders within seconds, all evidence of her past life removed.

Leon Cassell had been on his way to the kitchen to seek out a second portion of chef's excellent apple tart when he'd seen the altercation between doctor and nurse from the locker room doorway. He hadn't stopped for fear of being seen, but instead had pressed his large frame against the outer wall in order to hear the conversation. So, Mallery had been talking to Nurse Shepherd, had he? How interesting. Nothing had been mentioned about her at their meeting earlier.

The inspector had made a point of asking Cassell not to tell Doctor Lafoy that he knew about her having previously worked at the clinic where Enzo Roche was having counselling, but now to discover that Fran had also been under scrutiny, caused a stir inside him. Were both women police suspects?

Abandoning his mission to fuel up with a second dessert, Leon had quickly made his way back to the office and now sat tapping his fingers on the desk. Should he add fuel to the fire by telling Mallery about Fran Shepherd's very close relationship to Roche? Or were they already keeping a close eye on the nurse? Surely the officer on duty upstairs had overheard their conversations.

And what of Juliette Lafoy? Perhaps an impromptu dinner invitation might entice her to open up about her involvement with Enzo Roche and her reasons for wanting to follow him to the sanatorium. It would hardly be an unpleasant task to wine and dine the woman, would it? Not with her petite figure and impeccable fashion sense, not to mention that pert backside.

Cassell allowed a reasonable time to pass for Lafoy to get settled back at her desk, before lifting the phone and dialling her extension number.

"Juliette?" he purred, adopting a soothing tone. "I think it might be prudent if we get together to discuss the ongoing police investigation, on a professional level, of course. Perhaps you would care to dine with me tonight?"

He waited for the predictable sigh and moment of silence that always followed such conversations with the psychiatrist; it was almost as though she thought herself far too superior to be seen out with Cassell and was considering the invitation with either resentment or distaste.

Eventually, having feigned checking her diary, Juliette agreed.

"You're free? How splendid, I'll meet you in the lobby at seven."

"You're quite safe, I saw Commissioner Rancourt going out ten minutes ago," Luc told the team, as they assembled in the incident room.

"Good, at least we can get on with the briefing uninterrupted," Max countered, instinctively moving towards the old whiteboard.

"Boss," Jack winked, passing the inspector an iPad, "they're all connected to the main screen now."

"Mmm, of course."

Mallery spent a few minutes tapping at the device before he was ready to begin.

"Okay, Thierry, what did you find out at the agent's office?"

Marceau looked even darker than usual, having been out in the sun for most of the afternoon, and his brown eyes sparkled. "So, the cottage is owned by an elderly couple, as we found out earlier, but they're currently on a cruise. They've been letting out the property for the past five years, the last three of those to employees of the private hospital."

"So, who lived there before Fran Shepherd?" Max wanted to know.

Detective Moreau consulted his notes before answering, "Juliette Lafoy's predecessor, Doctor Florian Blume."

Mallery turned to Luc. "Where does Lafoy live?"

Martin clicked a few letters on his keyboard. "In Salbec, in a rented house. What's the significance?"

"I'm just wondering why Juliette Lafoy didn't take over the tenancy from Doctor Blume? After all, she was stepping into his professional shoes."

Luc looked up through his long, wispy fringe. "Lafoy arrived a month after Shepherd. According to personnel files, Doctor Blume spent the last month of his tenure in a self-contained apartment at the sanatorium."

Mallery was confused. "Why? I mean, why move out of the cottage and then have to move again a month later when he left his job? It doesn't make sense."

Jack Hobbs was looking pensive. "Thierry, who signed the tenancy agreement? Was it done by the individual or the hospital?"

There was silence as Moreau flicked through his notepad. "The hospital. In all three cases, Blume, Shepherd and Lafoy, the leases were arranged at the same time as the contracts."

"So, ultimately, the responsibility fell to Leon Cassell," Max noted.

"It looks that way, yes."

"Okay, something to keep in mind. Now, Gabriella, any news about Raymond Verdin's funeral?"

Gabi nodded, her blonde ponytail bobbing up and down. "Yes, it will be at two on Friday afternoon. Do you want me to go?"

Mallery wondered if the sombre gathering might be too much for the female detective, given the emotional turmoil she had suffered during their anti-terrorism surveillance a few weeks previously, but Gabriella was smiling and looked as though she was recovering well from the ordeal.

"Do you mind?" he asked.

There was no hesitation. "Of course not."

"Jacques, would you go with her?" Max requested of Hobbs. "You know what they say about murderers being tempted to go to their victim's funerals."

"What, you reckon the poisoner will be hiding in plain sight?" Jack scoffed.

"You never know, I've seen stranger things."

"Have you found out anything about Fran Shepherd?" Gabriella probed. "I mean, she was living at the cottage where the water-hemlock was found, so that makes her the prime suspect, doesn't it?"

A conspiratorial look passed between Mallery and Hobbs, Max biting the bullet and answering the question head-on. "It does, but both Jacques and I don't think she's involved. Call it a... Jacques, what did you say it was?"

"A hunch," the red-haired detective provided. "Yes, it just seems a little too convenient for her to be right where the poisonous plant is growing. I don't think she's involved, more like somebody is using the cottage to frame Fran."

Gabi's nose for detection was on high alert. "What makes you so sure?"

"As Max said, just a hunch, but one I'm prepared to stake my reputation on."

Fran entered the large open lounge and headed towards Enzo Roche, who was sitting at a table concentrating on a jigsaw puzzle with another middle-aged man. She had noticed the police officer sitting on a chair in the corner of the room and thought that at least Jacques Gibault looked as though he was carrying out his duties a little more discreetly today.

"Enzo, Rafael," the English nurse greeted her patients, "I'm going home now, so just thought I'd stop by and say goodbye. I'll see you both tomorrow."

Rafael turned his lopsided face upwards and half-smiled at Fran, the effects of a recent stroke preventing him from achieving a full grin. "'Bye, Fran."

Enzo slotted a piece of jigsaw into place and patted the chair next to him. "Sit down for a minute please, Frannie. I need to talk to you."

Nurse Shepherd was immediately concerned. It wasn't like Enzo to be so secretive; dramatic, yes, but not like this, speaking in such a hushed tone. She pulled out the chair and sat, dropping her bag onto the patterned carpet.

"What's wrong?"

Roche allowed his eyes to travel the full circle of the room before he felt satisfied that nobody, apart from Rafael, was in earshot.

"It's Doctor Lafoy," he whispered, clearly distressed. "I asked her again about signing my release papers, but she won't have it. According to her, I need at least another three months of therapy!"

Fran listened with incredulity. "Seriously? But three months ago, Doctor Blume said that you would be ready to go home in a month. What reason did she give?"

Roche placed his beautifully manicured hands in his lap and pursed his lips. "That's just it, she didn't give one specific reason, just said that staying here for a while longer was for my own benefit. Would you speak to Monsieur Cassell for me, Frannie? Please? You know that I'd be better off away from here, where I can try to start dancing again and recuperating in my own home."

Fran did think that Enzo was ready to go home. After all, his being at the sanatorium was not only of great personal cost to the former ballet dancer, but it prevented him from being rehabilitated back into society. However, on the other hand, she had to be careful not to get on the wrong side of Juliette Lafoy. The psychiatrist obviously had her own professional reasons for wanting to detain Roche as a patient and Fran's interference would no doubt be received with nothing but animosity.

"Let me see what I can find out," she said eventually, turning over the possibilities in her mind. "I can't promise anything, but I'll certainly try. Are you sure she didn't give a reason? I mean, you're not thinking of self-harming again are you, Enzo?"

The man brought his face closer, enabling Fran to see the fine lines beneath his make-up. "No, darling, I'm not. All that is behind me now, I promise."

The nurse was satisfied and reached for her bag as she pushed out the chair. "Okay, just bear with me, I'll get to the bottom of it, Enzo, I promise."

As Fran wheeled her bicycle to the end of the sanatorium's long gravel drive, a text message buzzed through on her phone. She leaned the handlebars against the hedge to read it and couldn't help but smile on seeing the familiar number.

Oh, Maurice, she smiled to herself, *of course I'll join you for a glass of wine.*

Quickly typing a response, telling the boulangerie owner that she needed an hour to get home and shower before going over to his house, Fran mounted the bike and pedalled away, the only visible sign of her troubled conversation with Enzo Roche now being a few taut lines on her forehead.

Juliette Lafoy's ears were not burning that afternoon. Having been completely unaware of the two conversations that had taken place with her as the main subject, she was now in the staff restroom reapplying her make-up.

"Not too much, Juliette," she told herself, dabbing at the pink lip gloss with a tissue, "you don't want Cassell getting the wrong idea."

There was a flush and a clatter from behind her as a toilet seat was slammed down, followed by the lock sliding back and Dorothy Ramos' cheerful face.

"Sorry, Doctor." The short, plump Filipino smiled broadly. "Did you say something?"

"No, no, just talking to myself," the psychiatrist replied, pushing the glittery tube back into her purse. "Nothing to worry about."

"That's the first sign of madness," Dorothy chuckled good-naturedly, "so I'm told."

Juliette caught the nurse's eye in the mirror as the shorter woman washed her hands. "Really? Well, I can assure you that I'm completely sane, Madame Ramos."

Dorothy shrugged as the doctor hurried out, letting the door bang to a close behind her. "I'm just saying you're in the right place, that's all!"

"Right on time, Doctor," Leo Cassell called at the top of his voice as Juliette descended the stairs into the foyer. "I thought we might drive into town."

Quickly calculating that the car journey into Bordeaux and back would add at least an extra forty minutes onto her evening, the psychiatrist grimaced. The last thing she wanted was to have to make small talk with the hospital manager as he navigated the winding lanes out of Riberon. At best, she had hoped for a glass of wine and a light meal before making her excuses for requiring an early night. It seemed that Monsieur Cassell had other ideas.

"Lovely," she replied, following the tall bald man out to his saloon car, a silver-grey Mercedes Benz which had been parked in full view of the dining room window. Great, not only did she have to endure the man's incessant pandering, but now they would be the talk of the whole facility, by staff and patients alike. As if to confirm her fears, several faces craned their necks forward to watch the doctor climb into Cassell's car, Dorothy Ramos amongst them. Juliette could just imagine the gossip.

Leon gracefully raced around to open the passenger side door and ensured that his date was comfortable before setting off. It was as though the pair were acting out some rather elaborate comedy, with Cassell determined that their audience should watch every step and gesture, whilst Juliette shrank down into her seat and turned away from the glaring eyes. Finally satisfied that the opening scene had been viewed by all, Leon started the engine, turned his beaming smile upon the doctor and guided the vehicle towards the open gates.

***

Fran Shepherd had showered quickly, rubbing the lotion all over her body while plotting what to wear. For goodness' sake, she told herself, it's only drinks in the garden, no need to go overboard. But the mental image of the interior of her closet wouldn't shift from the woman's mind as she conjured up possible outfits. The evening was warm, no need for a jacket or cardigan, but it might get cooler later. Long sleeves then? Or a dress and carry a pashmina to put on later?

By the time Fran had blow-dried her short dark bob, the decision was made. She would wear a simple navy shift dress and carry a cream shawl with her. Applying just the lightest touch of foundation and a nude lipstick, the nurse was pleased with the result. She looked refreshed, casual and, dare she think it, sexy.

The walk to Maurice Fabron's *maison du maître* took no more than a couple of minutes, being situated directly across the street from the boulangerie, yet Fran took her time and composed herself before entering the side gate to the garden. The house was vast, certainly the grandest building in Saint Margaux, with its three storeys and multiple windows, yet the baker was such a modest and unassuming man, certainly not the type of person to bring attention to his wealth.

There was something she needed to tell Maurice tonight and it wasn't pleasant. However, it was a task that needed to be got over with, tidied away and then forgotten about. Of course, Fran would have liked the opportunity to get to know Maurice much better before spilling her secrets but, thanks to her earlier conversation with Inspector Mallery, she had been left with no such choice.

As she reached the French doors leading to Fabron's stunning kitchen, Fran could smell freshly baked bread wafting through the opening and it reminded her that she hadn't eaten anything since breakfast, thanks to the police officer's unexpected tirade.

"Maurice, *bonjour*," she called, spotting the tall man at the kitchen counter.

"Fran, welcome," he returned in English, "I'm so glad you could come."

The couple embraced, Maurice holding Fran in his arms just a moment longer than necessary, but she enjoyed the smell of his aftershave and clean skin.

"Let's take a glass of wine outside," Maurice suggested, leading the way, "Telo has gone to play music with a friend tonight, so we won't be disturbed."

"I'm glad," Fran replied softly, looking into his eyes, "because there's something I need to tell you and it cannot wait."

Seated in a secluded corner of a Mediterranean restaurant, Leon Cassell made a great show of deliberating over the wine list, attempting to impress his dinner date with sharing the merits of a local Chenin Blanc over an imported Sauvignon. Juliette, to her credit, attempted to look interested, but found her eyes glazing over after the first few minutes of conversation.

"I'm sure the Chenin Blanc is wonderful," she told him, rather too sharply, turning her attention to the menu, "I'm not much of a wine connoisseur."

Casssell ordered a bottle after another moment's scrutiny and then turned his attention to his companion. "Is everything alright, Juliette?"

"Of course, why wouldn't it be?"

Leon stopped himself from blundering on, choosing his words carefully. "Well, you know, all this business with Madam Butler and Raymond, it's sure to put everyone on edge."

Doctor Lafoy seemed to look through the manager, rather than at him, letting her concentration sway slightly. "No, I'm perfectly alright. It's not as if I knew either of them very well."

"True, but to think we have a murderer in our midst…"

Leon let the words hang in the air, judging Lafoy's reaction carefully.

The psychiatrist's blue eyes continued to scan the meals, running her forefinger along the descriptions of each to read the accompaniments.

"Sorry, what were you saying…?" Juliette answered, eventually looking up. "Why don't you tell me what's really troubling you, Monsieur Cassell?"

Despite Inspector Mallery having asked the manager to keep details of Lafoy's previous employment between themselves for now, Leon was sorely tempted to push the doctor for answers. She intrigued him and perhaps, by divulging his earlier conversation with the detectives, he might be able to get Juliette onside.

The words were out before Cassell could stop them. "He knows about your previous position, at the clinic, where Enzo Roche received counselling…"

"Who?" The voice was high-pitched, panicked.

"Inspector Mallery, he's on to you, Juliette."

The bottle of Chablis was cold, chilling Fran's throat as she sipped and confessed all to her new beau. Maurice listened without judgement.

"I'm married, Maurice," she began, trying to control the slight quiver that was forcing itself out, "but the divorce papers are in, and it should be over soon."

"Do you want to tell me what happened?"

Fran felt unexpectedly warm in this man's company. Instead of being shocked at her confession, Maurice was giving her a choice of whether to go on or not.

"Yes. We were married for eight years. Happy, or so I thought, for most of them, except for one problem that couldn't be resolved."

She could feel Maurice's hand slide onto hers, gripping gently, encouraging.

"I was unable to get pregnant," Fran said quietly, hoping that the tears would stay at bay, "and that's what came between us."

"He couldn't accept the situation?"

"No. Although he said it was okay, we began to drift apart. Neil would make excuses and come home late, working extra shifts. We decided on a trial separation, a few months to clear our heads and possibly make a fresh start, but it turned into a year, and I just couldn't go on."

"Were you hoping for him to come back?" Maurice ventured.

"At first, yes, but then as time went on, I realised that our marriage was over. That's when I applied for the job here, in France. I needed to get away."

"Where is he now, your husband, back in England?"

Fran took a deep breath and a large gulp of wine. "I recently received a letter, my sister forwarded it to me. It was from Neil, telling me that he's met someone else and she's expecting his child at Christmas. He's having a baby with her!"

Tears bubbled, but Maurice was there, holding her tightly and kissing away the pain. "It's okay, no need to get upset. I'm so sorry. You didn't need to tell me this now, it could have waited. I can't imagine what you've had to go through."

Fran placed a hand on his cheek and stroked the smooth skin. "That's just it, I had to tell you tonight. Your friend, Inspector Mallery, he found out and threatened to tell you himself if I didn't. I hope you understand, Maurice."

Fabron gently pulled away. "Are you serious? Max said he would tell me?"

"Yes, I guess he found out during the investigation into the two murders, they must be checking everyone's backgrounds."

"But to threaten you, Fran? That's not right, and most inappropriate of Max."

The Englishwoman could feel Maurice's temper beginning to rise. "It's fine, he just said that if I didn't tell you, he would. I think he was just being a good friend, Maurice, trying to protect you."

"Wait until I see him," the baker grumbled. "Max had no right to upset you in this way. It's a very personal situation and he should have handled it better."

Maurice was on his feet now, pacing back and forth across the patio, one hand in his trouser pocket and the other ruffling his thick grey hair. He looked every bit the leading French actor with suave sophistication and natural good looks.

Oh crikey, Fran cursed inwardly, feeling her pulse begin to quicken, *I'm falling for him.*

Juliette Lafoy sat with her arms crossed tightly over her chest, staring out at the blurry evening as they drove past fields and villages. It was grating on her that Cassell insisted upon keeping a good ten kilometres per hour under the speed limit, and the psychiatrist suspected him of trying to prolong the journey.

"What do you want me to say?" she eventually snapped. "My being at the clinic at the same time as Enzo Roche is nothing more than pure coincidence. Don't try to make something out of it, I have nothing to hide."

Leon's large hands remained on the steering-wheel, focussed on the road ahead, although his eyes strayed to the side, weighing up the situation.

"My dear, I'm not saying that you're being secretive, I'm simply warning you that the police think you might have a motive for following Roche here. Come on, Juliette, we're friends, you can trust me. If there's anything I need to know in order to help you, don't hold back."

Doctor Lafoy wasn't warming to her employer. "There's nothing to tell."

"If you say so, I was simply trying to help. It's only a matter of time before Inspector Mallery and his team start looking at your work history and come to their own conclusions, whatever they may be, however right or wrong."

They were entering Riberon now and Cassell indicated right after a few hundred yards, towards Salbec and Juliette Lafoy's rented accommodation. It would soon be the end of their journey and time was quickly running out.

"How do I know I can trust you?" the doctor sighed, reaching for her bag which lay in the footwell. "I mean, if there was something I needed to share."

Leon supressed a smile, she was going to confide in him, at last.

"Of course, you can trust me. In my line of work I am entrusted with many different kinds of confidences, private information, confidential records. I just think you will feel a lot better if you get things out in the open. You know what they say about a problem shared, don't you?"

Juliette nodded. It was either trust Leon Cassell to help her or wait for Max Mallery to figure out what she was hiding and, from reading past newspaper reports about the inspector, it probably wouldn't take him very long to figure things out. The man was smart, sophisticated and very good at his job.

"Very well, Leon," she decided, as they pulled up outside her modest house. "Would you like to come in for coffee and I'll explain everything?"

Cassell had his seatbelt unsnapped almost as soon as the car came to a stop, flinging open the driver's door and swinging his long legs out onto the road.

Maurice Fabron clinked his glass against Fran's and proposed a toast. "To new beginnings, whatever they may bring."

Fran leaned back against the oversized striped cushions on the bench and sipped at her Chablis. It was ice-cold and slid down far too easily. The garden was quiet, save for a few birds singing in the trees, but then the tranquil moment was ruined by the sharp trill of the house phone.

"Excuse me, I'd better answer it," Maurice told her, reluctantly rising from Fran's side, "it might be important."

Fran watched him walk towards the open doors, thinking how lucky she was to find such a caring and sensitive soul. It didn't matter to her that Maurice was also terribly good-looking, with a sexy accent and toned physique. All of those attributes helped, of course, and she found it hard to take her eyes off him.

Within minutes, Maurice was back, a second bottle of chilled wine in his grip. "That was Telo, my son, he wants to stay over at his friend's house tonight. Apparently, they're watching horror films."

"That's a pity, I was hoping to see him."

Maurice looked down, trying to gauge whether Fran had genuinely wanted to spend some time with his only child. Her face was open and honest, and he believed her words to be sincere.

"There will be other days," he told her, "Telo really likes you."

Fran had only met the baker's son a couple of times over the past week, but on each occasion the young man had been polite and chatty, joking with her about village life in Saint Margaux being boring.

"I like him, too," she answered softly, kissing Maurice's cheek as he bent down to refill her glass. "He's very like his father."

Slipping the bottle into an ice-bucket, Fabron nestled back into Fran's side on the bench, "Would you like to stay over, *ma chérie?*"

The nurse felt her heart skip a beat, conflicting messages passing through her brain as though she were tossing an invisible coin into the air.

"It's very new, all this," she told Maurice. "You and me."

"Maybe, but it feels right. I haven't been this happy for a very long time."

Their lips found each other, locking together, at first gently and then turning into a much deeper passion as they lost themselves in the moment.

"What about Mallery?" Fran queried, pulling away slightly. "Aren't you worried about what he thinks? He's obviously been looking into my past.

"No, not at all," Maurice told her, gently tracing the curve of Fran's collarbone with his finger. "Our relationship has nothing to do with him."

"He was going to tell you about my husband…"

"And so, you told me yourself, which proves you have nothing to hide. Please don't let Max's mistakes ruin what we have."

Fran felt a weight lift from her shoulders as she slipped her arms around Maurice's torso, snuggling her head against his strong, muscular chest.

"In that case, let's finish our wine upstairs."

Max Mallery was a man on a mission that Thursday morning, determined to get to the bottom of the mysterious secrets that seemed to envelop the case like a dark shroud. It seemed to him that most of the likely suspects had something to hide and he didn't like it, not one bit.

"Jacques, do you feel like taking a drive with me this morning?" he asked Hobbs, as soon as the Yorkshireman entered the interview room. "I think we need to look into Doctor Lafoy's background, find out what she's up to."

"Yes, sure. I did a bit more digging into Fran Shepherd's history last night, and what she told you checks out. She worked for the NHS for ten years before coming here and by all accounts she's very good at her job. No complaints, great references and her personal life checks out, too."

"You mean about the husband?"

Jack nodded. "Yes, married to Neil Shepherd, separated last year. Divorce papers have been served. He currently lives with his new partner in Ipswich."

Max felt a great weight lifted from his shoulders. Fran had been telling him the truth and he dearly wished, now, that he hadn't pushed her so hard.

"What does Neil Shepherd do for a living?"

Mallery waited while Hobbs clicked open his computer and checked the file. "He's an IT engineer, for BT."

"What is BT?"

"Sorry, it's British Telecom, one the U.K.'s top internet and phone providers."

"I see, and does he have any previous convictions?"

"Three points on his driving licence for speeding, nothing else."

"Okay, great. It still doesn't put Fran in the clear," Max warned, "but it certainly doesn't push her to the top of our suspect list."

Jack was lifting a lunchbox from his rucksack and wandered over to the small fridge to put it inside. "So, you think Juliette Lafoy is more likely to be our culprit?"

Mallery wasn't sure of anything, but didn't like to show his frustration. "I think she's hiding something. Otherwise, why apply for a job at the exact place where Enzo Roche has been admitted and not divulge that information to Cassell?"

Before Hobbs could answer, Thierry and Gabi entered, closely followed by Luc, causing Max to turn his attention to the day's list of priorities.

"Thierry, did you manage to get access to the cottage? I'd like you to take a look around."

Moreau lifted a set of keys from his desk drawer. "I certainly did."

Luc Martin was hovering next to the coffee pot and looked expectantly at his boss. "I don't suppose I could…"

Max was quick on the uptake. "*Oui*, go on, you deserve some time away from your screen, as long as Thierry doesn't mind a passenger?"

The dark detective grinned. "There's a spare crash helmet in my locker."

"Okay, well, be sure to take a good look around," their boss instructed. "Look at any mail that might have arrived, in cupboards, everywhere. Uniform have cordoned off the water hemlock but check the rest of the garden for anything that doesn't belong there. You know the kind of thing, cigarette ends, bottles, rubbish, anything that could have been dropped accidentally."

"Got it," Thierry assured him.

Mallery was already turning his attention to Gabriella Dupont, eager to move swiftly on. "Gabi, see what you can find out about Daniel Baur, Roche's ex-lover. Find out if he had any family and, if possible, exactly what happened between him and Enzo."

"No problem. I'll get straight on to it. Max, what about Leon Cassell?"

"What about him?"

"Just something that Raymond Verdin's wife said yesterday. Apparently, Enzo had mentioned to Ray that he'd seen Cassell somewhere before, I mean other than at the hospital. She thought it was a bit odd, said that Enzo had been really troubled by it."

Mallery stood on the spot, thinking. "You have a point, we haven't really looked into Cassell yet, but resources are really stretched at the moment. I'll make an appointment to speak to Roche myself tomorrow, see if he can remember anything. You'll be at the funeral then, right?"

"Yes, I promised Chloe Verdin that I'd be there for support."

"Good. Thanks, Gabi, I'm sure she'll appreciate it."

Outside in the car park, Max walked straight past his own car, causing Jack to sigh and retrieve the Ford Mondeo keys from his trouser pocket. It was usually when his boss needed time to think that Hobbs was required to drive, and by the look on Mallery's face he had rather a lot on his mind.

As they drove south out of the city, the underside of Jack's wedding ring clicked against the steering-wheel as his fingers tapped in time to the Bee Gees. The Englishman could sense Max's shoulders tensing beside him but was determined to let the inspector pour out his troubles without being prompted.

"Turn left by the church," Mallery instructed, reaching for his cigarettes, and then pushing them back into his jacket again, remembering that his colleague wasn't keen on passengers smoking in his family saloon.

Jack indicated and navigated the road in silence, until an ambulance behind them prompted a significant reminder of something he'd witnessed earlier.

"I happened to see a certain dark-haired nurse sneaking out of Maurice's early this morning," he announced, a wry grin spreading on seeing Max's disbelief, "looks as though things are moving fast between them."

Mallery was shaking his head, unconvinced. "You must have been mistaken, they've only known each other a week or so."

"How long does it take? Maurice is a good-looking bloke."

Max worried the inside of his cheek, thinking. "He wouldn't, would he? Not when he knows that Fran Shepherd is under suspicion of murder."

"Come on, Max," Jack reasoned, "both you and I know that she's not involved, the evidence is purely circumstantial. Someone's trying to set her up."

"Until we have an arrest, we know nothing for sure, Jacques."

"She's a nice woman, fun and smart, and she's definitely smitten with Maurice."

Mallery frowned and shifted in his seat. "How do you know so much about her all of a sudden? I suppose that Fran and Angélique are best friends already?"

Hobbs could feel the tips of his ears burning. Max had hit the nail on the head. How did the inspector always manage to be so precise in his intuition?

Max hit the dashboard with his palm. "I'm right, aren't I?"

"Yes, they get along well. We bumped into her at the bistro the other night, Fran and Maurice were having dinner."

"Good," Max announced sarcastically, his mouth pulled into a sneer. "So Angélique will be able to keep a close eye on Nurse Shepherd."

"Oh no, you're not involving my wife…"

Max could feel the red-headed detective getting wound up tightly like a spring and he was enjoying every moment. "She will be undercover without even knowing it. All you need to do is ask questions. You know women as well as I do, Jacques, they can't wait to spill the gossip. How do you say in English, let the kitten out of the bag?"

"The cat. In Yorkshire we'd also say they were incapable of holding their own water."

Mallery mulled over the phrase, feeling slightly better about being kept in the dark over Maurice's private life. "It means they are always desperate for the bathroom?"

Jack laughed so loud that he had tears streaming down his face. "Not really, I'll explain later. Oh, Jesus Christ, Max, you crack me up!"

Unaware of his faux pas, Mallery pointed to a large white building standing back from the road. "Over there, pull over, that's the clinic."

A shiny gold plaque on the office door silently announced that the occupant was named Doctor Henri Huppert. The detectives stood back as the secretary knocked and entered, before introducing the men to a slightly built man in his sixties. Despite the doctor's lack of stature, being only five feet tall, he exuded an air of authority and spent several moments regarding the visitors through horn-rimmed spectacles before inviting them to sit down.

Inspector Mallery pushed his card across the polished surface of Huppert's desk, at the same time asking whether he would mind speaking to them in English for the sake of his foreign colleague.

"Of course," the clinician nodded, taking in the full measure of the younger detective, "I have no issue with that."

As if taking the cue to speak, Jack removed a photograph of Juliette Lafoy from inside his notebook and passed it to the doctor.

"We're here to ask you about a former employee, Doctor Lafoy. We believe that she worked here for a short period, as a psychiatric counsellor."

Henri Huppert passed the photo back almost immediately, having no need for the visual reminder. "What do you need to know?"

"We're informed that Doctor Lafoy worked here for just a few months, is that correct?" Max asked.

Huppert was nodding in agreement, the heavy folds of his eyelids drooping closed as he tilted his head. "Yes, four or months, that's all."

"We believe that her tenure here coincided with a certain famous dancer attending the clinic for counselling sessions, Enzo Roche."

Mallery had the doctor's attention now and the short man sat up straight in his chair. "Yes, I think that would be about right. Why?"

Max continued, determined to portray the gravity of the situation. "Is it correct that Doctor Lafoy left the facility straight after Roche terminated his sessions?"

Huppert consulted a file on his desk, lifting a few pages to scan for the information. "Yes, I believe so. Three months ago, to be exact. But Juliette had nothing to do with Monsieur Roche's counselling, so I'm at a loss to see where your enquiries are going."

Mallery was ready with the final blow. "Because Juliette Lafoy left your clinic to take up a position at the private hospital in Riberon, just outside Bordeaux. It also happens to be the same place where Enzo Roche is now an in-patient. Too much of a coincidence, don't you think?"

Henri Huppert got up from desk, flabbergasted. "Really? I had no idea! How very odd."

Jack Hobbs met the man's watery gaze. "*Very* odd, Doctor. Was it you who spoke to Monsieur Cassell about Lafoy's reference?"

Huppert ran a liver-spotted hand over his brow. "No, I believe I was on vacation at the time, so our Human Resources dealt with it. Juliette was a good psychiatrist, we had no cause for concern and, as I said, she wasn't responsible for Roche's counselling sessions. Could it not be mere coincidence that she's working at the same place where he's recuperating?"

Max jumped back into the driving seat to steer the conversation forward. "We don't think so, Doctor Huppert. Now, can you think of anything at all that might connect Lafoy to Roche? No matter how trivial, we need to know."

"Maybe you should speak to Doctor Manet. After all, he and Juliette were on good terms, professionally, and used to play tennis together after work."

"I hope we're not running around in circles," Max said under his breath as he and Jack followed the secretary across a courtyard and into the west wing of the building, "there are plenty of other things we could be doing instead."

Hobbs agreed. "Well, let's hope that Manet has something worth saying."

"If you wouldn't mind waiting in here until the doctor has finished with his patient," the secretary told them, opening the door to a stark white waiting room, "he won't be long."

As Jack sat down in one of the faux leather tub chairs, Max paced the room admiring the artwork that adorned two of the walls. He stopped in front of a large print depicting a reclining nude.

"Olympia," he told Hobbs. "Quite magnificent, isn't she?"

"Erm, aye, I suppose so, not what I'd choose to put on my walls though."

Max turned away, stepping towards a self-portrait of the artist. "Such talent."

A door opened suddenly and a man in his forties poked his head around the corner. "*Inspecteur Mallery?*"

With Hobbs close on his heels, Max greeted the doctor and set about explaining the reason for their unannounced visit.

"Ah, Juliette," the psychiatrist sniffed, shaking his head. "I wondered how she was getting on in her new position."

"Are you aware of any connection between Juliette Lafoy and Enzo Roche?" Mallery ventured. "Such as a reason why she might want to seek employment at the facility where he is recovering from his mental breakdown?"

Francois Manet narrowed his eyes. "You're joking! She followed him?"

Max gave a brief outline of the circumstances and waited for the doctor to respond.

"She was obsessed with him. I was Roche's counsellor and as soon as Juliette came to work here, she began hounding me. At first it was after-work drinks, then games of tennis, later excuses to meet at the weekends to discuss cases, but every time, all she ever wanted to talk about was Enzo Roche. No matter how trivial the information, his private life, likes and dislikes, she wanted to know. In the end, I refused to answer Juliette's calls and when Enzo left, so did she."

"But you had no idea that she had applied for the position in Riberon?" Jack asked. "Or that she had been accepted?"

Francois Manet seemed appalled at the very notion. "No, certainly not. Had I known about it, I would have tried to intervene. Juliette was taking far more than a professional interest in Roche, it bordered on fanatical."

Alarm bells were beginning to sound in Mallery's head. "I'm sorry to have to ask this Doctor Manet, but was your relationship with Juliette Lafoy purely professional? Or was there more to it?"

The man reached for a frame on his desk and showed it to the detectives. "This is my wife, Sandra and our two daughters. I'm a happily married man and would do nothing to jeopardise my home life."

Max was on his feet but turned in the doorway. "The prints, outside, by Edouard Manet, any connection?"

Francois Manet's shoulders sagged, glad that the rather distasteful questioning about Juliette Lafoy was over. "My great-great-uncle."

"Amazing," Mallery muttered, letting himself out as Hobbs followed. "*Au revoir.*"

The Ford Mondeo engine ticked over as Jack waited for a space in the traffic, in order to pull out. "Where to now?"

"Back to the station," Max decided. "We need to handle Doctor Lafoy very carefully. If we go charging in, making accusations, she'll run a mile. What we need, Jacques, is hard evidence to prove she tried to poison Enzo Roche."

"Maybe she's just an obsessed ballet fan," Hobbs answered, slipping in between two lorries. "You know, a bit star-struck."

"I don't think that's likely, do you?"

"To tell you the truth, Max, no I don't. It's one thing to ask questions about someone famous, but quite a different matter altogether to stalk them, and that's what she's doing. The woman needs psychiatric help herself!"

"What do you think she's playing at, Jacques?"

The Yorkshireman's eyes were fixed on the road. "I don't know, Max, but I don't have a very good feeling about it."

At the hospital in Riberon, Enzo Roche was sitting on a wooden bench in the private garden, a discarded copy of *The Count of Monte Cristo* beside him.

"What's up, Enzo?" Fran whispered, sneaking up behind him. "Bored?"

The slight figure jumped in fright. "Frannie darling, you nearly gave me a heart attack. For your information, I'm not bored, merely soaking up the ambience."

The nurse looked around, taking in the trio playing croquet and Joseph, the facility gardener, pruning the rhododendrons. "I see, and what is it that has captured your imagination?"

The ex-ballet dancer was picking at the hem of his cotton jacket with nimble fingers, nervous energy exuding from him.

Fran sat down and nudged him. "Come on, you can't fool me, what's wrong?"

Enzo abandoned the cotton threads and laid his palms flat on the top of his thighs, eyes closed in concentration. "Doctor Lafoy, that's what."

"I take it your session didn't go as well as expected this morning?"

"Oh Frannie, I don't understand the woman. Anyone can see that I'm perfectly well now and ready to go home, yet she still refuses to sign the release papers, instead keeping me here like a caged bird."

"Did she give you a reason?" Fran ventured softly, not wanting to step over the boundaries of doctor/patient confidentiality.

"That's just it. She says I'm getting better, but insists on asking questions about my past. I mean, what on earth do my dysfunctional parents have to do with my ability to look after myself at home? It makes no sense."

Fran Shepherd agreed. "No, it doesn't. I think you've come a long way during your stay here. Do you want me to talk to her?"

"Oh, Frannie, thank you, do you think she would listen to you?"

Fran stifled a laugh. "No, not really, but I've got nothing to lose."

Enzo squeezed the nurse's hand tightly. "Bless you, darling."

"I have to get back to my rounds," Fran told him. "I'll pop in to see you before I leave this afternoon. As for Doctor Lafoy, leave it with me."

From her upstairs office vantage point, Juliette Lafoy was watching the interaction between nurse and patient. It was obvious to her that Nurse Shepherd was forming more than a professional attachment to the facility's most famous patient, and she didn't like it one bit.

The morning's therapy session with Enzo Roche hadn't gone well. Juliette could have cursed herself for pushing Roche too hard, trying to regress him in order to relive memories from his childhood, but the dancer was strong-willed and had refused to comply, instead insisting that his younger days had no bearing on his later obsession with self-harm. As the psychiatrist watched Fran Shepherd move to sit alongside Roche, she imagined the intimate conversation that the pair were having, sharing secrets and making promises.

"Just you dare to try to meddle in Enzo's therapy sessions," Juliette growled between clenched teeth, her fingers gripping the windowsill so hard that flaking paint caught under her nails. "I will have you dismissed, Fran Shepherd."

Officer Jacques Gibault stood at the edge of the lawn, pretending to watch the excitement of the croquet trio as they putted the balls through steel hoops. He hadn't wanted to stand too close to Enzo Roche, despite being charged with watching him, especially now that the English nurse had appeared and was deep in conversation with him. Instead, Gibault looked upwards, noting the glare of the resident psychiatrist as she watched the exchange between Shepherd and Roche. If Jacques wasn't mistaken, there was a scowl upon Lafoy's face, one that told him she disapproved.

Continuing to hold his position as the nurse returned inside, the police officer subtly looked around the perimeter of the lawn and then back up to the doctor's window. She was gone, confirming Gibault's suspicions that it was Fran Shepherd whom she had the problem with. He vowed to keep both eyes and ears to the ground, especially when both women were in the same vicinity. As for Enzo Roche, he had been an easy person to take care of, but not knowing who had poisoned the dancer's birthday cake was driving Jacques Gibault to distraction. In his eyes, solving the case would put Officer Gibault on the road to joining Mallery's team of detectives.

Gripping the passenger's seat with both hands, a testament to his English colleague's erratic driving, Max Mallery was forced to let one hand leave its position of safety as his phone rang. The caller identity showed that it was Coroner Paul Theron and, intrigued, the inspector tapped the screen to talk to his friend.

"Paul, everything okay?"

"*Oui,* Max," Theron countered, "very good, although I'm just calling to warn you that Gerald Butler is on his way over to see you. I take it you are at the station?"

The inspector let out a low groan. "Really? What does he want?"

"Answers, I expect," Paul said honestly. "Are you still no closer to finding the person who planted the poison?"

Mallery glanced across at Hobbs. "We have a few leads, but nothing conclusive."

"Butler's keen to get his sister's service and burial sorted out, so that he can head back to England."

"Let me guess," Max huffed, "he's not going away anytime soon."

"Well, at least not until you've charged someone with Edwina's murder."

"*Merde.*"

"Alright, well let me know if I can help with anything."

"Oh, don't worry, I will, thanks Paul."

As he closed the call, Max made a circling motion with his fingers. "Change of plan, Jacques, let's go and get some lunch before we head back."

Hobbs raised an eyebrow, wise to Mallery's ploys. "Who are you trying to avoid?"

The inspector tapped the side of his nose with one finger. "Better you don't know, Jacques, that way you won't need to lie when the dirt hits the fan."

"Shit," Hobbs corrected.

"What happened?" Max asked, suddenly concerned, his face looking worried.

"Nothing, I mean the saying is, 'when the shit hits the fan'."

There was a wily look on Max's face as they pulled up outside a small café close to the river. "I knew that. I was just testing you."

Audrey Rancourt was ascending the front steps to Bordeaux Police Headquarters on her return from a meeting with the city's Mayor. Having sat through three hours of pomp and ceremony, listening to the self-righteous Mayor explain his vision for expanding on Bordeaux's tourism over the next five years, all she thought about was slipping off her new, tightly fitting shoes and allowing her feet to breathe. Instead, the commissioner was faced with an irate Englishman demanding to speak to the inspector in charge. The officer manning reception was trying his best to calm Gerald Butler, but no amount of cajoling in broken English would convince the man to leave.

Noting the pristine cuffs and collar of Butler's shirt, together with his neatly trimmed moustache and upper-class accent, Audrey smiled politely at the reception officer and stepped into the space between the desk and the visitor.

"Monsieur Butler," she smiled politely, having overheard the man introduce himself, albeit somewhat abruptly, "I am Commissioner Audrey Rancourt. I am so sorry for your loss, it must have been a terrible shock. Perhaps you would care to come up to my office, where we can speak in private."

Gerald Butler's demeanour changed immediately, going from one of being pompously outraged to that of calm intrigue. "Commissioner, eh? Well, yes, that would be most agreeable."

Rancourt tucked her cap under one arm and led the way up to the third floor, slowing her step as she heard Butler's ragged breathing on the second flight of stairs. As they reached the large and spacious office, she turned and offered the man a seat in the upright leather chair reserved for guests.

"Can I get you a coffee, or perhaps a tea, Monsieur Butler?"

Now, having almost completely forgotten his mission to get answers from Inspector Max Mallery, Butler nodded, mildly appeased. "Tea, please. This really is very good of you, Commissioner Rancourt," he supplied.

Audrey buzzed her assistant, ordered drinks and then slid behind the desk.

"Now, I believe you require an update," she said smoothly, flipping off her shoes one by one out of sight of her unexpected guest, "which I am unable to give you without the presence of Inspector Mallery. However, let us hope that by the time we have finished our refreshments, he will be back and able to bring us both up to date. Hopefully with some positive news."

Butler nodded, satisfaction sliding over him like butter on warm toast.

Having dissected the details of the investigation over a prolonged lunch, the two detectives headed back to the car, satisfied in their stomachs but still lacking clues in the case. As the car navigated traffic on the east side of town, Jack Hobbs glanced at his boss and raised a sensitive topic.

"Have you heard from Maurice at all this week?"

Max continued to look straight ahead. "*Non*, should I have?"

The younger detective cleared his throat. "It's just that I know you two usually meet up for a beer..."

There was the slightest twitch at the corner of Mallery's eye. "He's probably too busy, with his new lady friend."

"You're not jealous, are you?"

The question was met with mocking laughter. "Jealous? Whatever for? I'm very happy for him."

Hobbs was unconvinced. The way in which Max had his jaw set and avoided eye contact told him otherwise.

"Just asking," he remarked after a pause, trying to diffuse the tension in the air. "Fran's a really lovely lady, you should take some time to get to know her."

As they came to a halt in the car park, Max jumped out and slammed the door, striding ahead of Jack Hobbs with his head held high and cheeks burning.

In the incident room, Luc Martin was studying some data on his computer screen. A packet of cookies lay open on his desk and Mallery helped himself to one as he passed, heading determinedly towards the coffee pot.

"*Merde,*" he cursed, looking down at the melting chocolate on his fingertips and reaching for a damp cloth. "What a mess!"

"What's up with him?" Luc mouthed to Jack, who followed at a safe distance.

The Englishman shrugged his shoulders. "Not sure."

On the opposite side of the room, Gabriella Dupont dropped her cell-phone and let out a loud sigh. "Thierry's not answering his phone."

Max swung around, meeting the young woman's eye, "Oh? Where is he?"

Gabi stood and sauntered over to where Max was pouring thick, aromatic coffee, helping herself to a clean mug. "We went out to the cottage by the river, did a thorough search, and then he received a call. I'm not sure who it was, but he said he needed to check something out and would meet back here. That was three hours ago."

Mallery poured the steaming liquid into the outstretched mug. "Perhaps he's called for a late lunch somewhere."

"Without transport?"

"He didn't have his bike?"

Gabi shook her blonde ponytail. "*Non*, we went out in my car. Thierry walked off in the direction of the hospital. I told him I'd wait but he said it was okay, that he'd catch the train back."

Max smiled. "Well, don't worry, I'm sure there's a reasonable explanation."

High heels clattered down the corridor and all four detectives looked towards the footsteps. Audrey Rancourt stopped at the door with her arms tightly folded.

"Inspector Mallery," the commissioner said loudly, her voice carrying across the room, "so glad to see you are finally back. My office, please."

Without waiting for an acknowledgement, Rancourt turned around and headed back up to the second floor.

Slamming his coffee back down on the counter, Max followed, large hands reaching up to ruffle his unruly curls.

By the time Mallery reached his senior's office, she was already seated and looking perfectly composed, albeit with a flicker of frustration in her eyes.

"May I ask where you've been for the past few hours?" Rancourt inquired, pressing her fingertips together.

"Pursuing a lead on the investigation," the inspector replied without hesitation. "Is there a problem, Commissaire?"

"Gerald Butler," she answered, "has been here for the past two hours, waiting for you to return and provide an update on his sister's murder investigation."

Thoughts of his leisurely lunch with Jack Hobbs came to Mallery's mind.

"As you well know, Madame, in order to fulfil my duties effectively, I simply cannot remain in the office all day long. Detective Hobbs and I were following up on a couple of important background checks."

Audrey Rancourt looked unconvinced, but instead of retaliating she pulled open the top drawer of her desk and took out a set of keys.

"These are for the silver Peugeot estate parked downstairs. I've already had Luc arrange the necessary insurance papers."

Max stared at the logo on the keyring, confused. "Sorry, I don't…"

"For Jack Hobbs," the commissioner went on. "We simply can't have a member of the French police force driving around in an old Ford Mondeo with British number-plates. It's not ethical."

Realisation dawning on Mallery, he scooped up the keys and blinked.

"Thank you, Commissioner Rancourt, I'm sure it will be much appreciated."

Without letting him pause for breath, Audrey leaned forward and stared back. "Now, get this case closed, Inspector. I want results and I want them fast."

"Yes, Madame, we'll do our best. You can count on it."

The tightly-set line of Audrey Rancourt's lips told Mallery that he didn't want to face the consequences of failure, and he left the room feeling as though he were a schoolboy who had just received a severe spanking.

"Try Thierry again," Max told Gabriella, pointing at her phone, "he's got to pick up eventually, unless his battery is dead."

The female detective did as requested, but then shook her head as the line automatically connected to her friend's voicemail.

"Okay, then we'll reconvene tomorrow morning. Briefing at eight sharp, don't be late. Commissioner Rancourt wants this case solved as soon as possible, so let's try our best to catch this killer before he takes any more lives."

There was a unified murmur as the group nodded their agreement.

"Jacques," Max called as the team made to leave, "seems you've gained yourself a new car, so at least one of us has made a good impression on the new boss."

"Oh? Really?"

Hobbs followed Mallery to the corridor where the inspector pointed down to a gleaming silver car. "That's all yours, so you can take your old Ford to the scrap heap now."

"Wow, there's plenty of room for Thomas's pram and toys in there. Brilliant! Angélique is going to be thrilled."

Max handed over the keys and slapped his friend on the back. "Take her out for a drive this evening, but take it steady."

"Cheers, boss."

Watching the red-haired detective leave, beaming from ear to ear, Max felt a pang of guilt at his earlier mood and called out, "Hey, Jacques?"

Hobbs turned. "Yeah?"

"I'll make an effort to get to know Fran Shepherd, okay?"

"Great, Maurice will be thrilled."

Mallery stood with his hands in his pockets, waiting for the Yorkshireman to emerge downstairs in the car park. The fingers on both of Max's hands were still crossed as he watched his colleague get into the Peugeot.

"*Merde*, Jacques," Max cursed, "now I'm supposed to condone my friend's relationship with a murder suspect? Whatever next!"

***

Thierry Moreau lifted his head and groaned into the dark, damp space, the stench of mould and moss filling his nostrils as he tried to steady his breathing. As he lifted his cheek from the cold stone floor, a heavy throbbing in his skull caused the young detective to cry out, before laying his head back down to avoid any further unnecessary discomfort. The ground underneath Thierry's body was slightly wet, perhaps caused by the persistent dripping of a pipe in the far corner of the room, and he shivered as it penetrated his thin cotton shirt.

Licking his lips in thirst, the man rolled onto his side, trying to accustom his eyes to the dark. On the far wall he could just make out the rectangular shape of a doorway, although there appeared to be no handle or hinges. Slowly bringing his arms up in front of him, Thierry tried to raise himself off the ground slightly, but the searing pain in his head refused to let up, causing him to slump back down exhausted.

"Hello?" he called out, aware that his own voice sounded feeble and weak.

Nothing.

"Is anyone there?"

Still nothing.

Bile rose in Thierry's throat as the torturous agony began once more, causing him to feel that his head was splitting in two. This time he threw up, heaving onto the cobblestones with shaking breaths, before the blackness came, and Thierry plunged down into unconsciousness once more.

It was a couple of hours before Thierry woke again, this time sensing the passage of time from a drop in temperature. He managed to push himself up so that his back was against the lichen-covered wall, being careful to avoid banging his head on the uneven rock. The space was silent, save for the persistent drip of water, and the detective felt a strange sense of being deep underground.

His legs were still too weak for him to be able to stand, and he leaned back gently, breathing in and out. He had never feared small spaces before, yet now, trapped goodness only knew where, he felt claustrophobic and unnerved.

Think, he told himself. *How did I get here?*

The distant memory of raucous laughter filled his ears; a deep, throaty voice, followed by the loss of sight. That must have been when he lost consciousness. What happened? Bringing up a hand to his fuzzy afro hair, Thierry traced the groove of his skull, bringing away his fingers soaked in blood. Somebody must have hit him on the head, with something hard and heavy judging by the damage. He stretched out his legs, trying to stop the panic that was building inside him. Would somebody come for him? Yet how could they if they don't know where to look?

In Saint Margaux, Jack Hobbs strapped his young son into the padded car-seat in the rear of the Peugeot. His wife smiled at the pair as she climbed into the passenger's seat, a picnic basket having been deposited in the boot.

"This is much better than your old car," she told Jack, looking at the smart CD player and plush leather seats.

"We've got the new commissioner to thank for this," Jack grinned, ruffling his son's hair, "although I'm not sure Madam Rancourt would be too happy if she thought I was using it for pleasure rather than business."

Angélique waved a hand at him in mock horror. "What a thought!"

Pulling away from their cottage, Detective Hobbs glanced over at the large *maison du maître* across the square, immediately recognising a familiar figure heading around to the back garden.

"It looks as though Fran's got her feet well and truly under the table over there," he commented, nodding towards the nurse as she disappeared out of view.

"Leave her alone," his wife sniffed, "they're very happy together."

Jack smiled. "Yes, I know. It's great to see Maurice finally finding someone, despite what some people think."

Angélique picked up on the comment instantly, her senses tuning in to the note of irony in his voice. "Oh, somebody doesn't approve?"

Hobbs squirmed in his seat, "I shouldn't have said anything, Ange…"

"But you did, so….."

"Oh heck, it's just Max. I think he's jealous. Or at least he doesn't seem to like Fran very much. He'll come around."

Angélique flicked her long, dark hair over one shoulder, giving him a coy look. "Oh, I know he will, I'll make sure of it."

Jack groaned inwardly. He hated it when his wife took it upon herself to meddle in other people's affairs. "Can't you just leave it? Please?"

"No way! We're going to invite them all over this weekend. That way, Max and Fran will both be on neutral territory and can find out a little more about one another. It'll be fine, you'll see."

"You've got no chance until our current investigation is closed," Jack replied, thanking his lucky stars. "Besides, Max will get used to the idea in time, I think he's just missing having Maurice all to himself."

The seat squeaked next to him as Angélique shifted herself towards the open window. "Men! You're certainly a lot more complicated than women!"

Max stood under the pulsing shower, massaging his scalp with shampoo and allowing the suds to cascade down his toned and muscular body. He was trying to wash away the day's blues, but somehow it just wasn't working. In fact, the whole afternoon had been a shit show. Firstly, his lunchtime showdown with Jack had riled Max, bringing emotions to the surface that he hadn't even been aware existed.

Then there was the dressing-down from Audrey Rancourt. Mallery hadn't expected the new commissioner to exert her superiority so quickly, especially as the current murder investigation was less than a week old.

He wondered whether she was used to getting much faster results but, if that was the case, it would only have been due to the manpower. Perhaps Rancourt needed reminding that the team in Bordeaux was small and lacked resources. It was true that the commissioner had already managed to get funding for new technology, which was much appreciated, but it still didn't make up for the lack of feet on the ground.

Mallery switched off the water and grabbed a towel, wondering whether he should cut his new boss some slack. After all, she was just doing her job and had something to prove to her own superiors.

Now completely dry, except for his unruly curls, Max wandered into the living room with the towel wrapped around his midriff. Picking up his mobile, he called Thierry, wondering if the younger detective might like to join him for a beer at a local bar. The phone rang out, unanswered.

"Strange," Mallery muttered to himself, "unless he's got a date. Why the hell is it that everyone around me seems to be crazy in love these days?"

He threw the phone aside and walked to the kitchen, heading for the wine rack where a bottle of Malbec waited.

Stirring from unconsciousness, Thierry Moreau was vaguely alerted to the sound of a phone buzzing. He blinked into the darkness, looking around for signs of the device on the stone floor underneath him. The sound seemed further away, and he struggled onto all fours, following the vibrating to the other side of the room. Putting one hand out in front of him, Thierry touched a much rougher wall, its surface well worn but lacking the dark moss that riddled the far side of the space. He listened, straining his ears into the silence. The phone had stopped buzzing, if that's what it was.

Thierry traced his fingers along the brickwork, feeling for some kind of handle or opening. After a few minutes, he touched upon a deep groove that coursed all the way around in a rectangular shape. Surely this must be a door of some kind, he hoped; could it be a way out? Pressing his aching head against the cool stone, the young detective searched for a sound, anything that might suggest signs of life on the other side.

Scratch, scratch.

Down on his hands and knees, Thierry strained to see if there was a gap in the opening. Was someone there? The sound persisted for several minutes, followed by a loud squeak.

"Shit," he murmured, "rats!"

***

Fran Shepherd wrapped her fingers around the glass of wine offered to her by Maurice Fabron. She wasn't used to such gentle manners and watched as the Frenchman turned back to the stove, a bouquet of aromatic herbs wafting into the kitchen as he stirred a large pot.

"Thank you," Fran smiled, sipping at the ice-cold Chablis, "this is wonderful."

"It's a local wine, produced by my brother-in-law at the Saint Margaux vineyard. I'll take you to meet him very soon."

146

"I was talking about this," the nurse replied, waving her free hand around the room, "you cooking for me after a hard day at work. Although the wine is pretty good, too."

Maurice raised his own glass. "You have come into my life like a breath of fresh air, Fran. The very least I can do is feed you."

The pair kissed, already familiar with one another just a few days into their fledgling relationship, and both anticipated a second night of passion later that evening.

"Telo wants to meet you," Maurice said, gently pulling away. "I think it's only fair that he does. How do you feel about us going to the bistro together tomorrow?"

Fran weighed up the question, swirling her drink around the glass. "Yes, of course. I just thought it might be better to meet him here, on home ground."

The boulangerie owner reached over and stroked his lover's cheek. "I think perhaps a neutral place is best. Don't forget that this house holds memories of his dear mother."

"Have you told him anything about me?" Fran ventured.

"Just that you and I have become close and that I think we might be spending a lot of time together in the future."

"Was he okay with that? I mean, you said he has autism."

"Telo is highly intelligent," Maurice explained, "but he is… how to say?… awkward… in social situations. He sees things very black and white, which means if he likes you straight away, you'll be friends forever."

"But if he doesn't?"

The baker gave a wry smile. "Let's face that if we come to it."

Fran nodded, she understood. Having worked with psychiatric patients for most of her career, she knew how to be both patient and tactful in these situations.

"What about your friend, Inspector Mallery?"

Maurice brought a wooden spoon to his lips, tasted the sauce and added a pinch of salt. "What about him?"

"I think he's already taken a severe dislike to me."

"Then, *ma chérie*, we are going to have to change his mind."

Fran frowned, looking down into her glass. "I think it's because of the murder investigation, you know, because he hasn't got a viable suspect yet."

Maurice held his breath for a second. "Well, we both know you're innocent, don't we? So, Max will just have to get over it."

Fran continued to look down, a nod of the head her only commitment.

By eleven o'clock, the night temperature had fallen considerably, plunging Thierry's prison to an even deeper chill. The detective rubbed his arms, trying to get warmth into the skin underneath his thin cotton shirt. It had been several hours since the buzzing of the phone had ceased from outside the tomb-like room and he wondered whether the battery had died or if people simply weren't worrying about him – if indeed it was his own device. If it was the latter, he was in for a miserable night.

Pense! he told himself. Think! *Que s'est-il passé?*

Stretching out his long legs in order to keep the circulation flowing, Thierry rubbed at his head and tried to recall his last lucid memory of earlier that day.

There had been a phone call, he remembered it quite clearly, and then he had set off on foot to the sanatorium in search of answers. There was a conversation, he knew that much, but it was non-confrontational and gave no clues as to how he had ended up in this hellhole.

Touching the back of his head, where a nasty gash remained tender, Moreau retraced the footsteps in his mind. They had talked for ten minutes or so and then there had been a suggestion of clues in the hospital basement. Yes, that was right, he'd gone down there expecting to find some old patient files that might shed some light on the investigation. As it turned out, Thierry could neither recall seeing the documents, nor anything else after that.

He shivered, feeling goosebumps appearing on his arms, and doubted whether anyone would come looking for him now. Thierry could just imagine Max tutting at the morning meeting and presuming that Detective Moreau had overslept. The best he could hope for was his mother phoning the station, worried that her son had gone missing. Keeping that positive thought at the forefront of his mind, Thierry tried to rest, one ear trained on the incessant scratching outside where he was certain a horde of rats awaited.

Juliette Lafoy pushed her feet into soft sheepskin slippers and padded downstairs, cursing that she hadn't thought to bring a glass of water upstairs before retiring to bed. She was parched, her throat dry from a day spent conversing with some of the most vulnerable patients and, on reaching the kitchen, she gulped down a large tumblerful of ice-cold sparkling Perrier from the fridge. The room was dimly lit by the pale greyish moonlight streaming in through the one square window, illuminating Juliette in her nightgown like the figure of a ghostly woman in white. Having drunk her fill, the psychiatrist turned to the sink, rinsing the glass and staring out into the darkened garden beyond. The day had been long and mentally taxing, another fruitless conversation with Enzo Roche being the bane of her afternoon.

Juliette turned the glass over and placed it on the draining-board. She needed to find a new way to get the principle dancer to open up; everything depended upon it. Naturally, the psychiatrist had already suggested that Enzo allow her to try hypnotherapy, but he was having none of it, protesting that his mind was now sound, all signs of depression gone, ready to move on with his life. Juliette disagreed, and she had just three weeks left to get the desired results, otherwise both her career and financial stability would be in jeopardy.

There was a sudden flash of light, definitely something unnatural, and Juliet traced it with her eyes as the beam moved away and across a nearby field. She felt neither alarmed nor afraid as the yellow light source flickered back and forth across the land, but instead presumed it might be a farmer out to tend to an injured or pregnant animal. Leaning forward on tiptoes, Juliette watched as the flashlight disappeared suddenly, rubbing at her tired eyes as the landscape became a blanket of darkness once again. Whatever it was had gone, and she didn't intend spending another minute of precious beauty sleep worrying about it. Yawning, the doctor retuned to the warmth of her bed and within minutes had returned to slumber.

A rusted key turned in the lock, causing a clunking sound, loud enough to disturb Thierry Moreau from his fitful doze. The crusted brick wall suddenly moved outwards, creating a faint shaft of light as it did so, and the young detective scrambled to his feet, keeping his back firmly against the wall. Bright torchlight flashed in Thierry's eyes, momentarily blinding him.

"*Qui est là?*" he called into the void. Who's there?

Heavy feet shuffled forwards, giving the impression that their owner was a large man. Something slid across the slimy stone floor towards him and then the door slammed shut without word or hesitation.

Making his way across the cobbles with careful steps, Moreau reached out and touched the item that had been pushed inside. It was a metal tray laden with a few foodstuffs, causing the man's stomach to rumble. It had been many hours since he had last eaten. Fumbling around with clumsy fingers, Thierry reached out, his grip falling upon a bread roll filled with what instinctively smelled like fresh creamy cheese.

"*Dieu merci,*" he mumbled, bringing the food to his mouth and biting down, an exhalation of pure joy escaping from Thierry's lips. He chewed greedily, allowing the taste to satisfy his tastebuds, savouring the flavour for a few moments before opening his mouth wide.

"*Merde!*" he cried out, spitting the bread from his mouth as realisation dawned. The overpowering flavour of parsley caused him to gag in sheer panic as it settled on his tongue – the very same flavour that Max had described to them during the first briefing on the two murders. There was no doubt about it, whoever had brought his supper was attempting to poison Thierry Moreau with water hemlock, the deadly plant that had already taken two innocent lives.

Audrey Rancourt peered down into her empty coffee cup, the thick dregs of a cheap brand congealed on the bottom. She made a mental note to send her secretary out to purchase a machine, something state-of-the-art that would brew up a delicious blend to satisfy her caffeine cravings. Something like the one Max Mallery had in his office, she told herself, with its shiny knobs and capacity for frothing milk. Now, that was a commodity to look forward to in the mornings.

Suddenly, as though summoned by the mere visualisation of his office, there was a knock at the door and the inspector himself appeared.

"*Commissaire*," he said warily, waiting to be invited inside, *puis-je entrer?*"

Rancourt nodded, adjusting her chair into a position that gave her the full measure of her next in line. "*Oui, y a-t-il un problème?*"

Mallery closed the door, eager to keep what he had to say from the prying ears of the commissioner's secretary, and then took the vacant seat, ready to tell his boss about the disturbing phone call he'd received from Madame Moreau at seven that morning.

Ten minutes later, looking visibly frustrated, Max was back in the incident room bearing news. He leaned on Luc's desk as the team gathered around.

"Okay, so we have permission to enlist three uniformed officers, but only for today, so we need to cover as much ground as possible in the search for Thierry. Each of you will be assigned one officer and I want you to stay together. At no point, or under any circumstances, are you to go off alone, understood?"

There was a collective murmur as the detectives assented their agreement, each more concerned about their colleague's wellbeing than the fact that they were literally being minded by a street cop.

"Good," Mallery breathed, bringing up a map of Riberon and the surrounding areas. "So we know that Thierry was heading for the sanatorium, but what we don't know is whether he made it there. Luc, any signal from his phone, or a possible location?"

Luc Martin shook his head. "*Non*, nothing. I think the battery must have died."

"Okay, well, in that case, let's see… There are three possible roads leading out of the village." He tapped the screen for emphasis. "One goes past the church on a narrow lane to Salbec, the second heads out to the main Bordeaux highway and the railway station, and the third, towards Saint Margaux, is where the hospital is located. That one is our primary concern, but we can't discount the others, in case he was sidetracked or abducted elsewhere."

Notepads were brought out and pages hastily scribbled upon as the group prepared to head to their individual destinations. Max thrust his hands deep into the pockets of his chinos and let out a breath.

"Okay, uniform will be downstairs in fifteen minutes. If anyone needs me, I'll be at the sanatorium trying to find out if Thierry actually made it there. So far, Officer Gibault hasn't had any confirmed sightings from the staff, but it's worth a try. I also want to speak to Enzo Roche. It's about time we found out who is trying to poison him. I'll meet you all back here at four, unless we have news. Now, go and find Thierry. Good luck."

As the detectives filed out, Max pulled on Jack's arm, guiding him over to the window, which he opened wide before lighting up a cigarette.

"I thought you were trying to give up?" Hobbs said, moving away from the smoke that slowly snaked upwards as his senior took a drag.

"I'm stressed," came the curt reply.

"About Thierry, or the investigation in general?"

Max flicked ash outside, recoiling as a few flakes blew back in and onto his shirt. "Both. Of course, the case isn't going well. I thought we would be much further along by now, at least have a viable suspect, but Thierry's disappearance doesn't sit well with me, either. Madame Moreau called me first thing. Thierry's bed hasn't been slept in and his phone is going straight to voicemail."

"You don't think he's just nursing a hangover somewhere?"

"Do you?"

Hobbs rubbed his cheek. "No, I don't, actually. It's unlike him not to phone in or tell one of us his whereabouts, let alone ignore his phone."

Max nodded in agreement. "Exactly, but try telling that to Commissioner Rancourt. She thinks we're wasting manpower looking for him."

"What? Like we're going on a wild goose chase?"

Mallery choked on his cigarette, flummoxed. "What?"

"Never mind. I'd better get downstairs and meet up with my accompanying officer. Let's just hope he has a smattering of English."

The inspector groaned. He hadn't thought to remind Gabriella and Luc to ensure they left the most linguistically competent of the uniformed police to go out into Riberon with Jack. Instead of dwelling on the issues, however, he simply said, "Find him, Jacques. Whatever reason Thierry has for disappearing, I just need to know that he's alright."

The Yorkshireman tilted his head, blocking the glinting sunlight that shone into his pale blue eyes. "Don't worry, we'll find him."

A sliver of yellow sunlight crept through the stonework of Thierry's prison, approximately four feet above his head. It was no more than a quarter of an inch wide, yet that small amount of light and fresh air filled the detective with hope of escape. A short while earlier, he had heard heavy footsteps on the other side of the door, coming to a standstill before turning back the way they came. Thierry had remained silent, waiting to see whether his captor would venture inside. He didn't have a plan, or a weapon, but trusted himself to opportunity, hoping that he might catch the man off guard as he entered.

As it was, neither had presented itself, the unknown perpetrator going back the way he came instead, and Thierry had a good idea why. For hours during the night, the detective had held his stomach as it cramped, vomiting up the sandwich filling several times. The overpowering herby smell of the water hemlock still left a faint stench in the cell. Therefore, he was in no doubt that the man who had brought him here now presumed Thierry to be deceased, poisoned by the same means as Ray Verdin and Edwina Butler.

Satisfied that the stone door wasn't going to open any time soon, Thierry laid down his head on the cold floor and tried to rest, reserving the last of his depleting energy for the next time someone came to check on him. Looking upwards at the glimmering daylight, the detective made a quick calculation of the height above his head. It was too high to scale and the walls too moss-ridden and slimy to gain a decent grip. Besides, there was no guarantee that the brickwork up there was loose, it could simply have a few pieces of broken mortar. With this in mind, Thierry drifted off, nursing his aching skull.

Max put his foot down on the accelerator, determined to reach the private facility before breakfast was over. He knew that by nine, the patients would be undergoing their various therapies and counselling sessions and he wanted to catch Enzo Roche before he disappeared into his daily routine. What Max hadn't counted on was a heated discussion coming from the reception area as he entered the grand entry hall of the sanatorium.

"Why can't you just stop prying into his personal life? It's got nothing to do with his treatment here. Just lay off!"

Max recognised Fran Shepherd's voice immediately, her steady but irate voice speaking in English as she confronted a rather startled Juliette Lafoy.

"I am doing my job, Nurse Shepherd," the psychiatrist spat back, hands on hips in a defensive pose. "I suggest you mind your own business, or I will report your inappropriate behaviour to Monsieur Cassell."

Inspector Mallery stood in the open doorway looking from one woman to the other, fixated on the sheer contrast of their appearances. Fran was tall, dark and confident in her immaculate white uniform, her hair neatly blow-dried and complexion clear, without a trace of make-up. Juliette Lafoy, on the other hand, was petite, fair-haired and sporting a casual pair of grey trousers with a pink polo shirt, looking significantly more casual than when Mallery had seen her on previous occasions. The doctor's face was made up in full, with thick eyelashes, blusher and a dark scarlet lipstick, a look more suited to a night out than to counsel psychiatric patients, in the inspector's opinion.

"Ladies!" Max called out, raising his voice to make himself heard over the arguing women. "What seems to be the problem?"

Lafoy was the first to turn towards him, her eyes glowering at the intrusion. "Nothing, Inspector, nothing at all, just a slight disagreement."

Max glanced across at the nurse, his face placid. "Nurse?"

Fran shrugged her shoulders, but the red tinge on her face remained, a sure sign that her temper had yet to diminish. "Like the doctor says, it's nothing."

As if on cue, Juliette snatched a folder from the timid-looking receptionist and bid the detective good day, her high-heels clicking constantly on the black and white tiled floor as she made her way towards the sweeping staircase, the doctor's cold grey eyes narrowing at Fran Shepherd as she began her ascent.

Waiting until the doctor had disappeared from view, Max took Fran to one side and looked steadily at her blushing face.

"Are you alright? Can you tell me what that was about?"

Fran glanced at the reception desk, aware that the woman there was only pretending to tidy some papers and gestured towards the garden.

"Outside. Everyone else is in the dining room."

Mallery followed the Englishwoman into the fresh air, where he was immediately struck by the scent of a magnolia tree that blossomed close to the entrance and wondered how he had failed to notice it on arrival. They sat on a wooden bench, a couple of feet between them.

"We were arguing about Enzo Roche," Fran confessed as soon as they were settled. "Doctor Lafoy has been pressurising him into opening up about his past. A past, I might add, that Enzo would rather keep to himself. She's even suggested hypnotising the poor fella so that she can 'scourge his demons'."

"I take it Monsieur Roche isn't happy about the situation?"

"No, he's dead set against it. Enzo shouldn't even be here now, he's absolutely fine. He was vulnerable when he arrived a few months ago, but I honestly believe he would be better off back home now, getting on with his life."

"Have you spoken to Monsieur Cassell about this?"

The nurse bit her lip, looking at Mallery from under her soft fringe. "Yes, once, a few days ago, but he wasn't interested in my opinion. In Cassell's eyes, the sun shines out of Juliette Lafoy's…"

"Backside?" Max finished, a smile playing on his lips as he recalled Jack Hobbs using the phrase on more than one occasion.

"Exactly."

"Where is Enzo now?"

Fran pointed towards the upper floor of the building. "In his room. He took a croissant and some fruit upstairs after an early walk around the grounds. The rules are pretty flexible here."

Mallery rose, helped Fran to her feet and turned to face her. "I think a chat with Monsieur Roche is well overdue."

Jack Hobbs opened the boot of the Peugeot estate and took out a pair of old walking boots, swapping his smart work shoes for the more casual pair as the uniformed officer scoured the area with a pair of binoculars. The duo had been assigned to a back lane that ran alongside the churchyard and the ground on the adjoining fields was boggy from a combination of the morning dew and a herd of cattle that inhabited the area. Hobbs worked the heavy boots onto his feet, securing the laces with a tight knot before standing and slamming the car boot shut.

"Let's start over there," he told the tall, slightly overweight police officer at his disposal, pondering that if the lad could lose a few pounds, he would make a decent rugby player.

"*Quoi?*" came the response.

Jack rolled his eyes. It was typical that nobody had checked whether his new partner could speak English.

"There," he answered, pointing at the field next to the graveyard with exaggerated hand gestures. "*Comprendez?*"

The officer nodded and began tramping over the sodden grass until he reached the adjoining stone wall, head down looking for clues.

"Paul," Hobbs called, trying but failing to recall the French vocabulary that he needed in explanation. "I'll go that side."

He made a sweeping motion with one arm and set off towards the far side of the field in what he considered to be a fruitless expedition.

Jack had to concede that Max was usually right about most things, but on this occasion the Englishman's gut told him that they were nowhere near Thierry Moreau's current location. Fields stretched out on all sides, with only the occasional cottage or outbuilding blotting the landscape. Still, it was his duty to comply, and Hobbs rarely complained. He just hoped that Gabi and Luc were on more productive missions.

Enzo Roche sat poised with a mother-of-pearl-handled hairbrush in his hand, attempting to tame his thick, dark hair with soft sweeping motions, as Fran Shepherd knocked at the door of the ex-ballet star's private quarters.

"Frannie, darling," the dancer called out, smiling broadly. "Do come in."

The man's smile drooped slightly as he noticed the police inspector following on her heels and one perfectly plucked brow lifted in an arch.

"Good morning, is everything alright?" Enzo asked.

"Monsieur Roche, I was wondering if I might speak with you," Max explained, coming to stand at the dressing-table. "It would help greatly with our ongoing investigation."

Enzo glanced at Fran, who gave his hand a gentle squeeze.

"Yes, of course," the dancer replied. "Please, sit down."

Mallery lifted a silk kimono off the only available armchair and eased himself down, sitting forward with his hands clasped.

"As you are aware," he began, "we are still trying to find the person who poisoned Monsieur Verdin and Madame Butler, and it will come as no surprise that we believe the way in which the gateau was delivered, to your room, suggests that you were the intended target."

"Yes, yes, I realise that, but your officer has done an excellent job of keeping me safe," Enzo gushed in response, singing the praises of Jacques Gibault. "I don't know what else I can tell you, Inspector."

Max cleared his throat, an indication that the matter he was about to touch upon might come across as being slightly indelicate. "Monsieur Roche, could you tell me about your recent counselling sessions with Doctor Lafoy?"

Roche laid down the brush, bristle side up and extracted a few dark hairs from its grooves. "It has been quite stressful lately. The doctor is constantly badgering me about my past, wanting to know about my childhood and… erm, my… past lovers."

Mallery tried his best to remain impassive, prompting Enzo to go on. "Have you found it to be inappropriate?"

Roche brought a hand to his face, flapping it around as though to cool himself down. "Yes, exceptionally. She just won't let up. Every session is the same and Doctor Lafoy insists upon making me stay here, when the rest of the staff agree that I would be far better off in my own home now."

"Do you have any idea why Doctor Lafoy is pressurising you in this way?"

"No, no idea at all. I was hoping that I would be able to talk to your handsome young detective about it when he arrived yesterday, but it seems he was here on some other errand."

Mallery blinked hard. "Which detective? Was it the one who came here with me when we took the chocolate cake away?"

Enzo smiled proudly, he was gifted in never forgetting a single name. "Yes, as a matter of fact it was. Detective Moreau."

Max got to his feet, a dozen thoughts racing through his mind. "Do you have any idea why Detective Moreau was here? Or where he went to when he arrived?"

The dancer pressed a finger to his lips, creating a dramatic pause. "Oh yes, Inspector. He was on his way to see Doctor Lafoy."

Oxford brogues clicking on the polished wooden parquet flooring, Max headed straight down the corridor towards the psychiatrist's office, pressing an ear to the door before knocking. He could hear Lafoy speaking softly.

"*Rafael, décontractes-tu.*" Relax yourself.

There was the squeak of a leather chair as someone moved and Mallery swallowed hard, deciding that his questions for the doctor simply couldn't wait. He turned the handle and pushed the door inwards.

"Doctor Lafoy, I'm sorry to interrupt, but this is urgent."

A long-haired, skeletal young man blinked at the detective from his reclined position on a chaise longue. "*Bonjour.*"

Juliette stood behind her patient, her hands either side of his head, and she looked up, startled. "Inspector, this is highly unprofessional."

Max jerked his head towards the door, indicating for Rafael to leave. "Sorry, Doctor Lafoy will continue your session later."

The woman stood open-mouthed as her patient retreated, watching as the police inspector closed the door firmly behind the retreating figure.

"Doctor, this is a matter that cannot wait. I need to speak to you about the whereabouts of one of my team, Detective Moreau."

Gabriella Dupont pointed towards a low, grey-bricked outbuilding and tugged on her colleague's arm. "*Nous allons jeter un coup d'oeil.*" We'll take a look.

The officer obliged by stepping up his pace to keep abreast of the blonde detective's quickening strides, eyes focussed on the abandoned one-storey hut.

Having been out searching the rural district of Riberon for almost two hours with neither sight nor sound of Thierry Moreau, the officers were becoming frustrated at the lack of progress. Gabi had intermittently radioed both Jack and Luc several times during the morning but neither had found any clues as to their friend's whereabouts. Secretly, Gabriella was hoping that Madame Moreau would call her at some point, having discovered Thierry arriving home after a night on the tiles with a flat phone battery but, as the hours seeped by, her confidence in finding him began to waver. As she moved in the dark, the detective flicked back her hair and heard a skittering sound as one of her earrings rolled across the dirt, but it was impossible to see in which direction it had landed.

"*Attends. Qu'est-ce que c'est?*" her companion suddenly called out, getting down on his hands and knees in the dirt.

Gabi waded through a pile of dead leaves, keeping her eyes focussed on the slats of rotting wood that lay across the floor in one corner. It was too dark to see clearly, but what the detective could make out was a bolt, hooked through with a great, rusted padlock.

The uniformed officer reached over and tugged. "*Il n'a pas été ouvert depuis des annees.*" It hasn't been opened for years.

Detective Dupont's shoulders sagged. She felt deflated that they had no clues whatsoever and time was getting on, not to mention losing her earring. Pulling out her phone, Gabi looked at the time. It was midday and a reminder had flashed up on the screen and she vowed to return later.

"*Merde*," she exclaimed, "*nous devons y aller.*" We need to go.

The shorter officer raced to keep up as Gabi hurried back towards her parked car, breathlessly explaining that she had just two hours to get home and change her clothes before driving back to Riberon for Ray Verdin's funeral.

Juliette Lafoy sat with her hands clasped on the desk in front of her, eyes glowering like a feral cat's. "Inspector, I don't know how many times I have to tell you, Detective Moreau was here for less than five minutes before he hurried off. I don't know anything more and harassing me will get you nowhere."

"So, tell me again," Max growled, trying desperately to steady his voice despite the anger boiling up inside of him. "What did he ask you? What was it that caused him to go running off?"

The psychiatrist exhaled sharply. She seemed agitated. "He asked me about the lease on my cottage, that's all and, as I said, I told the detective that my rent is paid directly by the hospital trust, I had nothing to do with the contract."

Mallery processed the information for a second time, trying desperately to pick what clues he could from it. "Nothing else?"

Lafoy shook her head. "No, nothing."

"So, who is responsible for procuring properties for the staff?"

The doctor shifted in her seat. "Leon, I mean Monsieur Cassell, I suppose."

Mallery could feel the woman closing up, as though the very mention of the hospital manager's name had given her cause to become defensive. As he paused for thought, Max's gaze fell upon an oversized leather handbag at the side of the desk. A folder lay half in, half out of the unzipped leather and it was easy to read a name in bold black lettering on the front cover: *ENZO ROCHE.*

The inspector nudged the bag with his foot. "Are you in the habit of taking patient notes home with you, Doctor?"

"Those are not patient notes!" Lafoy snapped, swallowing hard as she realised her very grave mistake. "It's…"

"*Oui?*" Mallery urged.

"Private," she offered.

Max decided to call the woman's bluff.

"Madame Lafoy, Doctor… Enzo Roche spoke to me about some concerns he has a short while ago. He thinks that you are keeping him here unnecessarily."

Mallery watched as Juliette dug her fingernails into the palm of her hand, her face wincing with the pain, his eyes steady on hers.

"That is a terrible allegation."

"It certainly is, but I have concerns of my own, Madame Lafoy. You see, not only has a patient expressed his feelings towards your therapy, but you were also the last person to see my missing detective. It's only natural that I now feel bound to question you under oath."

"Under oath?" Lafoy's mouth had fallen open.

"Unless, of course, you would like to voluntarily tell me what's going on?"

Max let the words fill the space between them as Juliette weighed up her options. The inspector couldn't possibly have a clue what she was hiding, but to refuse to co-operate now might cause her a great deal of aggravation later.

The psychiatrist reached down into her bag and retrieved the folder, throwing it across the desk to Mallery. "Here, if it's that important to you."

As the thick cardboard wallet slid to a halt next to his hand, Max read the subtitled words underneath the patient's name.

"*Le Danseur Déchu.*" The Fallen Dancer.

As realisation dawned, Mallery felt a mix of surprise and disgust flow through him. Lafoy had been keeping Enzo Roche close at hand in order to write an unofficial biography, a task that was both deplorable and unethical. Now the suggestion of introducing hypnotherapy into Roche's counselling sessions made complete sense. Max was is no doubt that the doctor was going to try to regress the dancer to his troubled childhood and then use the information to fill in the gaps in her literary efforts.

He was unsure as to whether a crime had actually been committed, but he was damned sure that Lafoy was taking a huge risk, as, if she wrote anything defamatory, it could end up in a legal battle between her and Roche. He rubbed his chin and leaned forward.

"Why would you take such a risk? Monsieur Roche could drag you to court over this. What the hell happened to patient confidentiality?"

The doctor tapped her pink nails on the top of the mahogany desk, her voice beginning to show evidence of the cracks in her diminishing confidence. "Because I've already received a large sum from my publisher and can't afford to pay it back."

Max Mallery was a man on a mission as he headed down the long corridor to Leon Cassell's office. Determined to get to the bottom of Thierry's quest at the hospital, he had decided to put Juliette Lafoy's secret on the back burner, for now, and instead focus on finding the missing member of his team. He knocked and waited, feeling flustered after his heated conversation with the psychiatrist.

"*Entrez*," Cassell called in his rather nasal voice.

Max didn't hesitate and turned the handle immediately.

"Monsieur," he nodded, striding into the room, "I need to speak with you urgently."

Cassell slowly removed his spectacles, irritated at the intrusion. "Inspector Mallery, I'm afraid this isn't a good time…"

"Regardless, I'm afraid it cannot wait. I believe that you were the last person to see Detective Moreau here yesterday. Is that correct?"

The hospital manager made a great show of considering the question before shaking his head. "I'm sorry, but no, you must be mistaken."

"Now look here," Max seethed, raising his voice, "one of my officers is missing and he came here to speak to you about the staff accommodation contracts."

Cassell splayed his fingers and looked around the room. "Well, as you can see, Detective Moreau is not here now, nor has he ever been."

Mallery took in the other man's cool countenance, not a whisper of deceit in his calm voice, hardly able to believe that he had hit yet another dead end.

Cassell was watching Max as he mulled over his next move and pointed to a chair on the opposite side of his large oak desk. "Please, sit down. I'll order us some coffee and then perhaps, together, we can try to work out where your officer might be."

Mallery accepted the offer gratefully. A shot of caffeine might give him the inspiration needed to decide where to look next. Damn Thierry. If he wasn't in trouble, then Max would make darned sure that he worked extra shifts over the coming autumn. As Leon Cassell exited the room, the inspector fidgeted in his seat, eventually rising to pace the office. It was then that he noticed a small leather notebook pushed between two encyclopaedias on the bookshelf. Lifting it carefully, he flicked to the front page, noted the inscription there, and then pulled out his phone to call Jacques Gibault.

Gabriella Dupont discarded her muddy jeans in the laundry basket and pulled a pair of plain black trousers from the wardrobe. She had no time for deliberating over her outfit and reached for a crease-free cream blouse to replace her bright red t-shirt. Appraising herself quickly in the mirror, the detective brushed her long blonde hair and pulled it into a high ponytail. She reached up to her left ear, removing the earring and dropping it into her jewellery box. The stone sparkled, causing a pang of guilt. They had belonged to Roberto's grandmother and had been presented to her on their trip to Italy as a welcome gift from the family. Now half of the pair was missing, and Gabi was riddled with guilt.

She was sure that Max would understand her predicament and might even offer to return to the old building with her later to search for the precious stone. If that were the case, she could avoid telling Roberto and there would be no cause for concern. With a plan in her mind, the detective set off back towards the village of Riberon, ready to attend Raymond Verdin's funeral.

Thierry pressed his back against the damp wall and pushed with his legs, hoping to propel himself up onto his feet. The effort it took was incredible, he had never felt so weak; it was as though his muscles had lost all their strength.

Could this be an effect from the poisonous plant? he wondered.

The inside of Detective Moreau stomach felt raw. He had vomited five or six times during the night, each time retching until his throat was dry. The taste of parsley was getting fainter now, almost unrecognisable, but still the aroma of it pervaded the small, confined space.

Eventually making it to a standing position, Thierry edged his way along the wall, unsteady and slightly dizzy as he shuffled along towards the position of the door. Nobody had been near for hours and he reckoned that whoever had brought him here now supposed the detective to be dead.

Reaching the stone entrance, Thierry once again fell to his knees, weak from the exertion of traversing the cell, but also determined to find a way out of there. He pressed his face to the floor, trying to see if there was a gap under the door, and relaxed slightly on sensing a faint breeze. Maybe there was hope after all, he told himself, desperately digging at the soil with bare hands.

"Jacques, are you nearby? I mean, are you still in Riberon?" Max panted down the phone.

Hobbs lifted his leg over the low wall that circuited the graveyard and swapped the phone to his other ear as he waited for the uniformed officer to climb over. "Yes, we're at the church, no sign of Thierry out here, though…"

Before Jack could go on, Mallery was talking over him. "I need you at the hospital now. I've arrested Leon Cassell and need you to drive him back to the station."

The Englishman's mouth was working like a goldfish, questions bubbling on his lips. "What? Why?"

"Just get here as soon as you can."

The line went dead, and Hobbs motioned to the policeman standing next to him. "Apparently we need to go."

"*Quoi?*"

A group gathered at the doorway to the church, with Father Pelletier clearly visible consoling a woman dressed completely in black. Hobbs gestured to the officer with him to take a wide berth and keep to the outskirts of the consecrated ground. He'd completely forgotten about Verdin's funeral today and hoped that Gabriella would be joining the family in their final farewell.

The inspector had allowed Monsieur Cassell the dignity of remaining in his office while they waited for transport, Mallery's two-seater sports car being wholly unsuitable for taking the manager to Bordeaux for questioning, although Max's patience was wearing thin. Having read Cassell his rights, the man had refused to elaborate on how Thierry Moreau's notebook had found its way into his office.

"I told you, I know nothing about it," Cassell told Mallery, curling his lip in disgust. "Someone must have planted it there."

"And who do you suppose might have done such a thing?" Max retorted, walking the length of the room while Jacques Gibault stood guard at the door.

The large man shrugged, the padded shoulders of his suit jacket moving animatedly. "I really don't know."

Concern growing for the whereabouts of his missing team member, Mallery could feel his frustration intensifying. As soon as Jack Hobbs arrived, he would light up a cigarette to calm himself down.

In less than five minutes, the silver Peugeot estate car rolled up the hospital driveway, causing the patients that milled around in the garden to turn their heads in curiosity. Jack was halfway up the stairs when he caught sight of Max walking towards him, one hand on Leon Cassell's shoulder.

"Thanks, Jacques." He smiled weakly, pulling the leather notebook from his pocket. "I found this on Monsieur Cassell's bookshelf but, very conveniently, he does not recall how it got there. It belongs to Thierry."

Hobbs was genuinely taken aback. He had found the sanatorium manager to be completely compliant on their various visits and was surprised that Mallery had grounds to implicate him in Moreau's disappearance. With this key piece of evidence, he couldn't help but wonder whether Cassell was also involved in the poisoning of Verdin and Butler.

"I have a uniformed officer with me, if Jacques needs to stay here," he told Mallery as they walked outside. "We can check Monsieur Cassell in."

"I'll be right behind you," Max replied, flipping the lid on a packet of cigarettes. "In fact, I will probably arrive before you."

Jack smirked. It was just like his boss to turn everything into a challenge.

Driving with caution and watching as the red BMW reached the village church and disappeared down a country lane at speed, Hobbs saw a white Mini appear from the opposite direction. Jack raised his hand, acknowledging Gabriella Dupont with a flash of his car headlights as she searched for a place to park amongst the throng of mourners' vehicles come to pay their last respects to Raymond Verdin. The man had obviously been popular, as dozens more cars were now heading towards the church.

Hobbs glanced at Leon Cassell in the rear-view mirror, their eyes connecting for a fraction of a second before the bald man looked away. Jack was a usually a good judge of character and hadn't suspected Cassell of being involved in the murders yet now, seeing the wolf-like glint in the man's eyes, he understood that there was far more to Cassell than he had first thought.

Booking Cassell into the station and locating a vacant interview room took less than five minutes and, despite the humidity indoors, Mallery was gasping for a coffee. He glanced at Hobbs, who was taking off his jacket.

"I wonder if you would mind getting us some coffee," Max asked the duty officer, who stood in the doorway filling out information on a clipboard.

Jack held up a hand to stop him, whilst putting his jacket around the back of a chair with the other. "No, it's fine, I'll get it. Monsieur, coffee or tea?"

Leon Cassell shook his head and looked away, feeling considerably more uncomfortable now that he was in police custody. "Nothing."

Hobbs left the room, sidestepping the uniformed guard on his way to the canteen, in no doubt at all that Max needed a strong black dose of caffeine.

A couple of minutes after his colleague had left the room, Mallery heard a buzzing and looked down at Hobbs' jacket. The sound was coming from the pocket, so he reached down and checked the screen before answering.

"Hello, Jean? This is Max, how are you?" he told Hobbs' mother, walking over to the door away from Cassell and listening as the Englishwoman talked ten to the dozen in his ear.

It was several minutes before Jean Hobbs had relayed her message and by the time the call ended, Max Mallery's face was ashen. He asked the officer to watch over Cassell and headed towards the canteen to find Jack.

"Hey, don't you trust me to get you a cup of coffee now?" the Yorkshireman joked as Max approached. "I've made sure it's strong, just how you like it."

Mallery steered the red-headed detective over to a vacant table and pulled out a chair. "Jacques, sit down for a minute."

Hobbs set down the drinks and did as requested, his face screwed up in a look of confusion. "What's going on?"

"Jacques, your mother just phoned. I hope you don't mind but I answered it, thinking it might be important." He swallowed hard and went on, "It's your father, I'm afraid he's had a heart attack, they've taken him to Leeds General Infirmary."

Sending Jack upstairs to phone his mother in the privacy of his own office, Mallery popped his head into the Incident Room and was glad to see Luc Martin at his desk.

"Hey, boss," Luc grinned, "any luck?"

"I've got Leon Cassell downstairs in an interview room, do you want to join me in questioning him?"

Luc frowned. "Cassell? Why, what's he done?"

"I found Thierry's notebook in his office and the bastard won't tell me how it came to be there. He's definitely hiding something,"

Max looked around the room and went on, "Where's Gabi?"

"At Verdin's funeral, she should be back in an hour or so."

"Okay, great. Meet me downstairs, will you? Cassell's in Room Three, I just need a quick word with Jacques before we start."

Luc nodded and made his way downstairs, leaving Mallery to make a resolute decision to send Jack Hobbs back to England.

The little church at Riberon was packed to capacity. A few of the mourners Detective Dupont recognised from her door-to-door enquiries following Raymond Verdin's death, but most of them she had never set eyes upon. It was both heart-warming and a testimony to the hospital orderly's popularity, seeing the throng gathered in respect of a man whose life was taken far too soon. At the front of the church, Gabriella could just make out his widow, Chloe Verdin. The woman was dressed in an elegant black suit and had one arm wrapped around the shoulders of her fourteen-year-old daughter, Elise. Gabi recalled how grief-stricken the pair had been when they had broken the news of Raymond's demise.

The detective suddenly felt a tug on her jacket and tuned to see a sombrely dressed older woman in the pew behind her.

"Are you with the local police?" the lady asked, keeping her voice to a whisper.

"Yes, Detective Dupont."

"Would you wait for me outside after the service?" came the reply. "I think I may be able to help with your enquiries."

Max stood smoking at the second-floor window while he waited for Jack Hobbs to complete his personal phone call. It had been a crazy day, so far, and the bad news that the Yorkshireman had just received only intensified that feeling. The inspector felt that they were racing against the clock in the hunt for Thierry now, yet his gut told him that Leon Cassell was going to hold out until some a deal could be struck. He looked at his watch. It was almost twenty-four hours since Gabi had last seen Moreau and Mallery had no idea whether the detective had food, water, or shelter. He prayed that Thierry's natural instincts and physical strength would help him to survive.

Footsteps coming down the corridor told Max that Jack was on his way, and he threw the cigarette stub out into the fresh air, letting it fall to the warm tarmac of the car park below.

"How's your mother coping?" he asked softly.

"Not well. They've been married for nearly forty years and Dad has never had even a day in hospital."

"And what about him? What did the doctors say?"

"He'll pull through, he's as strong as an ox, but they reckon he's going to have to take it easy for quite some time. He's had a nasty shock to his system, but it could have been worse."

Max bit his bottom lip. "I suppose he has kept fit running the farm, *oui*?"

"Aye, he has, but that's going to have to change now."

"Have you booked a flight home?"

Jack shook his head. "Not yet, I wanted to make sure you're alright here. I mean, what with Thierry still missing…"

"*Non, non.*" Max was adamant. "You must go, be with your mother. We will crack this case before long. What is important now is that you go and be with your family. Now, go home and pack. If you need anything," he leaned forward, grabbing Jack's arm, "anything at all, just ask."

Hobbs coughed in an attempt to clear his throat as he started to well up at the thought of his strong, stubborn father having to abide by the doctor's orders, something that Peter Hobbs wouldn't take kindly to. "Thanks, Max."

Mallery steered the Yorkshireman towards the staircase. "Off you go, and give your mum a big hug from me."

Gabriella stood under the shade of a yew tree waiting for the woman to finish shaking hands with Father Pelletier. They seemed to be on very friendly terms, or so it appeared by the fond smiles and closely gripped handshake, causing Gabi to presume that she might be local to the area. Then, as the mourners made their way to the graveside where Raymond Verdin's body was to be interred, the tall woman broke away from the group and picked her way across the grass in soft leather pumps. She smiled on reaching Gabi.

"Thank you for waiting. My name is Selina de Gaulle."

Gabriella repeated the name in her mind. She had definitely heard it before.

"I let out two cottages to the sanatorium staff, a doctor and a nurse, I believe," Madam de Gaulle explained. "I did mean to speak to someone earlier, but I'm afraid that my husband was taken ill during our vacation, and I had to make arrangements... well, you know how it is..."

Dupont inclined her head, waiting for the woman to finish. "Of course..."

"Anyway," Selina sighed, "we were absolutely mortified on finding out that Raymond had been poisoned by a plant that was growing in the garden of one of our properties. It's unbelievable."

"Yes, I can imagine," the detective sympathised. "May I ask how you found out? We haven't released too many details to the press yet."

Madam de Gaulle pointed a finger at the graveside. "Chloe Verdin, she told me on our return, we have known each other for years."

Gabi could feel time pressing on. "I see. You said that you may be able to help with the investigation..."

"Yes, I mean it could be nothing, but we did find it rather strange at the time."

"Please, go on. Anything that might help is appreciated."

The woman glanced over to the mourners and then continued.

"You see, Detective, we knew that the water hemlock was there. My husband had called a specialist to have it removed, but when we told the man who came to sign the lease at the agent's office, he asked us to leave it, said that he'd sort it out himself. It was quite a relief, with us planning a trip, and we had no reason not to believe that he wouldn't deal with it."

Cold sweat began to trickle down Gabi's back. "What was his name?"

"Monsieur Cassell, the manager of the sanatorium."

"Thank you, Madam de Gaulle, you have been very helpful."

Selina pressed a clean lace handkerchief against the tip of her nose. "Not at all, Detective. It's just a pity that we didn't act sooner, or poor Raymond would still be alive, and that English lady, too. I feel so dreadful about the whole business."

Dupont rested a hand on the woman's arm reassuringly. "What you have just told me will help our investigation a great deal, Madame. Don't blame yourself, please. Now, if you could just give me your number and address…"

Jack Hobbs drove home, only just managing to keep the car within the speed limit, his mind racing ten to the dozen. As soon as he had spoken to Angélique, he would need to book the first available flight back to England. His mother had tried to sound calm, saying that his father was conscious and had managed to speak to the doctor, but her voice had been shaky, and Jack could imagine the worry she was going through.

Of course, there was also the farm to consider. Despite their conversations earlier in the year, when Peter Hobbs had told his son that he was ready to hand the reins over to a tenant, the stubborn farmer had done nothing about it. Jack wondered whether his old dad had been waiting for his son to change his mind about going home and taking over the family business, despite Jack's insistence that he wasn't cut out for it, instead coveting his new position with the Bordeaux police and being completely settled in St Margaux with his beautiful French wife and little son.

As Hobbs indicated to turn off the highway into Saint Margaux, the Vidals' vineyard came into view, reminding him of the very first case that he'd worked on with Max Mallery. A few years had passed since then and the men had become firm friends, but Jack could still recall those first few months when he hadn't known how to handle the detective inspector.

Thoughts of his family life and progressing career filled Jack's thoughts as he neared the village. Thierry was still missing and the investigation into the two poisonings was far from closed, yet Hobbs was torn between going back to Leeds where he was needed and staying put until the current case was closed.

Gabriella Dupont returned to her Mini and reached into the boot for her waterproof jacket. Slipping off the kitten heels that she'd put on especially for the funeral, she changed into a pair of trainers and glanced up at the greying sky. Gabi was relieved that the weather had held for the service. She had always felt that dark skies darkened the mood even further on such occasions, and poor Chloe Verdin and her daughter were having a hard enough time coming to terms with their loss already. The detective grabbed a torch and locked the car.

Setting off in the opposite direction from the church, Gabi straddled a fence and headed towards the abandoned stone building in the distance. She knew that she needed to get back to the station, and also that Max would be concerned if he knew she was out in Riberon on her own, but the simple truth of the matter was that she owed it to her fiancé to go off on this mission. The earrings given to her in Italy had been a family heirloom and to have lost one after only owning them for a few weeks would break Roberto's heart. So, despite the cold and the rough terrain, Gabi was determined to find the lost gem.

Arriving at the outbuilding twenty minutes later, the detective looked back towards the road and where her car was parked. It hadn't seemed so far away this morning but, she considered, she had been talking to the uniformed officer as they'd walked, and time must have passed more quickly. Apart from a few cows grazing near the hedgerow, the field was devoid of life and Gabi realised that it must be bleak out here for the farmers during winter months.

Pushing the rickety wooden door inwards, Gabriella switched on the flashlight, pointing it down at the floor before walking forwards. The rusted trapdoor with its rotting hinges lay off to one side and the detective moved towards it, positioning herself in front of it as she had been that morning, before trying to determine in which direction her precious earring must have fallen. Visibility was poor, despite it still being mid-afternoon, with the low beams and boarded-up windows offering no source of natural light. The beam from the torch moved in an arc, allowing Gabriella to scour the area with her eyes, stooping down amongst the dried leaves to search with her fingertips.

Off to one side, a mound of leaves had built up, perhaps blown by the force of the wind from outside, causing the woman to sigh at the thought of her daunting task. All at once, as if by some miracle, Gabi caught a glimpse of something shining in the torchlight and reached out, scooping up the earring in her palm. Tears of relief welled up as she pocketed the precious item and prepared to leave, but it was then that the detective heard the unnerving sound of something scratching from below the trapdoor.

Inspector Mallery slapped his palms down onto the plastic tabletop, causing Cassell to flinch. Max was in no mood for games and pushed his face close to the man in custody. *"Où est le Detective Moreau?"*

The sanatorium manager blinked, biding his time. *"Je voudrais appeler mon advocat."*

Mallery stormed from the room, slamming the outer door behind him in rage. It had taken Leon Cassell thirty minutes to ask for legal representation and during that time he had offered no hint of knowing Thierry Moreau's whereabouts. Max was aware of time ticking past, the hours creeping into late afternoon and the daylight beginning to show signs of fading. He looked down at the smart Tag Heur on his wrist, calculating that Thierry had now been missing for around twenty-eight hours. The inspector prayed that his team member hadn't come to harm, but the chances of Moreau now turning up of his own accord were looking slim.

Max leaned on the desk at reception, waited for the duty officer to finish his phone call, and then requested that Cassell's lawyer be contacted. He slid a name and phone number across the divide, adding that it would do no harm to phone the man in an hour or so. Mallery intended for Leon Cassell to sweat. As the phone trilled to life for a second time, Max walked away.

"Inspecteur," the uniformed policeman called as Max made for the staircase, *"c'est Détective Dupont."*

Lifting to the receiver to his ear, Mallery could hear the panic in Gabriella's voice. "Max, I think I've found something. You need to send officers out to me. I'm at the farm across the road from the church in Riberon."

The inspector frowned. "What is it? And why didn't you call my mobile?"

As he spoke, Max felt in his pocket for his iPhone, noticing that the screen was blank due to its battery being dead. He continued to listen as Gabi explained.

"I think there's someone underneath this trap-door, but I can't get it open. I can hear groaning."

"I'm coming, stay put, I'll be as quick as I can," he assured her.

Delaying his departure by only a few minutes, in which time he raced upstairs to collect Luc Martin, Mallery called the police storeroom requesting a set of bolt cutters, then headed there to collect them. Finally, after rounding up two squad cars to follow him, the entourage set off towards Riberon.

Thierry Moreau had collapsed in a heap in the dark. Having used his fingers to claw at the damp earth underneath the door for over an hour, he had finally managed to squeeze his body through the gap, albeit a painful exertion on his stomach, the lining and muscles of which were still raw from his constant vomiting. Now, still in darkness, the detective made his way along the moss-covered wall, hands gripping the wall to steady his weakening body. The passage smelled of damp, a cloying, mildewy stench that filled his nostrils and gave Thierry the impression that he was deep underground. Light was non-existent and the young man's pupils strained in the darkness to try to make out shapes or forms, to no avail.

About a hundred feet along, the little air that pervaded the underground changed, becoming more of a cool stream than the clagging, earthy stench that had threatened to suffocate its prisoner earlier. With the alteration in atmosphere came the end of the wall which the detective had been holding onto as his guide, the area opening up and becoming more of a greying darkness than the pitch black of the area he'd found himself in immediately after escaping his cell. Holding his hands out in front of him, Thierry determined that he had reached a fork in the tunnels structure, which left him two options. He could turn left towards the faint breeze, or right to where the air felt slightly warmer and smelled slightly of decay. He opted for the former option, treading carefully along the slippery, muddied ground to where the promise of freedom beckoned.

After what he deemed to be around ten minutes of stumbling along the same tunnel, Moreau's foot hit upon a large, solid object, and he bent at the waist to touch the obstruction. Stone, hard and chiselled, blocked his way. Thierry reached out blindly in the dark, allowing his fingertips to travel upwards slightly. More stone, rectangular, sloping. Realisation dawned on him and Thierry clambered upwards, carefully making his way up the crudely formed staircase, to where he hoped salvation awaited.

Suddenly, his head bumped against something, causing the earlier damage to his skull to re-start its cruel, stabbing pain. Thierry slumped down onto the topmost step, pressing his fingers against the wooden panel above, but he reckoned the strength of at least two men would be needed to shift the covering from its tightly fitted niche. Moreau reckoned he had one shot at breaking whatever restraints were keeping the covering secured over his head, and he breathed in and out slowly, summoning the strength and courage to go on. Dipping his head slightly and using the curve of his shoulders to press against the wooden slats, Thierry heaved himself upwards. The stones underneath his boots were wet, causing him to lose his footing and go tumbling down. Thierry's knees and elbows bumped against every crudely fashioned step on the way down and he landed in a heap, nursing new injuries that shook him to the core. Mindful of the serious damage to his skull from being hit over the head the day before, Moreau patted his hair and fought to stay awake, his eyes now beginning to blur in and out of focus.

A sound from above suddenly penetrated Thierry's subconscious.

"Bonjour, il y a quelqu'un en bas?"

He knew that voice. Or was it the voice of an angel come to claim him in his dreams? Thierry moved his mouth, trying desperately to shout out, but the noise that escaped from his lips was more like the sound of a cow braying.

"Uuuhhh," he called, descending into the abyss of blackness. "Uuumph."

Max jumped out of the BMW, lifted the bolt cutters from the boot and climbed the gate to the field with Luc hot on his heels. Fifty feet into the quagmire of boggy grasses and cow dung, Mallery cursed at not having thought to change out of his Oxford brogues. They would be totally ruined, he grumbled, and so be it on Gabriella Dupont's head if this was a false alarm. A quartet of uniformed officers was right behind the duo, the lead policeman prepared with a heavy-duty flashlight.

"Do you think it's Thierry?" Luc Martin panted, his slight frame struggling to keep up with the inspector's fitter form.

Max turned, raised an eyebrow and hurried forward. "Who knows?"

Martin knew when to keep his mouth closed; he could tell a shift in his boss's mood simply by the tone in which he responded and pressed on in silence.

Gabriella came into sight, standing at the rickety open door to the near-collapsed grey stone building. She waved an arm at the officers and stepped back inside as though keeping vigil on her discovery.

A few minutes later, Mallery was at her side staring down at the crudely constructed trapdoor.

"The bolt is rusted," Gabi pointed out, "it's completely jammed."

Max swung the bolt cutters forward and gripped the shaft in its vice-like jaws, forcing his hands to close around the handles.

"It's no good," he breathed, feeling a jolt up his arm from the pressure, "I can't do it."

A hefty officer tapped Max on the shoulder. He was built like a rugby fullback and held out his meaty paw for the implement. "Let me try."

Annoyed at his own failure but determined to get to the bottom of Gabriella's find, Mallery passed over the tool.

Three attempts later and the rusted hinges gave a final creak as they were worked free of their secured bindings. The heavier officer ripped at the wooden slats with his hands, flinging the covering open.

Max was on his stomach in seconds, directing the officer with the torch to shine it down into the shaft below.

"Thierry?" Mallery called, straining his eyes to make out shapes in the blackness. "Are you there?"

"Let me go down there," Luc suggested, coming to the inspector's side. "I'm the smallest, plus I have rubber soles on my trainers."

Max weighed up his options, which appeared to be very few. "Okay, but for goodness' sake, please be careful, it looks pretty slippery down there."

Sliding himself into the opening feet first, Luc carefully lowered his body into the gloom, taking the flashlight from the officer's outstretched hand and trying to get a good footing before climbing down.

A minute passed, but to the officers at the top of the shaft it was though time stood still as they waited for Luc Martin to report back with his findings. When the shout came, a wave of relief, panic and nausea washed over the group.

"Boss, it's Thierry, he's here, but he's unconscious."

Mallery gestured to Gabi to call for the paramedics before positioning himself at the trapdoor opening. "I'm coming down."

Max was a good fifteen kilos heavier than the techie and found it a tight squeeze to clamber down into the tunnel. As he neared the bottom of the steps, his smart but ruined shoes offering little grip against the slime, the inspector could see Thierry's prostrate body below. Luc had propped his friend's head up on his knee and was checking the dark-skinned detective's vital signs.

"He's breathing," Luc smiled weakly, "but only just."

***

Jack Hobbs tapped his fingers against the kitchen worktop as he waited to be taken off hold. He'd been phoning the airline for half an hour, with Angélique sitting at the computer searching for a flight to Leeds/Bradford airport.

"This is crazy," Jack seethed, shaking his head. "It's been ages since they put me on hold. I might as well just drive to the airport and wait, then catch the first one to anywhere in the UK."

Angélique bit her lip, feeling her husband's obvious frustration. "There's a flight to Manchester at eight tonight, but it's showing as no seats available."

The Yorkshireman slammed down the phone and drained the glass of water that he'd poured some time before. "I might as well just pack a bag and go then, see if there's a cancellation and take my chances."

"Are you sure you don't want me and Tom to come with you?"

Angélique's eyes were searching, concerned. She knew how much Jack's family meant to him, especially his stubborn old dad.

"No, love, it's alright. I don't know how long I'll need to stay, and Thomas is only just settled in nursery. I'll call you often, I promise."

Angélique reached across the table and grasped her husband's hand. "Tell your dad I wish him a speedy recovery and give your mum a big hug, okay?"

"I will, no worries. Now, have you seen my good pair of jeans?"

Leon Cassell wiped the trickle of sweat from his brow. The cell was stuffy and warm with hardly any ventilation, and he could feel the perspiration gathering in his armpits. The duty officer had taken away his shoelaces and watch, but Leon reckoned it had been well over an hour since he'd requested the presence of his lawyer. There had been a great deal of activity in the station when the guard had returned him to the cell, far more than he would have expected for one of its proportions, and Cassell wondered whether something was afoot. Whatever it was, he mused, was unlikely to affect him. There was no way that anyone would discover the body of that detective for years, if at all. Cassell considered the removal of Moreau to be a necessary but unpleasant step; the officer had gained far too much information and had to be dealt with accordingly. The dilemma now doing circuits in Leon's mind was how to wriggle his way out of his current situation. Usually, he was adept at escaping unscathed but, with Mallery's discovery of his team member's notebook, it seemed that this time the odds were against him.

Cassell thudded down onto the metal-framed bunk, clasping his hands together. How stupid he had been to leave to the leather pocketbook in plain sight. He had completely underestimated the inspector's keen eye and powers of observation. Still, the sanatorium manager told himself, keep your head up and your motives hidden, they have nothing to connect you with Moreau except for a shabby notepad. Had it been put there by Marcel, he wondered? After all, he was the last person inside the office.

Cassell toyed with the idea of apportioning blame to the domestic woman who regularly came to vacuum and polish his office. Yes, he smiled, it was completely feasible that someone else could have put it there. Smiling broadly, Leon could hear the 'Not Guilty' plea to his lawyer being taken into consideration, followed by his immediate release. *It won't be long*, he told himself, *before I'm out of here and able to finish the task of getting rid of Enzo Roche.*

Leon stood, making his way over to the metal door and called out in French, "I'm entitled to a phone call. You have to allow me that!"

After a couple of minutes, the shutter flipped up and a police officer pressed his face up against the mesh. "I have to check with the inspector, you must wait until I can get hold of him."

"Where is he?" Leon queried, genuinely interested in Mallery's whereabouts.

The shutter snapped shut, cutting off the conversation and leaving Cassell feeling frustrated. There was someone he desperately needed to ring and time was running out.

Max, Gabi and Luc sat on uncomfortable plastic chairs in the hospital corridor outside Thierry Moreau's room. Two doctors were in attendance and the loud beeping of monitors echoed out through a huge window which separated the ailing detective from his colleagues.

"What are they doing in there?" Gabi sighed, glancing through the glass to where her friend lay motionless under white sheets, his dark face partially obscured by an oxygen mask. "Why won't they let us go in?"

Mallery slipped an arm around the woman's shoulders, pulling her close. "They'll let us see him once he's been thoroughly checked over, let's stay positive, *oui*?"

Gabi nodded and allowed her tense shoulder to relax under her boss's grip. "Leon Cassell has a lot to answer for. What kind of monster is he?"

Before Max could respond, the door to Thierry's room popped open and Doctor Singh appeared.

"Inspector Mallery," he smiled weakly, "I didn't expect to see you here again quite so soon."

"How is he?" Max replied, desperate for an update.

"Well, Monsieur Moreau has received quite a blow to the head, so we'll be keeping him sedated until we've seen the results of his brain scan, but that's not our only concern, I'm afraid."

The trio of officers had presumed that the bleeding cut on Thierry's head had been his only wound and the three faces looked stricken as Singh continued.

"It appears that your colleague has been poisoned. Thankfully, due to the previous two cases that were recently brought in, I recognised the distinct smell right away. I believe that Thierry has digested water hemlock in one form or another. We're going to have to pump his stomach to be sure there's nothing left. His throat is red raw, so we can presume that he's already vomited quite considerably, so I'm hopeful that the worst of the plant has already left Thierry's system."

"You're certain it's water hemlock?" Luc asked, his eyes wide.

"As certain as I can be until we send his remaining stomach contents off to the lab."

Max turned to Gabriella. "Is Roberto working today?"

"Yes, until six," she confirmed.

Mallery took out his notepad and scribbled some details on it, ripping off the top sheet of paper and passing it to the medic.

"Roberto Mazzo is the lab technician who identified the poison in the previous two victims. If you call him on this number, he'll be able to arrange a courier to collect the sample. He'll also ensure you get a quick result."

Brijesh Singh took the details and tucked them in his top pocket. "Thanks."

"Can we go in?" Gabriella pleaded, staring at her friend through the window. "He'll want to know we're here."

The doctor smiled weakly. "Okay, but not for too long. Does Thierry have family?"

Mallery was already pulling out his phone. "I'll call his parents now." Stabbing at the screen, he remembered his battery needed charging and asked Gabriella for hers.

Singh made to return to his duties, but then hesitated. "Inspector, I hope you catch the person who has done this. Thierry could have died."

With the ringtone in one ear, Max laid a hand on Brijesh's arm. "He's already in custody."

Satisfied, the doctor retreated in search of his patient's scan results, leaving the police inspector to ponder over his own words.

Did they have the right man in custody?

Back at the sanatorium, Filipino nurse Dorothy Ramos was doing her final rounds before finishing for the day. The patients had been excitable during the afternoon, each ruminating over the presence of the police detectives and how they had escorted Monsieur Cassell off the premises in an unmarked car. Staff had tried their best to keep the gossip to a minimum, but nobody seemed to know why the sanatorium manager had been taken in for questioning, or when he might be expected to return.

"Are you almost done?" Fran Shepherd asked, pushing the drugs trolley into the secure storage room. "It's certainly been a long day."

Dorothy reached for a pair of surgical stockings and turned to face the staff nurse. "Almost. I just need to put these on Emiline, her legs are swollen again."

Fran made a mental note to check on the old woman before going home and turned the lock in the wooden cabinet. "Well, medicines are all done for the day, I'll be glad to finish today. Bet you will, too."

Dorothy glanced towards the door. She wasn't one for spreading rumours but curiosity was getting the better of her. "Do you know anything about Monsieur Cassell's arrest? Does it have anything to do with the deaths of Ray and Edwina?"

Fran frowned, brushing her fringe out of her eyes. "I should hope not, he seems a respectable man to me. Perhaps they just need him to help with enquiries. Maybe it has something to do with past patients."

"Oh, you're such a good person, Fran," her friend giggled, "always willing to see the good in everyone."

"I try to," the nurse admitted. "Monsieur Cassell has always been very fair with me."

"Unlike that stroppy Doctor Lafoy," Ramos commented. "I think if anyone's guilty, it's her."

Fran couldn't help but agree, although she refrained from voicing her opinion and changed the subject. "Anyway, never mind about the goings-on here, do you have any plans for the evening?"

"Not really." Dorothy shrugged. "Dinner, TV and an early night. You?"

Fran smiled to herself, anticipating the hours ahead that she would spend in the arms of Maurice Fabron. "Nothing much, same as you, probably."

Just as the nurses were about to close and lock the door, a voice called out from further down the hallway.

"Hold on, ladies, I was wondering if one of you could sign my timesheet before you go."

The women turned to see the bulky figure of gardener Marcel Caisse walking towards them.

Fran sighed. "I'm not sure that I can, Marcel, you know Monsieur Cassell deals with employee hours and pay. Can't it wait?"

Caisse shook his head. "No, I always have to put my hours in on a Friday and Monsieur Cassell isn't back yet."

Fran put out her hand. "Leave it with me then, I'll see if I can sort it out."

The gardener passed over the document and turned to leave. "Thanks, Frannie."

Nurse Shepherd continued to lock the storeroom door, then glanced down at the papers in her hand.

"I don't think this is right, anyway," she muttered, showing Dorothy the scribbled figures. "Marcel definitely wasn't here on Thursday afternoon. I remember quite clearly as Emiline pointed out that some tools had been left unattended in the garden, and when I went to find him, the tool shed was all locked up."

Dorothy was in agreement. "Yes, that's right. He was around at lunchtime, but after that I didn't see him at all. I remember thinking it was unusual."

"I guess he's just made a mistake," Fran continued, looking down the corridor to see if she could catch sight of the gardener. "I'll pop these on Cassell's desk, with a note to check it over with Marcel."

"Perhaps he's trying to get away with bunking off," Dorothy cackled, her round cheeks turning pink. "We've all done it from time to time."

Fran patted her friend's shoulder. "Not me, Dotty, not me."

It had taken the duty officer half an hour to contact one of Mallery's team, first getting through to Jack Hobbs who was at Bordeaux airport and finally to Gabriella Dupont, who explained that Max's battery was dead and had passed the call over.

"Cassell's complaining about not being allowed to make a call," the officer explained, "he's been going on for an hour."

"Did you get hold of his attorney? Mallery queried.

"Yes, all taken care of, he's been in court and will be here around six."

"Alright," Max replied, "I'll be back by then to meet him. Let Cassell make his call, but be sure to make a note of the number he's calling, okay?"

"Got it, thanks, Inspector."

Max handed Gabi's phone back to her and weighed up the situation.

"There isn't much we can do here, and I need to get back to the station to question our suspect. Do you want to stay until Thierry's parents arrive?"

"Of course, I'm not leaving until I know Thierry's going be okay."

Max turned to Luc Martin who had been unusually quiet. "You'd better come with me, we'll need both our brains to outwit Leon Cassell."

"No problem boss," the techie answered.

"When did either of you last eat?" Mallery questioned his colleagues. "Shall I get you something?"

Gabi shook her head. "I'm not hungry."

"Luc?" Mallery knew how unusual it was for the computer geek to go without snacks for any length of time. "Want to get something on the way back?"

Detective Martin sighed. "No, I'm alright. I'm too worried to eat."

Max was taken aback. He'd never known Luc refuse a meal in all their time working together. The young lad must be considerably stressed to knock back an offer of being fed.

"Let's go and see what we can get out of Cassell then. Gabi, tell Thierry's mother and father that I'll be back as soon as I can."

Thierry Moreau lay still under the covers, lucid dreams floating around in his head as the sedative took hold. He was barely aware of the dryness in his throat now and the pain in his head had subsided completely. As he allowed himself to go deeper into the dark, Thierry caught glimpses of the day on which he had been taken captive.

He vaguely recalled a conversation, easy, chatty. Then there had been a large, heavy object wielded at his head. As he'd fought to remain conscious, there had been strong arms pulling him, his legs scraping across the floor as the person had dragged him, firm hands underneath his armpits. Thierry could make no sense of the images, his confused state causing everything to become jumbled and blurred. One constant in his vision was a pair of green dungarees, the knees worn and patched, and the smell of fresh grass. Then later, the damp and cold of an underground cell, the bitter taste of parsley filling his mouth.

Where on earth had he been and who with?

Thierry allowed his mind to clear, letting sleep take over, the only sound in his ears the repetitive beep of a far-off machine.

Officer Petit ran after Mallery as he entered police headquarters, catching the inspector's arm and causing him to stop in his tracks.

"Sir, you asked us to note down the number on Cassel's call."

Max took the proffered paper gratefully. "Have you run it through the system?"

"Yes, I took the liberty of doing that myself. It was a cell phone registered to one Marcel Caisse, he lives in Salbec."

"Well done, I appreciate you taking the initiative, it will save us time."

Mallery passed the note to Luc Martin, who instinctively knew that his boss would require him to run Caisse's name through their records before commencing the interview with Cassell. Mallery always liked to be one step ahead of a suspect and any finer details that Luc could provide would be used wisely.

"I'll be ten minutes," he promised, heading towards the stairs.

Max turned towards the canteen. That was just enough time to get a coffee and some chocolate for Martin. No matter what the computer whizz had said earlier, he knew that Luc couldn't run on empty for very long.

Jack Hobbs typed quickly, determined to text his boss before the announcement came to turn off all electronic gadgets. The flight was only half full and he'd managed to get an exit seat where he could stretch out his legs.

ON FLIGHT. ARRIVE IN LEEDS AT 8PM.

A small tick appeared next to the text showing that it had been successfully sent and Jack turned the phone off before slipping it into his shirt pocket. He felt guilty at having to leave the team in the lurch, but the Yorkshireman knew they'd understand. Every one of his colleagues had met Hobbs senior at a summer barbecue and they'd all fallen for the great man's charm and wit, especially Max, who had later questioned Jack about his decision to join the force rather than take on the family business. The current situation at the station bothered Jack no end. Thierry was missing and they had only one suspect, who so far had refused to co-operate. He had no idea how long he would need, or be expected, to stay in England, but the thrill of closing a murder case was pricking at every sensory organ. He wanted to be there to catch the killer.

Luc Martin passed the information to his boss and reluctantly took the bar of chocolate that was being waved before his eyes. "Alright, if you insist."

"I can't have you fainting mid-interview," Max scoffed, "so eat it."

"What about you?"

Mallery raised his coffee cup, sipped and said, "I can survive on caffeine. Now, let's finish up and see what Cassell's got to say for himself."

Luc pointed at the canteen clock. "He's already been in custody for seven hours, you're going to have to charge him tonight or let him go."

"Well, I was hoping that Thierry would be awake and able to identify his assailant, but it doesn't look as though that's going to happen now..."

Max was reading the notes that Martin had given him as he spoke and suddenly stopped to recheck what he was seeing.

"What? Cassell gets one phone call, and he rings the sanatorium gardener?"

Luc's fringe was flopping up and down. "Yep, seems so."

"What do we know about this Marcel Caisse?"

"Not much, boss. He was employed at the hospital about a month after Leon Cassell arrived. No police record, in fact, I can't find any work history for him at all."

Max pondered the statement. "So why would Cassell employ someone to care for such a huge plot of land without being able to check references?"

"I guess you'll have to ask him," Luc answered, finishing the last block of chocolate and screwing up the wrapper.

"I intend to. Ready?"

The inspector drained his cup and placed it on the tray allocated to dirty crockery. It was going to be another late night, he could feel it in his bones, but there was no way he was letting Leon Cassell rest until they had some answers.

Bertram Boland was mentally exhausted. Having spent all day in the courtroom defending a client on a rape charge, he himself not being wholly convinced of the man's innocence, he had a blinding headache and felt mentally drained. Popping a couple of paracetamols into his mouth and swallowing them down with half a bottle of water, the lawyer climbed out of his car and pulled his briefcase from the rear seat. He vaguely recalled meeting Leon Cassell a year before at the inquest of his brother's death, but beyond a family similarity and Cassell's brusque manner, the memory of the man was hazy.

Climbing the police station steps, Boland was greeted by a man in his mid-forties, dressed in expensive but informal clothes. A chiselled jaw and head of thick, dark hair marked the man as handsome, carrying himself with an air of quiet confidence.

"Monsieur Boland? Inspector Max Mallery."

So, this was the infamous Mallery that he'd read about in the national newspapers, the lawyer mused. Wasn't it the inspector's team who had recently foiled a Taliban plot to place a bomb in the centre of the city?

"Inspector," he replied, shaking the strong, warm hand and noting the absence of a wedding ring, "I believe you have yet to charge Monsieur Cassell."

Mallery took the liberty of outlining the details, adding that Cassell had been found in possession of an injured detective's notebook.

"Apart from the notebook, you have nothing to connect my client to the murder cases?"

Max was non-committal, reluctant to admit that the case against Cassell was flimsy and weak. "*Non*, but how else do you explain him being in possession of Detective Moreau's private notes?"

"What does he have to say for himself?"

"Not very much all," Mallery confessed, "he's refusing to work with us."

Boland could feel the thudding in his temple beginning to return. "Inspector, you and I are both intelligent men. I suggest you let me speak to

Monsieur Cassell and then we'll see where we are, but I warn you, unless you have anything else to connect him to your colleague's unfortunate abduction, you're going to have to release him without charge."

Max led the way to the holding cell, fury burning up inside him.

Luc Martin couldn't explain why he had suddenly felt the urge to run back up to the incident room to do a further search on Marcel Caisse, but the techie knew when to trust his gut and had excused himself from Mallery's presence while they waited for Boland to speak with his client. Max had waved him away, knowing better than to question Luc's random requests, but had expected a quick return as time was pressing on.

Sitting at his desk, Martin pulled out his personal phone and clicked on the Facebook logo. It was just a hunch but he knew that most middle-aged people liked to keep in contact with their friends and family via social media, and he hoped that Marcel Caisse was no different.

Typing the gardener's name into the search bar, Luc found three people with the same name and clicked on each in turn. At the third profile, his mouth fell open. The photograph on the page was of a bald man with a thick, dark beard, but the eyes that stared back were unmistakeable, he had definitely seen them before.

Madam Moreau stroked her son's hand as she murmured soothing words and prayed for Thierry to wake up. Doctor Brijesh Singh had left the room a few minutes earlier, having broken the news that there would be no permanent brain damage and that the sedation could be slowly eased, bringing the detective back to consciousness. Thierry's father sat on the opposite side of the bed, his dark face a mirror-image of his son's apart from a few deep lines, albeit twenty years senior.

Gabriella Dupont was out in the corridor, wanting to impart the good news to Max as soon as possible. She also considered that this would now mean that Leon Cassell faced a charge of grievous bodily harm, as long as Thierry was able to identify his attacker, of course.

Under stark white sheets, Thierry began to stir, his short, soft eyelashes fluttering open before closing again under the glare of the harsh overhead lights. Monsieur Moreau quickly rose from his chair and reached for the switch to turn off the bright beam, immediately relieved that Thierry once again tried to blink.

"*Fils, nous sommes ici*," Moreau senior whispered, wiping away a tear of relief. "*Tu dois te reposer.*" You must rest.

Gabriella had sneaked back into the room and stood close to the bed. Opening her phone, she clicked on the photograph of Leon Cassell that Max had shared in their briefing a few days before. "Is this who abducted you?"

Thierry grimaced, the pain in his skull returning. "No, it wasn't him."

Bertram Boland slung his pin-striped jacket over one shoulder and dropped his briefcase next to the reception desk where Mallery waited.

"Well, he's denying any involvement," the lawyer said confidently, "so, I suggest you either come up with some evidence to prove otherwise or release Monsieur Cassell without charge."

The inspector was balling his hands into fists. "He *has* to be involved. That notebook didn't just find its way there by itself, unless Cassell is colluding with someone else."

Boland looked at his watch, eager to get home to a cooked meal and a glass of wine. "By my reckoning you have less than twelve hours. I have a court case to attend in the morning, but it shouldn't take more than an hour. Give me a call if you find anything substantial. If I don't hear from you, I'll presume that the case against my client has been dropped."

Max took the white card being held out to him, noting that the office address was in Aureillac. "Monsieur Boland, I hope you don't mind me asking, but you're new to Bordeaux, right?"

"Yes, that's right, ignore the address on there, my new cards are being printed."

Max ignored the explanation and went on. "So, if you're not local, why did Leon Cassell ask for you in particular? I mean, how does he know you?"

Bertram Boland considered the question, eventually deciding that he wasn't breaking any client confidentiality by telling the truth; after all, his connection to Cassell bore no relevance to the current allegations.

"Well, the truth of the matter is that my office was involved in the inquest into Monsieur Cassell's brother's death just over a year ago. Nasty business, so I recall, a suicide."

Mallery was intrigued. "Do you happen to remember the brother's name?"

"Burr, or Barr… no, Baur, that was it, Daniel Baur."

As Luc Martin joined the duo in their conversation, Mallery felt a chill run down his spine. "Daniel Baur? Are you sure, Monsieur Boland?"

"Yes. Of course I can check the files, but I'm sure that was the name. Why?"

"I think we've just discovered Leon Cassell's motive for murder."

The lawyer was confused, urging the detective to enlighten him.

"I need Luc to run a check," Max explained, "but Daniel Baur is the name of Enzo Roche's ex-lover. Baur killed himself after their affair ended."

"The ballet dancer?" Boland breathed incredulously. "He was mentioned briefly at the inquest, but Roche applied for an injunction to prevent the newspapers from mentioning his name. So, you think that Leon Cassell is trying to avenge his brother's death?"

"It would seem so."

Luc coughed to interrupt the pair. "Boss, I think you need to see this…"

The techie held out a printed sheet. The smiling face of Marcel Caisse looked back. Mallery was confused for a moment, failing to see the relevance, until Luc covered the lower part of the gardener's face with his palm, revealing the exact likeness to Leon Cassell.

"What the hell?" he stuttered.

Luc produced a second image and held it at arms-length. It showed a man with the exact same features as Caisse and Cassell, but with a full head of hair. The eyes, nose and long forehead were identical.

"Triplets?" Boland exclaimed, unable to believe his eyes. "Really?"

"It looks that way," Martin shrugged, feeling pleased with himself, "although why they all have different surnames is a mystery to me."

Bertram Boland stifled a yawn. "I'm sorry, but I really should be going. Please let me know when you find the answers, I'll be waiting for your call."

The detectives bade farewell to their visitor and headed back upstairs to the incident room. As they reached the doorway, Audrey Rancourt approached from the opposite direction.

"Working late tonight?" she asked, a large leather handbag hooked over one arm, a bright red raincoat at the crook of her elbow.

"Unfortunately, yes, we have a mystery to solve," Mallery told her.

The commissioner slipped her belongings onto an empty table and walked towards the whiteboard that took up most of the rear wall.

"What do you have?"

Max ran through the current situation in a record five minutes, focussing on the latest discovery of the connection between Cassell and the other two men.

"You look a little short-staffed," Rancourt commented, noting the lack of noise and the empty desks.

Max held up three fingers, counting off his absent officers. "Thierry's in hospital recovering, Gabriella's with him, waiting to see if he can positively identify the person who assaulted and abducted him, and Jack Hobbs has had to fly back to England, a family emergency."

Audrey trusted her next-in-line enough not to pry into what might have caused Hobbs to leave during an ongoing investigation, but she also recognised the dark lines under both Max's and Luc's eyes that told her the officers had been pulling long shifts for days.

"Okay, which desk can I use? Three heads are better than two."

"Seriously?" Mallery grinned, unable to hide his surprise.

The commissioner reached for her bag and plucked a bank card from her purse, holding it out to Luc. "I think you'd better order us some pizza or fried chicken to keep us going, don't you?"

Detective Martin was almost salivating at the very mention of food. "With a side of wedges and coleslaw?"

Rancourt laughed. "Yes, if you need to. Now, Max, show me what you want me to help out with, will you?"

***

Jack Hobbs pushed the toe of one foot against the heel of the other, trying to rid himself of muddy Wellington boots outside the kitchen door. Once inside, he collapsed into his father's chair at the side of the Aga, allowing the warmth from the stove to penetrate his cold fingers and toes. It was only just the end of summer, yet a biting wind had whipped at his face as he'd helped Simon, the regular farmhand, to round up the cows for milking. He had only arrived home an hour earlier, having hired a car at the airport and driven straight to the Leeds General Infirmary to visit his father, yet Jack already felt as though he'd done a day's work on the family smallholding.

Jean Hobbs placed a mug of tea on the table within her son's reach, and then went back to stirring a pot of soup. "Thank you so much for dropping everything and coming over, our Jack. I bet Dad was right pleased to see you."

The detective stretched out his toes, rubbing the ends of his socks against the heated front of the Aga. "Aye, he was. Although he insists that he'll be out in a day or two and told me I shouldn't have spent the money on a flight."

Jean moved away from the supper and came to stand behind her son, placing a hand upon his shoulder. "That's not what the cardiologist says. He told me your dad needs at least a fortnight's care in hospital, and then he'll have to take it easy when he comes out."

Jack turned to look at his mother. "What does that mean in real terms? That he won't be able to look after the farm?"

The farmer's wife looked away, trying to busy herself to avoid her son's eyes. "Yes, that's about the brunt of it. He's been overdoing things for months."

"What about all that talk of getting a tenant in to run the farm, with the prospect of selling it on? Was that just bullshit?"

Jean tutted. "Don't swear, Jack. You know your dad, he couldn't ever really let the farm go, it's in his blood."

The unspoken words that Hobbs expected to follow hung in the air between them. The farm was in his blood, too and it had hurt his parents no end

193

when he'd announced that he was joining the force instead of continuing the family legacy. Peter Hobbs was proud of the five generations of men who had bred cattle on the land before him, each passing down their knowledge and ethics to the next generation of Hobbs sons in turn. All that had stopped with his own son, the end of an era.

Jack sat in silence, thinking about the day when he'd come home with a handful of leaflets outlining the courses at police training college. His parents had acted surprised, outraged even, that he would consider such a career, but God knows he'd tried to drop enough hints over the years. It was true that Jack did have farming in his blood, after all he'd spent every hour after school helping with the endless chores around the farm, but it wasn't ingrained in him the way it was with his dad, and he'd always known that his true calling lay elsewhere.

"Penny for them?" Jean asked, setting down a bowl of oxtail soup.

Jack cleared his throat. "I was just thinking I'd better call Angie, say goodnight to Tom before he goes to bed, and then catch up with Max."

"Aye, alright, lad." Jean sighed, wondering how long her son would be staying but not daring to ask. "Eat your supper first though, they'll understand."

"We'll have to sort something out, Mum, before I go back to France."

Jean flinched. "What do you mean? With the farm?"

Jack could hear the denial in his mother's tone. It was the same with both of his parents, never wanting to face up to the prospect being incapable of carrying on with the dairy farm, always turning the other cheek and pretending they'd have their health forever. Either that, or clinging to the faint hope that their only son might have a complete change of heart and throw in the towel on his much-coveted police career in favour of spending his days up to his knees in cow muck.

"Yes, Mum, with the farm," Jack breathed, sliding his empty bowl onto the table. "You and Simon can't manage on your own, and goodness only knows how long it'll be before Dad will be well enough to work again, if at all."

Jean took the crockery to the sink and gazed out of the kitchen window into the fading light beyond. "Perhaps you could take a bit of leave, for a few weeks, or a month or so, just until we can sort something out, eh? There's a good lad."

And there it was, the uncomfortable silence, returned once more in the form of his mother's request. Jack knew that if he stayed longer than a fortnight, it would soon turn into a month, and then his mother would find every possible excuse under the sun for her son to prolong his trip indefinitely, until eventually she would suggest that he bring Angélique and Tom over to stay at the farm. Jack suddenly had the sensation of a great void opening up underneath his chair, waiting to swallow him whole. He got up and pulled out his mobile phone, moving to the privacy of the Hobbs' sitting room to call his wife.

"I need to ring Angie, Mum, we'll talk again in the morning, I promise."

With the cardboard buckets of fried chicken leftovers cleared away, the incident room smelled decidedly heady, with grease and spices adding to the warm air. The trio had worked in silence for almost an hour, only stopping to eat and refill their coffee mugs. Mallery was impressed with how Audrey Rancourt was letting him take the lead, asking what was required of her and then getting on with the task at hand without fuss.

It was on their third refuel of caffeine that Luc turned in his chair with a wide grin.

"I've just been on one of those ancestry websites," he announced. "You're never going to believe what I've found."

Max ran a hand over his face, as though to wipe away the tiredness that was tugging at him. "Of course you're going to tell us…"

Martin turned his computer screen around as the two senior officers got up to take a look. "So, according to Leon Cassell's birth certificate, he was born with the surname Proust. His mother, Lillian, was single at the time, no father is recorded. However, I checked the dates of birth for both Marcel Caisse and Daniel Baur, and guess what?"

"They're the same?" Audrey piped up.

Luc masked his disappointment by not pausing to acknowledge the question but instead continued, "They're exactly the same. The men were, or are, triplets, all born to Lillian Proust, who put the boys up for adoption within weeks of their birth."

Max peered at the computer. "So they were adopted by different families?"

"Exactly!" Luc was warming to his subject now and clicked onto an icon at the top of the screen. "I've pulled up an old newspaper clipping from eighteen months ago, look at the photo."

"*Triplets reunited after forty years*," Audrey read out loud.

"You see," Luc told them, "Leon, Marcel and Daniel had only just found each other again, six months before Daniel committed suicide. At the time of their reconciliation, Daniel must have been involved with Enzo Roche."

Max could hardly believe what he was hearing. "So Leon and Marcel cooked up a plot to exact revenge upon Roche for breaking up with their brother and, in their minds, causing him to commit suicide?"

"I would say that just about sums it up, yes," Luc finished.

Mallery glanced at the commissioner. "We need to handle Cassell very carefully, don't you agree? But we also need to pick up Marcel Caisse."

Audrey Rancourt was delving into her large leather bag. "Let me just change into my flat shoes, then we'll bring him in. One phone call will secure a warrant for his arrest based on Luc's evidence. Well done, to both of you."

Luc Martin was bouncing up and down on the balls of his feet. "Do you want me to come with you, boss?"

Max considered the question for a split second but shook his head. "You go home and get some rest, I'm going need you to help with tomorrow morning's briefing. We'll need all the facts laid bare so that neither Cassell nor Caisse can worm their way out of this."

Rancourt was speaking on her phone and raised her voice a couple of times, causing the detectives to look her way.

"Bloody paper pushers," she cursed, putting the phone away. "All sorted, we can pick up the warrant on the way. Your car or mine?"

Max waved his set of keys in the air. "I don't think Marcel Caisse will fit in my trunk, do you?"

For the first time in days, the officers witnessed their superior break out into a fit of laughter. "Oh, Max, you really know how to lighten the mood,"

In that split second, the commissioner looked a good deal younger than her fifty-five years and, had she not been his commanding officer, Max would have been sorely tempted to ask her out for dinner.

As Commissioner Rancourt headed for the highway in her sleek Mercedes, Mallery sat in the passenger's seat checking Marcel Caisse's profile on the new iPad.

"Caisse has learning difficulties," he announced, glancing at his superior, "so we might need to handle him delicately."

Audrey Rancourt always tended to err on the side of caution where disabilities were concerned and considered the eventuality of Caisse either not understanding what he was being charged with, or completely overreacting. "What's the name of the sanatorium's doctor? Do you think she can help?"

"Juliette Lafoy," Max confirmed. "I have some reservations about her, to be honest, but I guess we don't have any choice but to involve her. Waiting for another shrink to come out at this time of night might take hours."

He elaborated on the unethical practices that Lafoy had been using to extract information from Enzo Roche in the hope to gather scandal for her upcoming book.

Rancourt looked startled. "Seriously? Well, I suppose it will be up to Roche to press charges, once he finds out, but that sounds pretty underhanded."

"Do you still want to involve her tonight?"

Audrey nodded. "I don't think we have a choice. She can face the issues of malpractice after we've got Caisse in custody. I take it you will be telling Enzo Roche what she's been doing?"

Mallery snorted. "You try and stop me."

Rancourt indicated towards Riberon and asked for directions to Juliette Lafoy's cottage but, when they arrived ten minutes later, the building lay in darkness.

"Try around the back," the commissioner instructed, peering through the living room window for signs of activity, "but it looks as though she's out."

Max tramped through ankle-length grass and tried the rear door before cupping his hands through the frosted panel of glass. He could detect no shadow, light or sign of anyone at home.

"Nothing. What now?" he asked, returning to the front garden, brushing pollen from his jeans. "Do we speak to Caisse without her?"

Audrey shook her head. "No, definitely not. You know how the press jump on these situations. Before we know it, we'll have Human Rights activists protesting outside the station. We need to be sure that Marcel Caisse understands why we're taking him in for questioning and that he has an appropriate adult to accompany him."

"I would hardly call Doctor Lafoy 'appropriate'," Max smirked, making inverted commas with his index fingers, "especially after her recent behaviour." He pulled out his phone. "Maybe there's someone else we can call on."

"Who?"

"Fran Shepherd, she's a qualified nurse and works at the sanatorium."

Audrey raised an eyebrow, causing Max to add, "She's English, but don't worry, her French is good enough to communicate with the patients."

Fran stared at the Scrabble tiles in front of her, trying to find a five-letter word with two 'E's. Across the table, Telo Fabron was itching to help out and rubbed his palms together as he watched his father's girlfriend struggle. The young man had warmed to the nurse immediately and had welcomed her into their home as though he'd known her for years. Maurice sat at Fran's side, watching the interaction with a smile on his lips. He couldn't have been happier that the pair were getting along so well.

"*Plus de vin?*" he asked, accidentally dripping water from the ice-bucket onto the game board as he lifted out the wine bottle, causing Telo to shout out "Papa!" in mock horror.

Fran shuffled forward on the sofa whilst Maurice topped up her glass, excitedly laying out the tiles to spell '*FETES*' on the board.

"*Bravo, Fran!*" Telo clapped, consulting his own set of letters with a face set in deep concentration.

A familiar buzzing came from across the room and Fran struggled to her feet, rubbing at the pins and needles that had resulted from sitting with her legs tucked underneath her body. "Who on earth can that be? It's almost nine."

Maurice watched, feeling slightly concerned as she answered the call.

"That was the hospital," the nurse explained in English to avoid Telo becoming concerned. "Inspector Mallery needs me to help him with something."

"So late in the evening?" Fabron queried. "He's not chasing geese again, is he?"

"You mean on a wild goose chase?" Fran giggled. "No, not this time, he needs to talk to the facility gardener who has some learning disabilities."

"I guess it must be important, but why not call the doctor?" Maurice wanted to know, feeling slightly annoyed that Max had interrupted their perfect evening.

"Apparently, she's not at home. I'd better call a taxi, he's waiting."

The boulangerie owner sighed. "You have no chance of a taxi coming out here at this time of night, it's not worth their trouble from Bordeaux. I've only had two glasses, I'll drive you."

"Are you sure, darling?"

Fran kissed Maurice on the nose, silently wishing she'd switched off her phone.

"Yes, absolutely. *Telo, nous devons sortir, Max a besoin d'aide.*"

The young man swung around, alerted at the mention of his friend's name.

"*Max, est-il en difficulté?*"

Maurice tousled his son's hair. "*Non, Max va bien.*" No, Max is fine.

Or at least the baker hoped that his friend was fine. Only time would tell.

Marcel Caisse had worked himself up into a state of agitation. He hadn't seen his brother since late morning and Leon wasn't answering his phone, either. Marcel gazed out of the window of his self-contained apartment within the hospital. Leon had told him that only very special members of staff got to live on site, and Marcel liked having this space all to himself. The large man had felt concerned since finishing his tasks earlier in the day. Leon hadn't been around to sign Marcel's timesheet and the gardener had been forced to turn to one of the nurses to submit the hours. Marcel hoped that his brother wasn't in trouble.

It was unlike Leon not to tell him when he was leaving the premises. He wondered whether the manager had gone on another date with the pretty female doctor. He'd seen them leaving together a few nights before, Juliette Lafoy all dressed up with bright pink lipstick on. Marcel figured that it was three or four hours since Leon had called and told him to stay put, but his brother hadn't said why and the younger of the triplets was beginning to worry.

The bright beam of double headlights flashed against the windowpane, momentarily blinding Marcel, who had been too preoccupied with his thoughts to notice the car approaching. He blinked, watching as two figures climbed out of the shiny silver saloon. Caisse peered into the darkness, trying to make out who was approaching the building, but all he could see was long, thin shadows cast upon the gravel driveway. A second vehicle arrived, just a minute after, but this time Marcel could clearly see Fran Shepherd talking to someone in the front seat as the interior light came on.

"Everything will be alright now," the man murmured to himself, rocking back and forth on the side of the bed, "Frannie is here."

Marcel clamped a hand over his mouth, remembering how the nurse had told him not to call her by that name, although he'd heard Enzo Roche calling her 'Frannie' and, when the gardener had mentioned it to his brother, Leon had laughed and told him to carry on with the endearment, "to wind her up".

Juliette Lafoy shivered as she carefully navigated the stone steps, shining the flashlight around her as night owls and hawks cawed in the pitch-black night. A crypt was the last place that the psychiatrist had expected to find herself, but Leon had insisted she undertake the task of feeding the imprisoned detective and she presumed it was his way of implicating her should things go awry.

Juliette counted to seven, and then stopped; this was it, the seventh tomb along. She had only made this trip once before, guided by Cassell, but coming here alone was quite a different experience altogether. Her senses were on high alert, tuned to the silence in the space underneath the church, and she hurried to her task. Pushing hard, the doctor moved the stones surrounding the base of the tomb and climbed through the gaping hole that was revealed behind it. Her anorak caught on the craggy rock, tearing as she eased her shoulders into the space beyond.

"*Merde*," she cursed, dragging the torch in front of her before standing in the blackness of the freezing tunnel.

Placing one hand on the wall and the other grasping her only source of light, Juliette walked slowly forwards, bending her knees slightly as the passage graduated downhill and then levelled out into a muddy walkway.

It was hard to believe that monks had used this maze of tunnels to transport wine and weapons during the French Revolution but, by using very little imagination, Juliette could understand how the secret passages could act as a means of transport links between God's men and those fighting for the cause.

As the woman pressed on, she wondered what had happened to Leon Cassell, and whether the inspector had charged him. As far as Juliette knew, there was nothing to connect the sanatorium manager with the abduction of that snooping detective, but she reasoned that it was probably typical of Cassell's personality not to divulge everything to her. Now, she found herself on a thankless mission. The detective needed food and Leon was indisposed, leaving Juliette to venture below ground alone in order to check that the injured man received sustenance. Lafoy had no idea that Thierry Moreau now lay within the secure confines of Bordeaux General Hospital.

Walking steadily, placing her walking boots carefully on the wet ground, Juliette's thoughts turned to their dinner a few nights before. How Cassell had enjoyed watching her squirm when he'd confessed that he'd worked out why she was here in Riberon. Strangely though, it hadn't seemed to bother Leon that she was gathering snippets of scandalous gossip with which to create Enzo Roche's unofficial biography. Instead, he had encouraged her, asked if he could help, even offered her money in return for some tabloid-worthy exclusives. Juliette might have known that Cassell would both want, and expect, something in return, and later, after several glasses of wine, the truth had come out. Cassell wanted Roche dead.

Fran slipped off her jacket and knocked at the door of Marcel Caisse's self-contained apartment. He was pleased to see her and opened the door wide, not anticipating the steel-haired woman and handsome police inspector who stood behind the nurse's shoulders.

"*Marcel, pouvons-nous entrer?*"

The large bear of a man stepped back clumsily, knocking a book off the arm of the sofa, his face blushing pink.

"*Frannie….*"

Mallery stepped into the room behind Fran, followed by Audrey Rancourt, who stooped to pick up the volume of wild plants, turning it over in her hands, surprised. It was ear-marked at a page describing water hemlock.

Fran gently explained the reason for the intrusion, keeping her language simple and her tone even. Every now and again, Marcel glanced at the two police officers, but then returned his focus to the nurse who was speaking softly, asking if he knew anything about the dark-skinned detective's whereabouts. Mallery had briefed Fran on how he wanted the conversation to play out. Marcel must not know that Moreau was safe, but they did need to know what his brother had said during the phone call.

Caisse smiled at Fran, eagerly telling her that Leon was fine, but had gone out and might be late back. No, Marcel didn't know where or why, but his brother had told him not to worry. The nurse carefully turned the chatter around to the gardener's timesheets that he'd left with her earlier that day.

"Marcel, why did you write in your hours for yesterday afternoon?" she queried in French. "I know you weren't here, nobody saw you all afternoon."

Caisse began to get agitated, wriggling on the small leather stool that he perched upon, causing it to squeak. "Leon told me to write it in, like a normal day."

"But where were you really?" Fran urged, laying a hand upon the man's arm. "It's okay, you won't get into any trouble. After all, Leon said it was okay, didn't he?"

The large, bearded head nodded. "I had to take that policeman into a safe place, because his head was hurting."

"And this safe place, where is it?"

Marcel began to frantically shake his head. "Leon said never tell."

Fran looked up at Max for guidance, her eyes asking him what to say next.

"If you can't tell us," the inspector said quietly, "could you show us?"

Caisse bit the skin around his thumb, thinking. "Okay. I suppose"

Audrey Rancourt breathed out, relieved that they had been able to make progress. She made a mental note to personally thank Fran for her help later on, maybe even send the woman some flowers, if the conversation with Marcel led to strong evidence against his brother.

"Why don't you put on your jacket," Fran smiled, kindly, "it's getting cold outside. You go in the car with Inspector Mallery and Commissioner Rancourt, and I'll be right here waiting for you when you get back."

***

Leon Cassell paced his cell. He was still reeling from the earlier conversation with Bertram Boland and couldn't believe that the lawyer had now gone off and left him for the night. There would be stern words tomorrow, he could count on it. At least Marcel had sounded alright when he'd phoned, but Leon worried that his brother might begin to worry if he hadn't checked in by morning.

What the hell were these officers playing at? If all they had to connect him to Thierry Moreau's unfortunate accident was that leather notebook, undoubtedly picked up and put there by Marcel, then there was no case to answer. Leon would continue to deny all involvement, it was as simple as that!

Cassell thought back to his conversation with Inspector Mallery earlier that day. The detective hadn't mentioned Moreau by name, only saying that one of his officers had been abducted. For all anyone knew, the dark-skinned young man should be dead by now, he'd certainly laced the bread roll with enough water hemlock to kill a horse. By the time they found him, there would be no more than rotting bones to gather up.

Of course, he hadn't told Juliette Lafoy of his ploy to poison the detective. The psychiatrist would no doubt have turned him in, had Leon so much as hinted at it, and he wondered whether the foolish doctor might have ventured underground to take water and food to the incarcerated policeman. Even if she found his body, Juliette knew better than to open her mouth to anyone. Ten years of gambling debt, that's what Lafoy had to lose. The advance on her publishing deal had barely made a dent in the repayments and when Leon had offered her a way out, the psychiatrist had snatched his hand off.

Cassell found it quite ironic that he was paying Juliette to murder Enzo Roche with the money Cassell had received in a hush-hush payment from the dancer almost eighteen months before. Naturally, Leon had been clever, keeping his name and photographs out of the headlines when the inquest into Daniel's death went to court, and smarter still in asking for the funds to be paid in cash, delivered to a locker at the Gare de Bordeaux Saint-Jean.

When Roche had been admitted to the private facility following a nervous breakdown some months later, he hadn't a clue that the professional manager with his crisp linen suits and professional attitude was the brother of the man he'd caused to end his own life through their sordid liaison. As Cassell paced, up and down, up and down, he felt no remorse. Let Juliette Lafoy get her dirty pieces of gossip, and then she could exact revenge for Daniel Baur's death.

The psychiatrist shone the flashlight upwards, searching for the marks that had been etched into the limestone, just as Cassell had shown her the night before. The constant drip of water from an unknown source distracted her and Juliette swung the beam up and around her, wondering where the noise was coming from. Back up onto the wall now, shining at brick and trying to make out the deep grooves.

Was that it there? Or was that some sort of natural rutting within the stone? Left or right at this turning? How can I be sure that I'm following the right indentations? Why didn't he draw a plan?

Juliette blew on her hands. The temperature down here must have fallen to just a few degrees above zero and she was freezing in her thin sweater and single waterproof layer. An unnerving breeze ruffled the back of the woman's hair, causing her to swing around once more, the result causing her to become even more disorientated.

Why on earth did I agree to come down here alone?

The question was purely rhetorical. Juliette knew exactly why. Cassell had offered her enough money to clear her debt and the prospect of not having to flinch every time a red letter landed on her doorstep was enticing to say the least. All she had to do was keep her nerve, deliver the bottle of water and foil-wrapped sandwich to Detective Moreau and then she could return to the safety of her cottage and climb into a warm bed.

After that, Juliette reflected, she would be one task closer to being free. Her final task was to somehow ensure that Enzo Roche ate the poisoned food that Marcel was going to prepare. Despite that large man's rather backward demeanour, Cassell had assured her that the gardener was a genius when it came to handling and disguising poisonous plants. It had never occurred to Lafoy, up to that point, that Caisse might be involved, and it bothered her that Leon was taking advantage of the other man's inferior intelligence. She couldn't help but notice a strong resemblance between the two, but when she'd mentioned it to Leon over dinner, the manager had split his sides with laughter.

"Are you sure this is the right place?" Max asked Marcel Caisse as they shivered under the porch of Saint Magdalena's Church in Salbec, waiting for expert police dog-handlers to arrive. He was in two minds whether to venture into the depths of the tunnel but they needed evidence, if any existed, to prove that Leon Cassell had kept Thierry incarcerated below ground.

"Yes, this is the place. We have to go through the crypt to get to the tunnel."

Mallery glanced at the smart leather pumps on Audrey Rancourt's feet. "Why don't you wait in the car, Commissioner? The team might be a while yet."

Before she could argue, the roar of a van caused the police officers to turn in unison, watching patiently as the handlers opened the back doors and clipped leads onto two long-haired German Shepherds.

"*Commissaire, Inspecteur,*" the men called respectfully as they approached.

Max stepped forward, gently coaxing Marcel Caisse to lead the way inside. Once into the main tunnel, keeping their backs to the wall to avoid slipping in any large puddles, Mallery pressed a hand on the larger man's shoulder and told him to stand back, allowing the sniffer dogs to take the lead. Max shivered as he followed behind the trained handlers, having underestimated the freezing temperatures below ground, and called out to his superior who was bringing up the rear.

"Madam Rancourt, do you think it would be better if you went back and waited at the church? The ground here is unsafe, I don't want you to fall."

As soon as the last word had left his lips, Mallery missed his footing and skidded on wet moss, only righting himself when Marcel's large hands broke his fall from behind.

The commissioner pressed fingers to her lips to prevent herself from laughing out loud. "I'm fine, Inspector, perhaps you're the one we should be concerned about."

Max shrugged himself free from Caisse's grip and smoothed down his jacket. "Let's just go on, shall we?"

Ahead of them, one of the German Shepherds barked, causing his handler to tug on the lead and ask, "What is it, Nero?"

The dog's fluffy ears stood to attention, the animal turning its head this way and that, while its female counterpart let out a low whine.

"Easy, Freya," the second officer cooed in a low voice. "Go seek, girl."

Mallery heard two audible clicks as the dogs were let off their leads, prompting them to immediately lurch forward into the darkness.

"They've picked up a scent," the first dog-handler called, quickening his pace to keep up with his charge. "Could be an animal, but they're trained to track humans, so maybe they're onto something."

"Maybe they've picked up Detective Moreau's scent, from when he was trapped down here earlier," Audrey added, her face etched with concern.

Loud barking echoed from the passage beyond and all five ran on, uncertain of what they would find but trusting the canines to carry out their search effectively.

Juliette Lafoy could feel tears stinging in her eyes. She was a bloody fool for coming down here alone, she chided herself, but the last thing she wanted on her conscience was the death of that dark and handsome detective. The flashlight spun around, flickering off the crudely carved stone walls and confusing the woman even more. She was lost, all direction ceasing to make sense. If only Leon Cassell had asked her to do something else… anything but this. The doctor had lost all track of time, unsure whether she had been below ground for an hour or longer, having forgotten to look at her watch before venturing into the unknown.

"Steady your breathing," she told herself, taking the musty air in through her nose and expelling it orally. "Keep calm, don't panic."

A shiver ripped at Juliette's spine, fear clutching at her core as she heard what sounded like a bark.

What on earth is that? Is there something down here with me? It certainly doesn't sound human.

A second sharp, rasping noise had Lafoy letting out a sob as she chose the only option feasible and ran forward, her feet clumsily skidding into action and stirring up the sodden earth on the floor of the tunnel.

"Argghh," she cried, her hands breaking the fall as her left ankle twisted.

The patter of feet raced closer, more footsteps following behind, this time much more familiar than the canine clawing that threatened to come upon her.

Scrabbling to her feet, wincing with the agony of putting her foot to the ground, Juliette turned to catch the glimmer of lights coming towards her. Fear was paramount. The animals were close, barking, snapping their jaws. Edging her back against the only solid surface she could feel, the psychiatrist closed her eyes and prayed.

The German Shepherds came to a halt, trained to seek but not touch unless commanded, their constant deep howls loud in their quarry's ears.

"Nero, Freya, good boy, good girl, stand down."

The handler bent to stroke the soft, downy, brown fur on the dog's heads, his fellow officer producing treats to reward the find.

On hearing the man's calm voice, Juliette opened her eyes, blinking into the dog's eyes, and then glancing upwards, terrified of what she might see. A uniformed officer in a dark padded gilet looked down at her, with a familiar figure closing in just a few steps behind.

"Well, well, Madame Lafoy, what a surprise." Mallery sniffed sarcastically, his head shaking at the irony of their discovery. "I suppose you're going to tell me that you were just out for a stroll?"

Max opened one eye and allowed his vision to adjust to the morning sunlight, squinting at the bedside clock. It was six o'clock, meaning that he'd slept fitfully for just four hours. The phone on top of the cabinet continued its circling, vibrating on the lacquer surface, both as a reminder of the reason he'd woken and to urge him to pick up.

"*Oui, Mallery.*"

Using his right hand to fling the Egyptian cotton sheet back, the inspector swung his legs over the side of the bed and listened, smirking as the caller revealed their identity.

"Jacques, good to hear from you," Max yawned, "although why are you calling so early? It's only five there, isn't it?"

"I'm afraid the cows can't tell the time," the Yorkshireman told him, "they still need milking before going out to pasture and then there's the stalls to muck out. I've been up two hours already."

"Muck out?"

"Sorry, I mean clean up, get rid of their shit, shovel it out of the milking stalls."

Mallery screwed up his nose at the thought of Hobbs' task and politely inquired after his friend's father to avert the conversation slightly.

"Aye, Dad's doing alright," Jack replied. "Mum's not so good, though, she's worried sick. I think I might have to stay on a bit, at least until the old man comes out of hospital. I'd forgotten just how hard it was running the farm."

"I'm sorry to hear that," Max told him, full of genuine concern, "but take your time, your parents' health is the most important thing right now."

Sensing an awkward pause between them, Jack went on, "Anyway, any news on the investigation? Have you charged Leon Cassell yet?"

The inspector wished there was more positive news. "No, not yet, but we found some items in the underground cell where Thierry was held that might give us some much-needed evidence. Luc's taking them over to the lab this morning."

The detective's voice sounded dejected, causing Jack to wonder what his friend had omitted. "That's positive though, right? What aren't you telling me?"

He heard Mallery breathe out heavily and the sound of double doors opening as Max walked out onto the balcony, followed by the click of a lighter and a sharp intake of breath as his boss sucked on a cigarette.

"We've wasted time," the older man admitted, blowing smoke out through his nose. "I should have made sure that the place was searched before now. We were so caught up in getting Thierry to hospital that it was overlooked. I didn't think for one minute that someone had actually been going down there to feed him, but as it turns out, we caught one of his captors in the tunnel last night."

"Seriously? There was someone in there? Bloody hell!"

"*Oui*, Jacques, it was the psychiatrist, Juliette Lafoy. I can tell you it was a surprise for us, she looked like an owl caught in the headlights."

Hobbs coughed to hide his own laughter. "Rabbit, it's a rabbit in headlights."

Mallery was inhaling smoke again. "Oh, *non*, she definitely looked like an owl."

"Whatever you say, Max. Any idea what she was doing down there?"

"Hah, the doctor says she was visiting Saint Magdalena's and got lost!"

"A likely story! Creeping around inside a crypt's hidden tunnel at night?"

"Yes, that's what we thought, too but, unless we find something to incriminate Lafoy, we will have no other choice but to release her without charge."

"Seems you've got one heck of a lot on your plate right now," Hobbs sympathised. "Is there anything I can do to help out from here, like?"

"*Non*, Jacques, just take care of your mother and tell Peter to make a speedy recovery. I'll ring you later, okay? Look after yourself, my friend."

"Cheers, Max, good luck with finding that shred of evidence. I know you will, our team's the very best. Remember, the early bird catches the worm, yeah?"

Mallery said goodbye and sat looking at the phone in his hand for a few minutes afterwards. Despite having worked with the Yorkshireman for a couple of years, the English language was still a complete mystery to the police inspector.

Birds and worms? What on earth was Hobbs implying?

On the outskirts of Leeds, Jack Hobbs' posture and gaze was in symmetry with that of his boss over eight hundred miles away. He wanted to be a part of the current murder investigation, despite his difficult personal situation. Despite having only arrived home the night before, he felt the walls of the farmhouse closing in on him, as though he was in a wet cardboard box that threatened collapse. One more week at the farm, he told himself, just until Dad's out of hospital, and then back home. Rising to make a pot of tea, Jack realised that he was now thinking of France as home, a sign that his life had moved on.

Luc Martin took a bite of the fresh croissant he'd picked up on his way to work, dropping crumbly flakes onto his jet-black t-shirt. Brushing the front of his top only intensified the buttery mess and across the room Gabriella shook her head in disgust, although she was pretty close to bursting out laughing, too.

"You eat like a pig, Luc," she said in a pretence of scolding, narrowing her eyes. "Look at the mess on the carpet around your desk."

"I can't help it," the techie whined, still chewing on the last mouthful of warm pastry. "Anyway, Madame Misery, what's wrong with you this morning?"

Gabi Dupont stood up and stretched, her shoulder-blades clicking from the tension. "Thierry failed to identify his attacker, he seems to have slight memory loss. The doctor said it would probably return, but we've only got until midday to charge Cassell. I swear, if he did this to Thierry and gets away with it…"

"The best thing you can do to help Thierry right now is to ring Roberto and ask him to hurry up with the prints on those items I just dropped off at the lab. That, my dear Gabi," he pointed with sticky fingers, "is the best chance of finding evidence that Cassell was keeping Thierry captive in that awful dungeon."

Dupont shuddered but picked up the phone on her desk as requested. "It makes me sick just thinking about it. *Allo? Oui? Roberto Mazzo, s'il vous plaît.*"

Luc returned to his seat, forgetting about the crumby graveyard around his feet, and focussed on reading Mallery's report. According to the time on the uploaded document, it had been sent at one-thirty in the morning, a good hour after the computer whizz had gone home. Martin wondered whether Audrey Rancourt had stayed to keep Max company for a while on their return to headquarters, but he certainly wasn't nearly brave enough to ask.

At the sanatorium, Fran Shepherd put her head around Enzo Roche's door, calling out a cheery greeting before asking, "Have you eaten breakfast?"

Roche pointed at an empty plate on the side-table. "I had fruit, Frannie darling. Any snippets of gossip for me?" he asked, cheeks glowing as he patted the bed for the nurse to sit down. "Is Monsieur Cassell still under arrest?"

"Enzo," Fran tutted, "you know I don't like to talk out of turn, but actually, no, he's not here this morning, so I suppose we can presume…"

"I knew it!" the dancer snapped, clicking his fingers animatedly. "Cassell is involved in that detective's disappearance. Oh, I say, does that mean gorgeous Inspector Mallery will be back to question us all again?"

There was a knock on the door and Dorothy Ramos' pretty round face appeared. "Sorry to interrupt, but have either of you seen Doctor Lafoy this morning?"

Fran was on her feet, steering the other nurse away from Roche's prying ears. "Keep your voice down, love. Isn't she in her office, Dotty?"

"No, I've just tried the door and it's locked. Monsieur Grimond has a session with her about," Dorothy consulted her watch, "well, ten minutes ago, actually."

"That's very odd," the staff nurse considered. "Let me check at reception, I can get them to call her. It's certainly quite unusual for her to forget a session."

As Fran descended the main staircase, she reflected upon the events of the previous day. Half of the residents and staff had seen Monsieur Cassell being escorted into the back of a car with police escorts, the rounds of gossip were still echoing around the building's high ceilings and long corridors, but Fran was pretty certain that nobody had noticed Mallery's visit to Marcel Caisse. Despite the inspector's insistence that her help was no longer needed after the initial introduction to the gardener, Fran had invited Maurice inside and made him a cup of tea, while they waited for their return. As it happened, after an hour of deliberating over different scenarios, the boulangerie owner had persuaded Fran to go home with him, promising to call Max for an update at a reasonable hour in the morning.

"Any sign of Doctor Lafoy this morning?" she enquired of the weekend receptionist. "I know it's Sunday, but she booked a couple of patients in for early sessions today and the first one is upstairs waiting."

The woman shook her head. "I'm sorry, but no, I haven't seen her."

Returning to her duties, and to report back to Dorothy Ramos, the staff nurse considered the chances of Juliette Lafoy being involved in something connected to Leon Cassell. It was very odd that she had failed to show up for the counselling sessions, usually being punctual and meticulous about her appointments, but Fran had never liked the woman and wondered if the psychiatrist had been manipulating Cassell in some way. It still didn't explain why Marcel was still missing, though. She was worried about him.

Max Mallery slipped past the incident room door, feeling slightly guilty that he was going to fetch himself a top brand coffee from the state-of-the-art coffee machine in his office. Although the team had never complained about the instant granules of sludge they drank from the continually dripping pot in their own work area, he wondered whether a reward for their hard work in the form of quality beverages might be in order. He couldn't help but notice the delivery to the commissioner's office, a few days before, of a shiny new silver machine, which was an exact replica of his own, although he would bet his month's salary that it had been funded by his own department's resources.

Traipsing back to catch up with Gabriella and Luc, Max lifted the double espresso to his lips and winced. It was still boiling hot and burned the inside of his mouth, perhaps retribution for his selfishness, the inspector mused.

"*Bonjour*," Luc chirped, followed by a wave from Gabi as she continued to speak into her phone's receiver. "Everything alright?"

Martin noted that Max looked exhausted, the dark circles under his eyes now reaching to the inner side of his boss's nose.

"*Oui, oui*, but I'm not looking forward to interviewing Juliette Lafoy today. We also need some hard evidence to implicate Cassell, or he walks free before midday. It just seems as though we get a lucky break and then, what is it Jacques says, the fan hits the shitter?"

"The shit hits the fan," Gabi supplied, finishing the call, "but I might just have a reason to put the smile back on your face, boss."

Blowing on his dark, unsweetened coffee, Max raised his eyes, indicating for the detective to do away with the suspense. "Go on, get on with it."

"The water bottle found inside that underground cell has Leon Cassell's fingerprints on it. Of course, Thierry's are there too, but Roberto has managed to extract a clear thumbprint, it should be enough to prosecute. He's sending the full report over by email now, together with the toxin count. There was enough water hemlock in the leftover sandwich to kill a horse, let alone the part of it that poor Thierry had already eaten. No wonder he feels so terrible."

"Fantastic!" Mallery grinned, punching the air. "But is Thierry still adamant that it wasn't Cassell who knocked him out?"

Gabi clicked on the photo image of the hospital manager on her iPad, and it instantly appeared on the larger screen on the wall. "No, I showed him this when he first came around, and again last night when I visited with Roberto, but he says it definitely wasn't Cassell. He thinks the man had a beard."

Luc's fingers began tapping across the keyboard, bringing up a second image on the shared screen. "I've just sent you this, it's a photo of Marcel Caisse, one of Cassell's brothers. There's a chance it was him who assaulted Thierry."

Mallery slapped a palm against his forehead. "Of course, Gabi, you were at the hospital all day yesterday and missed out on Luc's discovery. Cassell, Caisse, and Roche's ex-partner Daniel Bauer, are all triplets. They were separated at birth and only reunited a short while ago, just before Bauer committed suicide after his affair with the dancer ended."

Luc supplied Gabi with the newspaper report detailing the men's long-lost search to find each other. "Crazy, isn't it?"

Gabi's eyes were wide. "Wow, what a find! So, the attempt to poison Enzo Roche was nothing more than revenge for their brother's death?"

Max tapped the screen with his finger. "It would appear that way. Thierry must have discovered Cassell's involvement in securing the properties for staff, including the fact that he insisted upon dealing with the water hemlock problem at Fran Shepherd's cottage. Can you get over there now, Gabi, see if Thierry can identify Marcel Caisse as the man who knocked him out?"

Dupont was already collecting her jacket and handbag, eager to get a resolution to the horrific assault and attempted poisoning that her friend had undergone.

"Luc, let's go, I think it's time we spoke to Cassell about his antics, don't you? Meet me in Interview Room Three, I'll just need to get hold of his lawyer."

Standing in an empty incident room, Max extracted a white card from his jacket pocket and punched the number into his phone.

"Monsieur Boland? I'm sorry to call you on a Sunday, but it looks as though we have enough evidence to charge Leon Cassell with murder. Are you able to come in?"

The inspector could hear Boland cursing under his breath, something about a planned fishing trip with his son, followed by air expelling from his lungs.

"I'll be there within the hour, Inspector."

Mallery stood at the police headquarters reception desk, watching the duty officer peel a pain au chocolat from its greaseproof paper wrapper. He glanced up at the clock, which showed it to be just after nine, and then back at the overweight bald man.

"Arnaud, you'll burst one of these days," he joked, signing the ledger with his indecipherable scrawl. "Let me know if anyone calls to find out about our trio of guests, okay? And you say nothing to the press."

"Of course." Arnaud smiled, lifting his bushy eyebrows. "You have your hands full today with three suspects to interview. Do you need some help, Inspector?"

"No, it's alright, you just keep your eyes and ears peeled out here, but I'm serious. Any enquiries at all and you let me know."

Arnaud fashioned his sticky fingers into a mock salute and said, "Yes, sir," leaving Max to decide whether Cassell, Caisse or Lafoy should be first on his agenda.

Juliette Lafoy was biting the quick around her perfectly manicured nails. Worried about the implications of her recent actions to help Cassell, and also Mallery's discovery that she had been trying to extract information from Roche in order to write his unofficial, rather steamy, biography, the psychiatrist hadn't slept a wink and now looked nowhere near her usually glamorous and composed self. As a heavy key turned in the lock of her cell, Juliette was told to stand back from the door, and she rose in anticipation of news.

"This way please, Madame Lafoy," the guard told her, tilting his head towards the corridor, "Inspector Mallery is here to interview you."

The doctor walked slowly forward, trying her best to appear unfazed by the circumstances, although without her usual layer of top-range make-up and fresh clothes, Lafoy looked more like a woman doing the morning walk of shame after a night on the tiles than a respectable professional. She was led into a stark white room where a milky, sugary coffee awaited.

Mallery entered the room soon afterwards, his face stern and his eyes honing in on Juliette as she shifted around trying to get comfortable on the hard plastic chair.

"Doctor." He nodded in greeting, slapping a thin folder on the table between them. "You have met Detective Martin," he turned to acknowledge Luc, "now, perhaps you would be so good as to explain exactly what you were doing in that tunnel last night. The same underground tunnel where one of my officers was held captive, assaulted and poisoned."

Juliette swallowed, reached for the warm coffee, and stared down into her lap. She owed Cassell no loyalty, but should he walk free, then neither would he cough up the promised cash. Mallery was no fool, she reflected, but he looked the type of man who might just fall for a woman's charms. Lafoy decided to hedge her bets and deny all involvement. If Cassell threw her to the wolves later, then at least she would have the satisfaction of seeing him go down for attempted murder.

"As I told you, Inspector, I was out for a late walk and, having heard about some archaeological remains in the area, decided to take a look for myself."

Max smirked, clasped his fingers together and sat back as though waiting patiently for a storyteller to begin. "And where did you hear about these 'remains', Doctor Lafoy? As it seems that even Father Pelletier, curate of Saint Magdalena's, has never heard of such a thing."

Already the medic could feel her account of last night's events falling to shreds, and she placed the cup back on the table, hands shaking. "I, er… it must have been one of the locals who told me, I really don't recall."

Luc Martin watched as his boss prepared to change gear, transforming himself from the mild-mannered inspector into a defendant's nightmare. "You really will need to do better than that, Juliette. Perhaps we could start with some names? Or have you conveniently forgotten those, too?"

Satisfied that he had pressed enough proverbial buttons to evoke the required reaction, Max allowed himself to sit back in the chair, feeling smug.

Lafoy bit the inside of her cheek, biding her time.

"Fuck you, Inspector Mallery," she suddenly raged, "I want a lawyer, now!"

Mallery was still feeling smug as he watched the guard escort Juliette Lafoy back to the cell. There was no doubt in his mind that Leon Cassell, being held in the room two doors down, would have heard the psychiatrist's ranting as she swore at the officers and demanded they call in a local attorney. He could imagine the panic in Cassell's mind, his heart beating ten to the dozen, as the sanatorium manager sat brooding over Lafoy's testimony. The pair could be played off against one another, but now he had Marcel Caisse to worry about.

"Luc, can you see if social services can send over an appropriate adult to sit in with Caisse during our interview? Given his learning disabilities, he's vulnerable, and I don't want any accusations of inappropriate measures coming back to bite us on the arse."

"I'll get on to it now," the techie promised, heading towards the front desk. "Any chance of a quick drink while we wait for Boland to show up?"

"Great idea," Max smirked, heading towards the upper floor where his pods of delicious coffee awaited. "I'll get you a Coke from the machine on my way."

Martin nodded appreciatively. That was what he loved about working with the inspector; no matter the time of day, he always knew what particular food, or beverage, would hit the spot with his team members.

It was another half hour before Bertram Boland arrived to consult with his client, giving Max and Luc plenty of time to go over their interview strategy.

"Let's cut to the chase," Inspector Mallery began, holding Cassell's eye. "We know about your brothers, we know of Daniel's involvement with Enzo Roche and of his subsequent suicide. We also know that you were solely responsible for acquiring property for your staff, including Fran Shepherd's cottage where the water hemlock was growing. Doctor Lafoy was apprehended in the tunnel where my officer was kept captive, thanks to your brother and, as if that wasn't enough, your fingerprints are on the water bottle found in the cell where he was imprisoned. I suggest you start talking, Monsieur."

At the mention of his sibling, Leon's lids flickered, a hand coming up to his brow as he bent forwards. "You have involved Marcel? Where is he?"

"Don't worry, Marcel is fine, we're taking good care of him," Luc offered kindly, stepping into his part of the good cop, bad cop routine.

Max took the opportunity to up the tempo slightly. "Leon Cassell, I am charging you with the murders of Edwina Butler and Raymond Verdin, the attempted murders of Enzo Roche and Thierry Moreau, and with obstructing the course of justice. I suggest you take a few moments to discuss your plea with Monsieur Boland and we will be back to take your full statement in fifteen minutes."

Cassell worked his mouth ineffectively; he had no words.

As they left the interview room, Luc Martin punched the air, hopping around on his squeaky trainers. "Boom, straight for the jugular, brilliant, boss!"

Mallery wasn't feeling quite so enthusiastic. "Let's see if he crumbles first."

The buzz of Max's phone brought the conversation to a halt. "It's Gabi."

It was only a short while until a cheerful-looking woman arrived at reception asking for Inspector Mallery and Max was pleased to see that the social worker walked with the air of a professional with years of experience under her belt. Maxine Perdeau was in her early fifties, broad-hipped and rosy-cheeked, with an unflappable disposition, especially under difficult circumstances.

"Call me Maxine," she told the detectives, having been given a formal introduction by the duty officer. "Now, what do you have for me?"

"Marcel Caisse, forty-three, Asperger's, we're told," Max replied, giving the briefest of explanations. "He's implicated in his brother's murder case and unfortunately is the most likely person to have assaulted one of my officers."

Maxine was unperturbed. "Okay, let's go and see him, shall we?"

She followed the men down a long corridor to where Marcel was being kept under supervision, slightly apart from Cassell and Lafoy. The woman's hips and briefcase swung in perfect rhythm as she walked, reminding Mallery of Dominique Fabre, the Saint Margaux gift shop owner who was continually trying to entice him out on a date, encouraged by his friend's wife, Angélique.

As the door swung open, a wide-eyed Caisse jumped to his feet. Sweat dappled the man's forehead and he was continually wringing his meaty hands.

"Hello, Marcel," the social worker smiled, making herself comfortable on the end of the narrow bunk, "my name is Maxine and I've come to sit with you while the nice police officers ask you some questions. Now, what can we get you to drink? How about a nice glass of juice? And a biscuit perhaps?"

The gardener warmed to Maxine at once, dropping both hands into his lap and visibly relaxing. "Orange please, and yes, a biscuit too."

Luc retreated to the canteen to fulfil the order, leaving Max to watch in wonderment as the two strangers began conversing in companiable low voices as easily as if they had known one another for decades.

Jack Hobbs rubbed his face, attempting to keep himself awake while they waited for news. Having received a phone call from the staff nurse an hour before they were due to leave the farm to visit his father in hospital, explaining that Peter had suffered a second heart attack, the flame-haired detective was trying his best to stay strong. At his side, Jean Hobbs was sobbing silently, a lace-edged cotton handkerchief balled up in her fist. Footsteps echoed down the corridor towards the family room in which they sat, and Jack looked up as they stopped directly outside the door. His heart sank on seeing the silhouette of a slim woman, not the cardiologist he been expecting, and he averted his gaze.

"Alright, our Jack, Aunty Jean?" a familiar voice trilled, coming closer to the pair, and reaching out her arms to envelop Mrs Hobbs. "How's Uncle Peter?"

"Rachel!" Jack gasped, standing back to look at his cousin. "Wow, I hardly recognised you."

Instead of the lanky tomboy teenager that Hobbs remembered from his childhood, who had morphed into a robust young woman who had left rural Yorkshire to pursue a career in photography overseas, he was now looking at a very attractive thirty-five-year-old with cropped blonde hair and wearing an outfit that wouldn't have looked out of place in a fashion magazine.

"Give us a hug," his cousin answered, "Dad's just parking the car."

Jack wrapped his arms around his close relative, inhaling her expensive perfume and then stepping back to take in the unexpected weight loss. Rachel had been a strapping teenager and hadn't lost any of her bulk in the years that followed, so this new, slender, model-like Rachel was a revelation. He wondered whether it was her life overseas that had changed the young woman so significantly, with daily square meals giving way to irrational eating trends and work-related stress.

"I didn't even know you were back in the country," he began, shaking his head in disbelief, at both Rachel's transformation in the past five years and also the fact that she was standing right there in the Hobbs' hour of need.

"Well, I had to come back eventually," Rachel admitted, "but I'm not staying long. You know me, Leeds never did hold any real appeal."

"Where are you off to next?"

"I'm not sure, to be honest, I'm open to suggestions."

The door opened a second time and Jean's brother, Terry, entered the room, taking off his flat cap as he walked over to embrace his sibling.

"What news?"

Jean shook her head. "Only what I told you on the phone. We're waiting for the cardiologist to come back in."

Before Terry could answer, Jean was looking over his shoulder at the man in white standing outside. He seemed hesitant and only entered when he realised that the family were all looking in his direction.

"Mrs Hobbs, Jack," he looked around at the other two family members, eyes filled with genuine regret, "I'm so sorry, there's nothing more we can do."

"But he's still here?" Jean gabbled, panicking as she stood up and began shaking. "I want to see my Peter."

"Of course," the cardiologist told her, speaking softly, "but I'm afraid that Peter has suffered a very severe heart attack and his body is incredibly weak."

It was Jack who suddenly asked the question that was on all of their lips.

"How long does he have?"

The doctor dipped his head, almost as a sign of respect as he prepared to break the news. "Only a matter of hours, maybe not even that long."

Max Mallery had warmed to Maxine Perdeau immensely. Not only had she put Marcel Caisse at ease before the interview, but she was now sitting quietly at his side, doing no more than utter the odd word of encouragement. Max felt certain that there would be no comeback on the gardener's statement and he glanced over at Luc Martin as the detective made concise notes. Caisse spoke honestly, admitting that his brother had explained that they needed to get revenge for Daniel's death, inciting fury in the mentally challenged sibling, and convincing him to help, no matter what needed doing.

"Marcel, do you understand that what Leon was doing was wrong?"

The large, bearded man seemed to consider the question, scratching at his bald head before answering, "Yes, I do. I didn't want to help him, but Leon said it was the only way to let Daniel rest in peace."

"And was it Leon who told you to hit Detective Moreau over the head?"

Caisse twisted his fingers together, thinking deeply. "Yes, but he said it was only because the policeman had found out about him renting the cottage, where we got the herbs from."

Mallery stooped forward slightly, wanting to be sure that they captured everything on tape. "You said 'we' got the herbs. So, you went with Leon, to pick the plant from Fran Shepherd's garden?"

Marcel seemed to brighten, suddenly faced with a topic that he knew a lot about. "Of course. Water hemlock is very poisonous, it has to be handled carefully, you shouldn't get it on your skin, and if you eat it, it can kill you."

Luc was intrigued. "Did your brother tell you that?"

The gardener smiled broadly, finding the question amusing. "No, don't be silly, Leon doesn't know anything about plants. He asked me to tidy Frannie's garden before she moved in, and I found the water hemlock near the riverbank. I told Leon it was dangerous, but he told me not to tell anyone. My dad was a botanist, he taught me everything."

Max hesitated, recalling that the triplets had all been adopted by different families, and wondering how much Marcel knew about his brother's upbringing. He decided to press for just one more answer.

"Marcel, did you put Detective Moreau's notebook on Leon's bookcase?"

Caisse glanced at Maxine, who gave his arm a short squeeze in support, saying, "It's alright, you can tell them."

"Yes, I did. It must have fallen out of his pocket when I put him into the back of the van, but I didn't see it until later when I went to put the tools away. I thought Leon might keep it safe for the policeman, until he let him go."

"And did Leon tell you that he intended to let the detective go?"

Marcel's eyes were wide, as innocent as a child's as he spoke just one word.

"No."

The inspector sat back, causing his chair to thud against the tiled floor.

"Thank you, Marcel, you've been very helpful. I'll see if we can get you something to eat now, okay?"

The gardener seemed pleased with that idea. "Great, but I can I go home soon?"

"Not yet," Max gulped, "and to be honest, it could be a while until you can."

The rhythmic sound of the heart monitor ceased suddenly as a staff nurse began unclipping the tiny wires connected to Peter Hobbs' chest.

"I'll leave you with him," she said quietly, wheeling the equipment towards the door as the family gathered around the farmer's bedside. "If you need anything at all, I'll just be over there, at the desk."

Only Terry turned his head to see where she was pointing, the rest of Peter's visitors more concerned with his sickly grey pallor and lack of response.

"Wait," Jean called, suddenly having the urge to speak, "can he hear us?"

The nurse smiled faintly. Despite having been in the same situation with dozens of families before, the pain of these final hours, and the feeling of helplessness, never got any easier.

"I like to think so. Talk to him, Peter's still in there somewhere."

Jack watched as his mother attempted to pull one of the plastic chairs up to the bedside and quickly moved to help her, feeling the trembling of her slight form.

"Sit down, Mum," he whispered, kissing the top of her head before raising his voice to say, "Now then, Dad, what's going on? I thought you had promised to get better."

Peter Hobbs weak body didn't react, despite all four sets of eyes watching for even the slightest flicker of movement.

"Shall we leave you alone for a while?" Rachel offered, her voice cracking.

"No, stay," Jean told her, more sharply than intended. "Peter loves you like a daughter. He would want us all here, together, wouldn't you, sweetheart?"

There was a rasping in the farmer's throat as his body began to close down, and Jack moved to hold his mother's hand. "How about we say a prayer?"

Jean chuckled, squeezing back. "Your father's not religious!"

"Well, in that case, let's remind him of the story of how you two met? Eh?"

Jean squeezed Jack's fingers tightly. "Aye, son, let's do that."

With one hand on Maxine Perdeau's lower back, Max guided her out of the cell and into the corridor, waiting for the familiar click of the lock before speaking.

"Well, it looks as though Marcel will need a lawyer now, he's going to be charged with accessory to murder and actual bodily harm."

"He was duped by his brother," the social worker replied tartly. "I don't believe for one minute that Marcel Caisse would hurt someone intentionally. I also believe that he must have assaulted your officer in a moment of panic."

Mallery watched the woman rummage in her handbag for a handkerchief, noting that her eyes were watering, a sign that Madam Perdeau took her job to heart.

"I'll make sure that he gets a lawyer with experience in mental health, then at least he might have a chance of being detained in a secure hospital rather than prison."

Maxine shuddered. "He wouldn't last two minutes in jail, you can see how frightened Marcel is."

The inspector glanced backwards at the cell door. "Yes, I can. Please rest assured that I will ensure his case is handled sympathetically."

"Do you need me for anything else?"

The question caught Max off guard, and he paused for a moment, mid-thought.

"It's just that you look as though there's something else bothering you," the woman continued. "What is it?"

"Do you know, Madam Perdeau, I'm not really sure. There is still one question that remains unanswered within this investigation, but for the life of me I can't figure it out."

As they reached the reception area, the social worker pulled her handbag up onto her arm and patted the detective on the shoulder, a motherly gesture that felt incredibly unfamiliar to Max. "You will get to the bottom of it, Inspector Mallery, I can tell that you are a very experienced officer. Now, please call me if I can be of any further help, no matter what time of day or night. It's important to me that Monsieur Caisse is understood. Far too many people in his situation, vulnerable and afraid, get thrown into prison and terribly abused. It would be tragic if he became just another statistic."

"You have my word, Madam Perdeau, and my sincere thanks."

Max stood watching as her dark auburn hair bobbed across the car park and disappeared from view, all the while feeling niggled that there was one final part to the puzzle for which he lacked clues.

"Everything alright, sir?" the duty officer queried, looking up from a stack of documents. "You look a bit perplexed there. How about one of my wife's home-baked muffins to perk you up a bit?"

The lid came off a flowered tin and it was handed across the counter as Mallery let the words sink in. *Home-baked muffins.*

"*Merde.* Sergeant, you're brilliant!" he cried, grabbing a chocolate sponge cake and dashing towards the stairs. "Absolutely brilliant."

Luc Martin looked up from his desk as Max offloaded the muffin onto his desk. "What's this for?"

"Think," the inspector teased, moving across to the steaming coffee pot. "What have we missed in this case? Or who?"

Luc peeled off the paper case and took a bite, his eyes still locked on his boss. "I haven't a clue what you're talking about."

"Who baked the cake that poisoned Edwina Butler and Raymond Verdin?"

"Oh, well, I presumed it would have been Cassell, or Caisse."

"Maxine Perdeau has just had a long chat with Caisse, and he can't boil an egg, let alone make a sponge. He and Cassell both had private apartments at the hospital and, according to Marcel, they used to eat on the premises, him in the kitchen with the domestic staff and Leon in the dining room with the patients."

Martin's jaw was looking rather slack as his mouth fell open. "Shit, so it must have been Juliette Lafoy who created Enzo Roche's birthday cake."

"My thoughts exactly, Luc." He turned to face Gabriella who was typing up a report. "Gabi, do you want to help me interview Doctor Lafoy? Maybe having a female present might soften her a bit, she's a tough nut to crack."

"Sure, I seem to have been missing out on the fun lately."

"Oh, how's Thierry? Any news?"

The smile returned to Dupont's face. "He's being discharged tomorrow. Doctor Singh has given Thierry the all-clear, but he'll need another week off work."

"That's great!" Max grinned. "I bet Madam Moreau is going to pamper him like a baby when he gets home. Poor chap will be glad to return to the office by the time she's finished fussing over him."

Gabriella wrinkled her nose. "Maybe he should be confined to desk duties for a while when he does come back – you know, just in case."

Mallery shrugged. "Maybe, but this investigation is coming to a close, we'll charge all three of them today, so unless you've been looking into your crystal ball and foresee any other murders coming our way, I think it will be pretty quiet around here soon."

Luc finished the muffin and wiped his lips. "What about Jack? Have you heard anything?"

"Not since this morning," Max admitted, looking at his watch, "but don't they say that no news is usually good news?"

At the hospital in Leeds, Jack Hobbs was gently escorting his mother down to the car park, flanked by his uncle Terry and cousin Rachel. Jean clutched a small leather holdall, her fingers gripped around the handle like raven's claws on a branch.

"Wait here, Mum," Jack said gently, trying to gently prise the bag from her, "I'll go and fetch the car."

"It doesn't feel right leaving him here," Jean whispered, the final word catching in her throat as she sobbed, "Dad should be coming home."

Jack turned away, pretending to feel in his trouser pocket for the keys as he tried in vain to hold back his own tears. He wasn't ready for this, not now, not with Thomas still young and looking forward to spending many summers with his grandpa. Everything had happened so quickly, his father giving a final sigh as life exited his body, nurses coming in, gathering Peter's belongings, and offering words of sympathy as they went about lowering the hospital bed and closing his father's gaping mouth.

"Are you alright, lad?" Terry asked, coming up alongside his nephew. "We'll follow you home, make sure you're both alright. It doesn't seem fair, does it?"

"No, Uncle Terry, it's not bloody fair at all."

Rachel zipped up her leather jacket against the sudden draught of wind and placed an arm around her aunt's shoulder. "I'll come back and lend a hand at the farm, Jack's probably out of practice by now."

Jean dabbed a tissue to her nose and supressed a laugh. "He's not doing too badly, lass, but I dare say he'd appreciate an extra pair of hands today."

Rachel, a head taller than her older relative, rested her chin on top of Jean's curly hair. "We'll get through this, Aunty Jean, together."

As the two cars pulled up alongside them, the women moved forward, both giving one last glance up towards the ward where Peter Hobbs' body lay and gasping in unison as a single white feather drifted down and landed by their feet.

"See?" Jean smiled through relentless tears as she stooped to pick it up. "My Peter's here, watching over us."

Interview Room Three was stiflingly hot but, despite the discomforting stale air, Mallery had insisted on the single window staying shut. He didn't want to do anything that might put the psychiatrist at ease, not now that they'd realised there were still missing answers. Still inwardly cursing himself for not thinking about the practicalities of creating a poisonous sponge cake, Max was determined to get a signed confession out of Lafoy by the end of the day.

"Oh, no, you are not pinning that on me," Juliette snorted, tilting her chin upwards in defiance, "I had nothing to do with that damned birthday cake."

The inspector watched Lafoy's body language with interest. The arms folded tightly across her chest showed defiance and negativity, but her face gave nothing away. Deciding that a different tactic might be necessary, he nudged Gabriella Dupont's foot under the table.

"So, Madam Lafoy," Gabi began, taking up the gauntlet from her boss, "if you didn't create that rich fondant cake, do you know who did?"

As the female detective's silky-smooth voice delivered the question, the doctor visibly relaxed, unfolded her arms and sat forward in the chair. Max tried to hide his pleasure at seeing the ploy to unnerve her work.

"Look, Detective Dupont, it must have been Leon, or Marcel, it honestly wasn't me. I don't bake."

"And you expect us to believe that?"

The psychiatrist's attorney gave a short cough and whispered to his client that it might be in her best interest to comply with the line of questioning.

"It is the truth. Look, yes, I took money from Leon to pay off my debts. In exchange, I helped him out with a few things, such as taking food to the police officer he was keeping captive, but I never set out to kill anyone, I swear."

Max studied her face, feeling that they were finally getting somewhere. "Did Cassell give you information about Enzo Roche? I mean, in addition to the medical file that you already had access to?"

Juliette's cheeks flushed pink. "It's hot in here, can I get some water?"

"Soon, Madam Lafoy, but first answer the question," Gabi insisted, glancing at her boss. "What did he give you in regard to Enzo Roche?"

Waiting for a nod from her lawyer, the doctor ran a hand over her throat and swallowed hard. "He knew all about Enzo's relationship with Daniel, Leon's brother. There were personal letters written by Roche, explicit ones, Leon promised to give them to me when this was all over."

"All over?" Max repeated, "You mean when Roche was dead?"

Juliette nodded her head slightly, lips tightly sealed.

"Please answer out loud for the tape, Madame Lafoy," Dupont ordered.

"Leon Cassell said that he would give me Daniel's letters from Roche after Enzo's death. That way, I would be able to complete the biography without being sued for libel."

"A win-win situation for everyone." Mallery sniffed sarcastically. "Cassell gets revenge for his brother's death, and you get your dirty gossip."

"Inspector…" the lawyer warned.

Max raised his hands in defeat. "I think we're done here, Detective Dupont. Please escort Madame Lafoy back to her cell, out of my sight."

"Doctor," Juliette told him. "It's Doctor Lafoy."

Mallery was in no mood to be taunted. "Believe you me, by the time the judge has finished with you, you won't have a single credential after your name."

Jean Hobbs was in the farmhouse kitchen making sandwiches, while her brother stood next to the long landscape window waiting for the kettle to boil.

"Look at that pair," he told Jean, nodding towards two figures as they herded the cows through the gate and into the wide cobbled yard for milking. "Farming is in their blood. How long's your Jack been in the force now? Fifteen years?"

"Yes, I think it must be," Jean confirmed, coming to stand next to him.

"And our Rachel has been travelling the world since she was nineteen, yet they both still have the knack for handling cattle, it's as though they were never away."

Jean turned back to the bread, waving a butter knife at her brother. "Well, I expect Jack will be wanting to get back to France as soon as the funeral's over, his life is over there now."

"Surely he'll stay on for a bit longer. What about the farm?"

"We'll manage. Simon has a friend who can lend a hand. He came over in the spring for calving. Of course it's an extra wage, but what can I do?"

"You don't reckon your Jack could be persuaded to move back?" Terry sighed, reaching up to the top cupboard for mugs. "The farm's his now, by rights."

Fresh tears prickled as Jean turned away. "He's not interested, Terry, believe me, I've tried. The lad's happy in his career and who am I to stop him?"

Before Terry could respond, the back door was flung open and two flushed faces appeared.

"By 'eck, that wind's getting up," Jack cursed. "Any chance of a cuppa?"

"Here, put those muddy boots on here," Jean told the pair, rushing towards Jack and Rachel with a folded newspaper in her hand.

As Jack placed a hand against the doorjamb, the toes of each foot prising the boots off one by one, his mother spread out the tabloid pages in a neat line, the bold headlines uppermost. Rachel closed the door behind her and did likewise, pulling off her woolly hat in one swift movement.

"Simon's taken over, Aunty Jean, says he'll stay on a couple of hours."

"Oh, he's a good lad. An excellent farmhand. I'm going to have to ask him to take on a lot more, I suppose."

The heavy hint hung in the air like damp washing, but the farmer's son was too distracted to take notice of his mother's words as she waited for him to react.

Jack bent to place the boots neatly to one side and caught sight of the main article on the paper below his feet, curiosity getting the better of him as he leaned in to read the feature. "What the hell…?"

"I can come and help out, too," Rachel offered, breaking the awkward silence. "I'm home for a bit now, at least until I hear about that job I've applied for."

"Oh, where is it? In England?" Jean inquired hopefully. "It would be lovely to have you home again, dear."

Rachel shook her head, ruffling her hair with one hand as she struggled out of the borrowed oversized coat. "No, actually it's in France, Bordeaux. I thought it might be a good chance to catch up with our Jack, but then… well, you know, I hadn't anticipated Uncle Peter…"

Jean frowned at her distracted son. "That'll be nice won't it, Jack? Having Rachel nearby?"

"What? Yeah?" he mumbled, continuing to stare at the newsprint.

"Are you even listening?" Jean tutted. "Whatever's the matter with you, lad?"

Jack carefully lifted the Wellington boots and retrieved the sheet of newspaper from underneath. "Where's page five?"

"What, why? It's here…" Rachel answered, sliding out the required double page spread and handing it to her cousin. "What's wrong, Jack?"

"Sorry, I need to call my boss, urgently," he told her, racing into the living room with his phone in one hand and the sheets of newspaper in the other.

Jean Hobbs shrugged and turned to her brother. "Do you see what I mean?"

Terry continued to pour tea into the mugs, watching his sister's shaking hands as she pulled a carton of milk from the fridge.

"He'll never leave the police force," Jean announced stoically, "no matter what my feelings are towards Jack's responsibilities here at the farm. You mark my words, though, I'm proud of him, and so was Peter, but you can't deny it's tragic to see the work of five generations of Hobbs men come to an end."

After receiving the call from England, Max Mallery paused just long enough to communicate Jack's news to Gabriella and Luc before stepping into the corridor to phone one of his closest friends. Scrolling through to the number with one hand, he reached for his cigarettes with the other, simultaneously switching the phone to his left ear and flicking the lighter. On the third ring it was answered, and he quickly inhaled and exhaled the nicotine before speaking.

"Maurice, it's Max."

Before the boulangerie owner could ask why Mallery was calling on a Sunday evening, the detective ploughed on, trying his best to use discretion.

"Is Fran with you tonight?"

"No. I mean, she was up until an hour ago, but then someone called from the hospital, and she had to rush off, they're very short-staffed with both the manager and Doctor Lafoy being in custody. Why, what's the matter?"

"Maurice, I'm coming over, I'll be there in twenty minutes."

"What's going on?"

Max pinched his temples, not wanting to lie but reluctant to tell the whole story over the phone. "There's something I need to tell you, just wait for me."

Luc Martin peered at his boss around the doorframe. "Are we coming with you?"

"No, I need you two to head to the sanatorium. Shepherd's there, so don't let her leave. I'm going to meet up with Maurice and check over the apartment."

Luc rubbed his hands together and walked back to his desk to pick up his worn leather jacket, "You were right all along, boss, who would have thought it!"

As soon as Max's red BMW pulled up outside the *maison du maître*, Maurice was at the door, his face looking totally perplexed.

"Are you going to tell me what's happened, Max?"

"Look, this is going to be hard to hear, Maurice, and I'm sorry to break it to you in this way, but Fran's ex-husband died last week. He was poisoned with water hemlock, the same poisonous plant that killed the two victims at the hospital."

The bakery owner's eyes widened. "That's terrible news, but surely you don't think that Fran was involved? She hasn't left the country for months and besides, she is no more capable of murder than you or I. It's absurd to even think that she would do such a thing."

"Walk with me to the boulangerie. Do you have the apartment key?" Max pressed, already starting to cross the road. "I got a call from Jacques a short time ago. Neil Shepherd was poisoned with chocolate cake, sent to him via express delivery from France. The British police have been trying in vain to trace the source."

Maurice was scurrying to catch up with Mallery, his face indignant. "And so you presume that my Fran is behind it? You already have Monsieur Cassell in custody. Hasn't he been charged with poisoning those two unfortunate people?"

Max waited for his friend to catch up, placing a hand on Fabron's shoulder. "Yes, that's true, but we couldn't figure out who it was that had baked the chocolate cake for Enzo Roche's birthday. I'm afraid that this is too much of a coincidence for Fran not to be involved."

"Why do you want to look inside the apartment?" Maurice demanded, his voice rising. "It's not right to go in there without a search warrant."

Mallery turned on his heel, skidding slightly on the cobbles underfoot. "No, you're right, Maurice, I should have a search warrant. But would you rather we waited until tomorrow morning when I can get one issued, or take a look inside the apartment now to put an end to this once and for all?"

"Max, as much as you have been a good friend to me, and to Telo, you have refused to accept my relationship with Fran from day one, and now you are willing to go as far as accusing her of murder in an attempt to tarnish her name. Isn't that correct?"

"No, honestly, I…"

"Max Mallery, I believe that you are jealous, and for that reason alone I will open the apartment and allow you to look inside, if only to clear Fran's name."

Mallery could feel the heat rising in his cheeks and a trickle of cold sweat was now running down the back of his shirt. He watched as Maurice opened the boulangerie door and retrieved a set of keys, wondering if at least on one factor his friend might be right. He had been jealous of Maurice and Fran, and it hurt him no end to think that his actions were now going to rip them apart.

Fran was making herself a second cup of coffee in the staff room when she heard a vehicle pull up outside. After three glasses of wine with Maurice earlier in the day, she was in no fit state to be administering drugs to the patients, but with Dorothy Ramos pulling double shifts and two of the orderlies off with flu, she had been given no choice but to answer the call for help when it came.

Setting the steaming mug to one side, Fran looked down at the white Mini, wondering who would be arriving at such a late hour. Visiting ended at eight, and many of the residents were either without family or lived too far away to receive regular callers, but there was something about the car on the drive that she recognised. A ball of tension began to knot itself inside her gut, twisting and pulling as she walked out into the corridor to quell her curiosity.

"Nurse Shepherd," a voice called, as she neared the staircase, "could we have a word, please?"

Now she knew who the car belonged to, the blonde detective who worked with Inspector Mallery. Fran had also seen the skinny, long-haired man before and knew that the two of them here together spelled trouble.

Damn those police officers, she told herself, pasting a smile on her face.

"Detectives, good evening, what can I do for you?"

Gabriella took the lead. "Is there somewhere we could speak in private? We have a few questions we need to ask you."

Fran smoothed her uniform, subconsciously wiping her clammy palms on the fabric. "Could it wait? I'm just about to give the patients their medication."

"No, I'm afraid it can't" Gabi replied tersely. "Let's not make a scene, nurse."

"In here," Fran told them, pointing to the staff room, "it's pretty quiet tonight."

As they closed the door, the Englishwoman reached for her coffee mug and took a sip to help soothe her dry throat. She felt uncomfortable with the tone used by the female officer.

"Sit down, Nurse Shepherd," Luc told her. "We would like to ask you what you know about the murder of your ex-husband."

There was a loud crash as the porcelain mug smashed into sharp fragments and Fran's legs buckled underneath her as she mouthed, "Neil's dead?"

"I'm sorry, Maurice, I don't know what else to say, Fran's obviously covered her tracks well. I'm going to join Gabriella and Luc at the sanatorium, see what Nurse Shepherd has to say for herself."

Monsieur Fabron was indignant. "You're going to be very sorry indeed when you find out that Fran had nothing to do with her ex-husband's death. I don't know how you could possibly jump to such a conclusion. Even now, after searching her apartment, you're still off on some… some witch hunt!"

"Please, let me just do my job, this isn't an easy situation, believe me," Max sighed, pulling open the car door. "I'll be in touch soon."

"Papa, what's going on?" Telo called from the front gate. "Max, are you coming inside? We're playing a board game, and you could join us."

Maurice gritted his teeth as Max started the engine. "Nothing, just a misunderstanding, Telo. Max can't stay, he has to go back to work."

Mallery's eyes creased at the corners. "I'll call you as soon as we know more."

"I'm going to call my lawyer," Maurice grunted. "At least I still believe in Fran and she needs help."

"This can't be happening!" Fran sobbed, taking the glass of water from Detective Dupont's outstretched hand. "I wouldn't kill anyone, let alone Neil."

"Were you still on speaking terms?" Luc coaxed, taking a seat beside the distraught woman. "When was the last time you had communication with Neil?"

Gabriella caught her colleague's eye over the top of Fran's head, her eyebrows raised, and Luc waited patiently for the nurse to respond.

"About six weeks ago, he sent me a letter," Fran managed between gulps of water. "Neil wanted to tell me that he was expecting a baby with his girlfriend."

"Did the news upset you?" Gabi asked softly.

"Yes, it did. We couldn't have children together, we'd been trying for years." She looked up into the detective's kind face. "Of course it upset me."

"Enough for you to want to take revenge?"

"What? No, of course not! I was emotionally drained after receiving the letter, it cut me to the core, but since meeting Maurice… well, I've moved on, we're really happy together. You have to believe me. I couldn't hurt a fly."

"I think perhaps we should continue this conversation at the station," Luc suggested, hearing the roar of Max's sports car on the driveway. "Inspector Mallery will have questions of his own to put to you."

Back at police headquarters, with Fran Shepherd settled into an interview room, Max pulled his detectives to one side in the corridor.

"Well? What do you think?"

"I think she was genuinely shocked on learning of her ex-husband's death," Luc admitted. "I would bet a month's worth of chocolate that she's telling the truth."

Mallery turned an inquisitive eye on Gabi.

"I agree with Luc," she admitted. "The shock was real. I reckon somebody is trying to set her up."

"But who?"

Gabriella walked forward and pointed a finger at the cell in which Juliette Lafoy was being held. "I'd place my money on the doctor."

"I need to ask you where you were on the night of September eighteenth, which was Saturday of last week," Max stated in clear English.

Fran ran fingers through her bobbed hair and looked up at the ceiling. "I think I must have been at Maurice's house. I've been spending most of my free time there lately."

Max turned up the volume on the tape recorder. "Madame Shepherd, would you mind explaining to us why you decided to leave the cottage that was being rented for you? Why did you move to Saint Margaux, which was further from your place of work?"

"It was Doctor Lafoy's suggestion," Fran told him without hesitation. "She said that it was possible to take a cheaper place and the management would pay the difference on my rent allowance, so I would end up in pocket."

Max was confused at the unfamiliar phrase. "In pocket?"

"Yes, it means that I would benefit from getting a place with a lower rent as the hospital would still pay the higher rate, so the extra money would end up in my pay cheque each month."

"I see. Madam Shepherd, the cake with which your ex-husband was poisoned was chocolate, the same type as was delivered to Enzo Roche. In fact, there was another similarity. The box in which it arrived was tied with a green ribbon. Don't you think that is a very strange coincidence?"

Fran stared at her hands, thinking back to Roche's birthday and the sudden appearance of the large box. "Yes, it is. Enzo's cake was also tied with a green ribbon."

"Ah, so you remember it clearly?"

"Yes, I do. Actually, I recall thinking at the time that whoever had sent it didn't know Enzo Roche very well."

Mallery leaned forward, fingers clasped. "Oh, and why was that?"

"Because everyone who knows Monsieur Roche is aware of his great dislike of chocolate cake and his hatred of the colour green. That's why he gave some of the cake to Edwina and Ray. Enzo wouldn't touch it himself."

Max pinched his nose, feeling a headache looming as the questioning began tying him up in knots. "So it was commonly known amongst both patients and staff that Monsieur Roche didn't like chocolate gateau?"

"Yes, that's right, and that's the reason that cook made a vanilla sponge for Enzo's birthday."

Gabriella decided to jump in, taking a chance on the outcome. "Was Doctor Lafoy also aware of Roche's preferences?"

Fran's mouth opened to speak and then she quickly covered it with her hand as realisation dawned. "Yes, she was. In fact, it was Doctor Lafoy who asked me to make a list of Enzo's likes and dislikes. She said it would help in their therapy sessions!"

Max exhaled deeply, wondering whether Juliette Lafoy had used the information both to antagonise Roche and frame Shepherd for murder.

"I'll drive you back to Riberon," the inspector told Fran, making a spur of the moment decision against his better judgment, "unless you want to go back to Saint Margaux? But please let us know where you will be… just in case we have further questions."

"I need to get back to the hospital," she said steadily, although internally Fran felt as though she had been in the spin cycle of her washer. "They're short-staffed and I still have responsibilities."

"Are the hospital management team sending help?" Mallery asked softly, trying to empathise with the Englishwoman. "I believe they have been advised of the current situation."

"Yes, a temporary manager has been assigned and should be here first thing tomorrow. I'm guessing that they'll be hiring a new psychiatrist, too."

The last sentence was delivered with the irony with which it was suggested, Fran being perfectly aware that Juliette Lafoy had tried to frame her, but she also felt a modicum of relief in knowing that Inspector Mallery had chosen to believe her own side of the story.

"I just have one last task to attend to," Max announced, sliding back his chair with a screech, "and then we can go."

"Would you like a coffee or a glass of water while you're waiting?" Detective Dupont asked gently, her features creasing into an embarrassed smile. She felt sorry for what the nurse had been subjected to, but knew that her boss had been given no choice but to bring the nurse in for questioning. At least now the full picture of the recent tragic events was becoming clear.

"No, thank you. I'll be fine here."

The women's eyes met for a few seconds, in which both wondered if they might have become friends under different circumstances.

"Right, okay," Gabriella sighed, following Mallery and Luc out of the room.

Max turned to face his detectives as soon as the door was closed behind them. "I want you both to go home now, get a good night's rest."

"What about you?" Luc questioned, concerned at the obvious exhaustion on Max's face. His dark-rimmed eyes and pale face were giving him a ghostly appearance.

"I have to contact the British police, with a request," he answered, tapping his nose. "I have an idea that might bring this whole investigation to a close."

Jack Hobbs was up early on Monday morning, the mundane tasks of milking, filling the troughs with feed and collecting eggs from the chickens keeping his mind away from the bereavement that threatened to tear open his heart. His mother had been silent as he'd left the kitchen at five, her cup of tea sitting untouched on the table as she huddled next to the range. Jack wondered how she was going to cope without her husband of forty years. The pair had been inseparable, and the loss would no doubt turn Jean's whole life on its head. He contemplated asking his mum if she would go back to France with him, for a short time at least, but he needed to test the water with Angélique first. It certainly wasn't a palatable experience for most wives to find themselves sharing a home with their mother-in-law. Yet he had a duty to his mother. She needed to be cared for, not left alone on the large expanse of farm in rural Leeds, her only company being two hired hands who were decades younger than her.

Emptying the last sack of grain into a steel feeding trough, Jack felt the familiar buzzing of his phone. It was barely six-thirty, yet Max was awake and calling in.

"Hey, Max, what's up?"

"Is there any chance you could help liaise with the police over there for me? It's too early for the labs to be open and I have two depositions to handle."

"Yes, sure, what do you need?"

Mallery reeled off his requirements, barely pausing for breath.

"Okay, that shouldn't be a problem," Jack answered, the biting chill of a bitter wind whipping around his one uncovered ear. "I'll let you know as soon I can get hold of someone."

"Oh, I'm sorry, Jacques," Max faltered, "how is your father? Is he recovering?"

The silence that followed told Mallery that he had hit a raw nerve and he instinctively cursed himself for using such a tactless phrase.

"He passed away yesterday," Jack told him. "There was nothing they could do."

"Oh, look… I'm so sorry, forget about that request, Jacques…"

"It's fine, Max," Hobbs continued, "I'm glad of the distraction. Call you later."

Jack dropped the phone in the hay, fell to his knees and sobbed uncontrollably.

It was three hours later that Inspector Mallery received the call he had been waiting for. Having requested that Luc upload Cassell's, Lafoy's and Caisse's fingerprints into the database, the information had been sent across to Cambridgeshire Murder Squad, the unit with which Jack Hobbs was now communicating. The wait had been unbearable, with copious amounts of coffee acting as Mallery's only stimulant and a means of keeping him awake.

When the phone finally trilled into life, he snatched it up and grasped a handful of curly hair with his free hand. "Max Mallery."

Despite Max's weary features and stooping shoulders, his face brightened and by the end of the conversation he was punching the air.

"We have it! Cambridgeshire Police have a match!"

"On what?" Gabriella queried, moving from her seat to the front of the room.

Luc was already bouncing on his toes in anticipation.

"The label on the package that was delivered to Neil Shepherd bore a clear thumbprint, it's enough to convict. A definite match to Juliette Lafoy. Madam Shepherd was right, the doctor was trying to frame her."

Gabi was confused. "Okay, but I don't understand why she would want to do that. What would she gain from putting Fran behind bars?"

Max was happy to elaborate. "Doctor Lafoy was planning to write Enzo Roche's unofficial biography, right? She was jealous of the dancer's close relationship with Nurse Shepherd, even to the point of obsession. I've seen her notes and, believe me, they're pretty damning."

"What's that English saying that Jack uses? Money is the root of all evil?" Luc interjected. "It seems that the doctor would stop at nothing to get some dirt for that book of hers."

Mallery agreed, the techie had hit the mark exactly. "She'd already used the advance from the publisher to pay off gambling debts, then Cassell had topped up her funds in exchange for some help. Some people are just born greedy."

"I feel sorry for Roche," Gabi told them. "Not only did he feel responsible for his ex-partner's suicide, but even now there are those that would use his past for their own personal gain."

"What about Fran?" Luc suddenly asked, turning to his boss with a sheepish grin. "I guess we owe her one hell of an apology. Not only did she get brought in for questioning twice, but both times she was accused of murder."

Mallery grunted. "I doubt if Maurice will forgive me so easily, either. I've made a right hash of handling things. He even accused me of being jealous."

The words 'Are you?' were on the tips of both Gabi and Luc's tongues, but they stayed silent, not wanting to antagonise Max when he was already feeling low.

"Why not drive over there now?" Gabriella suggested, trying to lighten the mood. "You could fetch us a well-deserved lunch and speak to Maurice at the same time."

"Okay, but I need to order some flowers first."

"For Fran?"

"No, for Jacque's mother. Oh, shit, I'm sorry, guys, we've been so busy, it slipped my mind… Peter Hobbs died yesterday."

Gabi put a hand over her mouth as Luc went to put his arms around her. "No! How terrible, he was such a lovely man."

"He certainly was. Peter was a real gentleman," Max concluded, rubbing his colleague's arms. "Jacques and his mother will need our support."

"I'll order the flowers," Gabi offered, a tear rolling down her cheek. "You go and smooth things over with Fran and Maurice."

"Fran is upstairs in the apartment, sleeping," Maurice told Mallery on arrival, "I'm guessing that's why you're here, to talk to her."

The baker's words were abrupt, leaving no doubt in Max's mind that his friend was mightily pissed off.

Max placed the bouquet on the top of the boulangerie display counter. "And also to you, Maurice. Sometimes my job forces my hand, giving me no choice but to pursue certain lines of enquiry. It might not always seem right, or just, but circumstances dictate my actions. I don't know how I can make it up to you both, I wouldn't blame you if you hold Fran's arrest against me for a lifetime, but I am truly sorry. Please forgive me."

Maurice turned his back, taking a loaf of bread from the basket by the till and wrapping it in waxed paper. As he moved, the man's shoulders seemed to stiffen and then relax, as though Maurice had made up his mind on a course of action.

"You could take this up to her," he suggested, holding out the parcel. "Fran asked me to wake her at twelve. She was exhausted, but still needs to attend a meeting at the sanatorium this afternoon."

Mallery took the loaf and picked up the flowers, wondering what kind of reception he would get when the nurse opened the door.

"I will make it up to you, to both of you," he reiterated.

The baker wiped his hands on a muslin cloth, contemplating his next move. "There is something you could for us, Max, if you would."

"Of course, anything…"

"I have asked Fran to marry me, and she has accepted. We're going to plan the wedding for Christmas. I wonder, if you feel it appropriate, would you be my best man?"

Trying to work his mouth to find the right words, Max gently placed down the items in his arms, moved behind the counter and grasped his friend's hand. "Maurice, wow, that's fantastic! Of course, I would be honoured to stand at your side on the big day."

"Now go and call on the bride-to-be." Fabron smiled. "She's got a big heart and doesn't bear a grudge against you."

The police inspector stepped into the back room and let himself out into the courtyard to the entrance of the apartment above, feeling incredulous at how the day could turn from rat shit to sunshine in a matter of minutes.

Jack Hobbs placed a glass of sherry in his mother's hand, kissing the top of her grey curls as he did so. Jean looked up, doe-eyed, proud at how her only son was managing to hold himself together in such tragic circumstances.

"I've spoken to Angélique," he said, taking the vacant chair next to the fire, "and we both think it would be for the best if you come over to France after the funeral. Uncle Terry has offered to lend us one of his labourers, just until we decide what to do in the long-term, and Simon can take charge."

Jean brought the liquid to her lips, the faraway look in her eyes confirming that the farmer's widow was deep in thought. "What about after that, Jack? What will happen to the farm? This place was your poor old dad's whole life, and mine too. I can't just see it sold off to the highest bidder."

"Let's face that decision when we've both had time to grieve, eh? I don't have any answers right now, Mum, but perhaps in time we can sort something out."

Jean's short lashes were wet with tears. "I'll only be in the way in France. Angélique doesn't need me under her feet."

"Angie will welcome some help," Jack soothed. "I would certainly appreciate you teaching her how to make your Eccles cakes."

Eventually, the woman's head tilted slightly as she whispered, "Alright, son."

Then, leaving his mother to finish the sherry in peace, Jack Hobbs climbed the stairs to his bedroom and made the call to his wife. He had no idea how Angélique would handle the news that her mother-in-law was coming to stay indefinitely, but he hadn't had the heart to risk a rebuttal and now the deed was done. Jack just hoped that his dad was looking down on him as he started to take the reins for what might be a long and arduous time ahead.

Maurice Fabron stood inside the darkened church porch, his suit as sharp and bespoke as that of his best man. Max Mallery was only slightly less jittery than the groom and adjusted the red rose in his friend's lapel in an attempt to busy his own slightly shaking fingers.

"We should go inside soon," the police officer commented as the last of the guests filtered inside, many of them wrapped in thick woollen coats and fur hats. Father Claude had been requested to turn on the ancient heating system, but the parishioners knew that it was a fruitless venture. Trying to fill the large stone building with warmth was as useless as putting up an umbrella during a monsoon. As people settled in the pews, Mallery could see them through the partially open door, rubbing their gloved hands together and shivering slightly.

"How have things been at the sanitorium?" he asked, turning to look at Maurice head on, "I guess there has been a real shake up with the staff."

"Poor Fran has worked some long hours over the past couple of months, she's been exhausted, but thankfully the new manager has recognised all that she's done and, as well as a generous salary increase, he has reduced her hours to a four-day week."

"That's great news. I heard that Enzo Roche got his release assessment too, has Fran kept in touch?"

Maurice smiled, reflecting upon the leaving party that had marked the patient's return home, "Yes, they've become very close. We were both quite emotional when he left, you know, and thankfully Monsieur Roche is dancing again. It's early days yet, but he has a small part in a production in Seville next summer. We're hoping to fly out there for the opening night."

Max blew on his cold hands and nodded, "Splendid, I'm truly happy for him, but most of all my heart is filled with joy for you and Fran."

On the street a dark limousine pulled up at the kerb, causing the men to turn their heads as the driver got out and opened the back door. A flash of violet appeared, causing a sharp contrast to the foggy white afternoon.

'Monsieur Roche?' Maurice questioned, straining to make out the figure who was being helped out of the back seat, a feathered trilby on his head.

'It certainly looks like him,' Max smiled, glad that the dancer was back on top form since his release from hospital under the new psychiatrist.

'Fran said she'd invited him,' the baker explained, 'but we weren't sure if he would come.'

'He thinks the world of Fran, you can tell by the way in which his face lit up every time she entered his room. It's actually quite strange seeing Enzo away from the confines of the sanatorium.'

Maurice cleared his throat as the figure put a hand on the latch of the gate. 'Fran says he should have been released months ago, that Doctor Lafoy was keeping him there for her own benefit, to get that book finished.'

Mallery agreed. 'I think that's definitely the case, my friend, the poor fellow must have been so frustrated. The attempt on his life was harrowing enough without Lafoy trying to glean every last detail of his private life, too.'

'Gentlemen,' Roche enthused, pale fingers appearing from the folds of his purple-lined cloak. 'What a chilly day, but surely the happiest of your life, Monsieur Fabron!'

'Indeed.' Maurice grinned, silently wondering how long it would be until his bride-to-be would be escorted to the church by Telo.

The trio shook hands and made small talk for a few minutes until the final group of guests arrived at the edge of the churchyard. Enzo followed their eyes and touched the inspector's arm. 'I'll see you inside, dear.'

Jack Hobbs and family were last to arrive, on account of Thomas's last minute temper tantrum, a bout which could only be soothed by a slice of his grandmother's sticky lemon drizzle cake. Max turned to greet them, noting an unfamiliar and unexpected addition to the group.

"Maurice, Max," Jack beamed, grasping the men's hands in turn, "good to see you. I must say, you both look very dapper."

"Just a little number from the back of the wardrobe," Mallery joked, still keeping one eye on the tall, short-haired woman at the edge of the group.

Hobbs followed his gaze and coughed. "Sorry, Max, this is Rachel, my cousin. I forgot you two haven't met."

Mallery took a step forward, lifting the woman's outstretched hand to his lips. "It's a pleasure to meet you."

"Likewise, Inspector." Rachel smiled, trying to ignore the butterflies that danced in her stomach on spying the charismatic detective whose soft lips were lingering just a little too long on her pale skin.

"Perhaps you would give me the honour of the first dance later?"

There was a twinkle in the Englishwoman's eye as she held Max's gaze. "I can't think of anyone I would rather have spin me around the floor."

As Mallery watched the party enter the church and find their seats, Maurice took his elbow. "Your turn next, perhaps?" the groom whispered.

"Maybe, Maurice, who knows. Sometimes life is insane."

THE END

Printed in Great Britain
by Amazon